'What seems to be a novel about generations of
a family swiftly becomes much deeper and more
intriguing. Kate Mahony deftly weaves past and
present, reality and the supernatural into a richly
textured story of the effects of colonisation and war
on communities, families and individual identity.
An engrossing, wonderful read.'

— *Catherine Robertson*

'*Secrets of the Land* draws parallels between the
domination of Ireland by the English in the 19th
century and colonialism in Taranaki, New Zealand.
The stories range from 1864 to 2018 through
characters who fight over farming rights, past hurts
and secrets, and those who try to make peace with
the present. Kate Mahony is a skilled writer and
blends well-researched historical facts with vibrant,
believable fiction to create an engrossing novel.'

— *Sandra Arnold*

SECRETS

of the

LAND

KATE MAHONY

CLOUD
INK

Published by Cloud Ink Press
c/o Southside
1/110 Symonds Street
Auckland 1010
www.cloudink.co.nz

First published 2023

ISBN: 978-1-7385943-0-6 (paperback); 978-1-7385943-1-3 (epub)

A catalogue record for this book is available from
the National Library of New Zealand.

Cover design by Keely O'Shannessy
keelyoshannessy.com

Internal design by Arotype

Printed in New Zealand by Ligare

Cover image: Taranaki by Arthur Bothamley, circa 1880,
from Collections Te Papa, Wellington, New Zealand

For Michael, Hannah, and Sophie

Acknowledgement

I acknowledge Taranaki maunga and the iwi that connect to it. They were deeply affected by the historical events that are the backdrop to part of this novel.

A note about place names

This novel is set in coastal Taranaki and I have used some of the actual place names found in this beautiful region's coastline. However, I have also made up place names. The district of Wexford under the maunga and its inhabitants and incidents as well as the Boulder River are imagined. This is to underline the fact this is a work of fiction inspired by events of the past.

IMOGEN
Melbourne 2018

I didn't see the man at first. He must have approached me while I had my head down reading a text from Simon and, when I looked up, I saw him close by. Instinctively, I pulled back.

I recognised him as the same man I'd seen earlier in the morning. He'd been standing outside our offices. He appeared to be in his twenties, had black curly hair that waved in the light breeze and a small beard. He could have been a Cillian Murphy lookalike but for his slightly derelict appearance due to an oversized jacket that hung loose on his body.

I'd wondered if he might be a beggar setting himself up here on our side of the river. Some of the ones in the city had become even more aggressive in their demands for money. A band tightened across my chest, making it harder to breathe. Was he going to ask me if I had any spare change? My wallet was tucked away in the bottom of my backpack, and I didn't want to stop and pull it out in full view of him.

When I had seen him on my way to work, I'd had a strange sense he was watching me. It had been unnerving. Now I began to hurry towards where Simon would be waiting at the other end of the small cobblestone street. The man stepped in my way. This time I noticed distinctive blue eyes, set back in his face, staring directly at me. I touched my hand to the gold necklace around my neck, something I did when I was nervous.

'Miss Maguire Baxter?' His formal approach brought me to a halt.

He had it wrong. It was just Maguire. My business partner Zoe was the Baxter. I remembered our business name was listed as Maguire Baxter on the directory outside our building. He must have seen it. 'It's only Maguire,' I said aloud.

'Good.' His eyes crinkled and he sounded relieved. 'I've been trying to find you. And it hasn't been easy.' He spoke with an accent, Irish I thought. He had an old-fashioned air about him. When he looked down, his gaze seemed to rest on my chest. My heart skipped a beat. I pulled my jacket closer.

'Look, I'm sorry,' I said, perplexed, glancing around in the hope Simon had decided to walk down to meet me. 'I don't know you. What's this about?'

He paused, as if searching for the right words. 'I've come about your grandfather.'

This was where he was wrong – it wasn't me he was after. I was instantly relieved. 'I don't have a grandfather.'

The man waited patiently.

'Not alive,' I amended my statement. I could have added that I didn't have a father, either. 'You've got the wrong person, sorry.'

He glanced down at me again as if he were checking I was the right person. I wasn't sure what I should do. Turn and run from him?

'No,' he said. 'I have the right person. I believe this to be so.' He seemed to stare at my chest again. 'Your grandfather's name is Jack. He lives in …' He said a long name quickly. I vaguely recognised it.

'In New Zealand?' That was where my mother had grown up.

He nodded again.

This was getting even stranger. Simon and I had a trip to New Zealand coming up. It'd taken me ages to get him to agree to go away together. At first I had suggested other places in Australia to visit but whenever I went to book flights, there was always some activity coming up for his boys that he had to be there for. I thought of New Zealand. It was more definite and would take a really major event to cancel. When I told him I'd book the harbour bridge climb and a vineyard tour of Waiheke Island with lunch at a world-famous restaurant, suddenly he was all on board. The boys would be fine with their mum.

He had asked me if I wanted to check out the place my mother had come from. I said no. 'Aoife only lived there for a short time years ago, before she and her mum went to Australia. And anyway, it's further down the island off the beaten track somewhere.'

Even if it were closer to where we were going, would I really want to visit there? Aoife had said all those years back that it wasn't a good place and had hinted it likely had a bad spirit. She had shut down any further questions pretty quickly.

Now I stared at the man in front of me, waiting for him to explain further.

'Your grandfather needs your help. Desperately. Time is of the utmost.' This quaint expression had a certain sincerity. It was then I had a horrible inconsequential thought – could it be this man had escaped from one of those psychiatric places in the community? He let out a long breath. 'You must help.'

'You all right?' a voice behind me asked. I turned to see a man in the uniform of the hardware store on the next street. He had narrowly avoided bumping into me. I realised I had stopped in the middle of the footpath.

'Yes.'

When I turned back the strange man who'd accosted me had gone. The man in the store uniform must've thought I was talking to myself. I began to walk faster towards the end of the street and was relieved to see Simon standing outside the café. He was checking his phone.

'Did you see a guy who looked a bit odd?' I asked. 'In baggy clothes? Approaching people?' I didn't say he'd only approached me.

He looked up from the screen. 'No. Was he begging? Are you getting beggars down here now?'

I was unsure how to explain the conversation. 'Not that I've seen before. I'm not sure what it was all about really. It was so weird I don't know what to think. He said he knew someone I knew in New Zealand but ...' I shook my head. 'I don't know anyone there.'

Simon ushered me into the cafe. 'Well, your mum did live there for a while, didn't she? And her family, I guess.'

'Yes, but like I told you she and her mother left years and years ago. She was still a child. And my grandfather is dead. That's why it was so strange.'

'A crazy guy. Lot of them around. Or someone hoping to scam you.'

'Yes, that's what I guessed, too.' Relieved we had thought the same thing, I pulled out a chair at one of the tables.

'Do you want to order food?' Simon glanced around for the waitress.

'No.' I realised I had lost my appetite. 'Just a coffee.'

The waitress came and took our orders. I asked him how he was getting on with a work project that had been stressing him out (he was a project manager for a finance company and there'd been a rushed deadline). The team had managed to get it done, he said. They'd worked till midnight the night before. After that, he was quiet. I sensed he was feeling uncomfortable, or maybe he was tired from the previous night.

'So?' I said at last. 'What's so important you wanted to meet up today?' I nearly added, 'At lunchtime.' Simon was so work focused this was out of character for him. Most of the time it was either work or his kids that he concentrated on.

'Look, I'm sorry,' he began.

The waitress brought our coffees. We both said thanks almost at the same time. After she left, Simon reached out to take my hand, pulling it towards him across the table.

'What?' I said, worried now. 'What's up?'

'You know I really like you,' he began.

I was stunned. Was he going to suggest we move in together? It could hardly be a marriage proposal, he still wasn't divorced from Nicole, but maybe the divorce papers were on their way? He'd always said it was an amicable separation. Except of course, he had cheated on her with someone else. A girl from his work. He'd told me this when we met. I'd told Zoe what he had said. She'd asked me if I thought it could be all that amicable with Nicole knowing about her.

'And I like you,' I said. What else was he going to say? Now I was feeling nervous. 'And …?'

His fingers tightened on mine. 'This is really difficult. Look …'

Spit it out, I wanted to shout. This wasn't like Simon, normally he was calm and confident. 'Are you ill? Is it one of the boys?'

He saw a lot of his family. For the sake of the boys, who were now aged seven and nine, he'd moved into a studio flat in a suburb within easy reach of his family home. He helped out with the boys. He even did maintenance jobs around the house.

'No,' he said. He shut his mouth firmly and appeared to be thinking of what to say next.

While I waited for Simon to go on, a comment Zoe had made

one time popped into my mind. Although she had never spelled it out exactly, I could tell even from the beginning she'd been a little suspicious of him. She observed one time that he clearly preferred to keep our relationship – she meant me, I decided – on the sidelines. I replied it worked for the both of us to spend time apart. 'You and I need time to expand the company, so if he's busy with the boys I can focus on that.' Zoe looked unconvinced but I was pleased when she didn't try to argue. Zoe and I saw things differently, I had told myself. That was all.

Simon cleared his throat. 'No, no,' he said finally. 'It's … well, Nicole has asked me back. We're going to try again.'

'What?' I could feel my face crunch into a mask of horror. 'But you said …'

What had he said? He'd indicated it was definitely all over, hadn't he? I was sure he didn't even like her that much. The boys' wellbeing was all that mattered, that's what he always said. They had to be happy.

'I know but I made a mistake. I made a big mistake and I didn't think Nicole would ever want me back but she's willing to give it a go, and, well, I want to be there for the boys.'

I stared at him, my cheeks becoming hot. 'You've been sleeping with her? That's what.' I just knew. 'And more than once? How long has this been going on?'

'How …? What …?' Simon was looking at me in horror as if I were a witch who could read minds. Or someone's deepest intentions.

'I knew it,' I said, removing my fingers from his grasp. 'I just didn't want to see it. Of course.'

I thought of all the Saturday Scouts' meetings and the mid-weekly swimming lessons he had to take the boys to. All the times he'd had to help Nicole – a roof tile that had come off, her car needing a new battery. I'd been okay with all this but why hadn't I seen he might still have feelings for her? Or, and this was a bitter thought, that he might be deliberately finding time to be with her? What a fool I had been. I breathed in harshly, prepared to speak my mind.

Simon beat me to it. 'Look, I feel really bad, but, well …' He stopped. He'd run out of anything to say. He avoided looking at me.

I glared at him some more as angry tears ran down my face. 'You're a bastard, did you know that? A rotten stinking bastard.'

Simon looked embarrassed. 'I'm sorry. If I could've … We weren't that serious, were we? We hadn't taken the next step.'

'That was because you were so worried about your precious boys and how they would take their dad having another woman in their life, that's the reason.' And maybe, a little voice in my head said, because I liked having time to myself. I hadn't minded it wasn't a full-time relationship. I told my conscience to shut up. This wasn't about me, it was about Simon cheating on me.

'You cheated on Nicole before and now you've been cheating on me. With her. You haven't changed, have you? You make me sick.' My voice grew louder as I said the words, more bitter. There were worse names I could've called him but I didn't know where to start. I managed, 'Scumbag.'

His face reddened and he gave me an annoying shamefaced little-boy look. 'Look, I'm sorry. That's all I can say.'

'What about our trip to New Zealand? I guess you can't go on that now. What would Nicole say?' I didn't care how childish I sounded.

Simon avoided my gaze. 'I'm sorry,' he repeated.

I stood up then and walked out of the café leaving him to pay the bill. I was sure he wouldn't follow me.

I had barely walked the length of the street when the stranger was there again.

'Go away,' I said viciously, raising my hand with the palm open and almost slapping him on the chest. I wasn't in the mood. 'Get out of my way.'

'Look, Miss, I'm sorry to have frightened you.' The man seemed genuinely apologetic. 'It's just that – you need to know. I am unable to help him. But you are his kin.'

His kin? What about my mother? Why didn't this weird guy know the old man had a daughter, also here in Australia? This was getting even more ridiculous. The most sensible thing would be to turn my back on him and go away.

'Without your help, I fear for him.' He sighed, a mournful sound. 'You are the only one who can do so. He does not have the strength on his own. You have the power.'

I looked around to find we were the only two people in the street. I wasn't sure what to say. That I wasn't swayed by his old-fashioned language and fanciful ideas? That he was talking rubbish?

I went to walk away, remove myself from this weird conversation. He put out his arm as if to stop me, but then dropped it. His blue eyes gazed into mine. 'You will do the right thing,' he said. 'I know you will. You will not allow your own flesh and blood to be in great danger, as I fear he may be if nothing is done.'

Even though the sun was shining I felt a chill go through me. I took a breath. 'Listen,' I began, determined to put him in his place but what if the elderly man really was my grandfather? And – a thought came out of nowhere – was there the faintest chance this 'grandfather' in New Zealand might have an idea who my father was?

It wasn't impossible. I'd been born in Australia, yet I'd been conceived when my mother met my father on a kibbutz in Israel. Could my mother have written to her father when she was travelling overseas? She might have mentioned her new boyfriend's name and where he was from.

The man before me now appeared to be waiting quietly for me to say more.

'Has someone threatened him?' I asked.

He didn't respond directly to this. 'You must believe me. He needs help,' was all he said. 'There are people who must know what has happened. Even a person from the newspaper asked him questions … I heard her.'

Now I was interested. 'What newspaper? Who asked questions?'

The man just shrugged. 'She said she was from the newspaper. Jack was angry, that is all I know. Someone tried to steal his calves, he said, and hurt them.'

I was silent, considering his words. 'So are you a friend of his then?'

He hesitated then he shook his head. 'I've known him a while. That's not important. What matters is you must go to the farm.' He moved from foot to foot, a kind of nervous reaction, as if he'd run out of energy. 'I cannot stay here long, Miss. I've stayed too long as it is. I must leave.'

He looked towards the end of the lane. A tram rattled by, startling him even further into more odd foot tapping. 'Now I must go. Your grandfather needs help. He is in desperate need of it. He needs help now.' He said it in the same patient tone, as if I were a child, and repetition was good, but there was no mistaking the urgency.

'All right.' There could be no arguing with him, whoever he was. 'Leave it with me.' Sometimes I liked to say that, especially to clients who were being demanding. It sounded commanding, in control, even if this wasn't at all true.

He smiled. Relief flooded his features. 'You understand the

importance. I believed you would. That is a good thing. If nothing is done …' He glanced around. 'I have stayed too long. I must go.'

'You haven't told me your name.'

The man seemed to hesitate. 'It's Michael Flynn. I …' He didn't finish the sentence.

Footsteps approached us. It was the same guy from the hardware store coming now from the other end of the lane. He looked closely at me but said nothing this time. I moved out of his way and let Michael Flynn go.

Zoe was out at a meeting all afternoon. She'd left a courier package on my desk, marked urgent and with my name in large letters. It was illustrations for a university textbook we were publishing. Although I'd been waiting on it, I was not inclined to even open it. I closed my eyes and willed myself to forget Simon, forget what he'd told me, forget what it all meant.

I concentrated on looking out through the big window to where the Yarra River meandered away in the distance. Up here all was quiet apart from the rattle of a tram passing by the end of the street. My mind zipped back to the strange Michael Flynn and our conversation, and I ran over it again to see if I had missed anything, any clue. Another weird happening on a day that was proving to be one of worst days of my life.

I kept mulling over what he had said. It was possible I had a grandfather living in New Zealand and he was in trouble but why should I believe a stranger who had accosted me on a street? The weird homeless-looking man, Michael Flynn, seemed convinced of it though that didn't mean it was true. What if he were right about him being my grandfather, and the old man knew the identity of my father? Perhaps he could answer the questions that had nagged away at me over the years – questions like did my father and I have much in common? Were we similar in any way? People often said how unalike my mother and I were, both in looks and personality. Aoife was classic Celtic Irish with her pale skin, reddish hair, and blue eyes. I had dark brown hair, hazel eyes and olive skin – more Mediterranean. I was taller than she was, but despite her lack of height she had a strong physique from working outdoors.

Aoife had always been reluctant to divulge any details of her past but I decided I would try at least one more time so I picked up my phone to call her. Not surprisingly, her phone registered as out of range. It probably meant she was working on a farm in the outback with no Wi-Fi around for miles or she had once again dropped her phone in a water tank. I did have a number for the people who owned the farm where she was working. I called that number only to be told she had moved on, gone further south. I tried the number they had for the next place and there was no response. I would hear from her when I heard from her.

I sat and stared at my phone for a while. What had I intended to ask her anyway? Is my grandfather alive? Was there any point asking her this? Had she ever been honest with me about any-thing? In the classroom when we had to draw a picture of our families, I would include a tall man with long legs in the corner of the painting, like the other kids did. Other kids had fathers even if some saw them every second weekend only or during the school holidays.

One evening when I was older and watching a Father's Day commercial on television – I really liked those ads – I asked her, 'Who was my dad?'

That was when Aoife had told me he was someone she had met when she was working on a kibbutz in Israel. He hadn't known I was born. He liked studying things, she said, like fish.

I decided he was a marine scientist. I told one of the new girls in my class that my father was travelling in places like Norway and Greenland, in the Arctic, on a big boat checking out the marine life. 'Whales,' I said, 'and sharks.'

When the girl's mum asked Aoife one day how Imogen's dad, the marine scientist, was getting on and when was he due back, she decided to have a chat with me. I learned he may not have been a marine scientist and he wasn't coming back to us.

'But can't you get in touch with him?' I asked. 'Write to him?'

The problem, it turned out, was his surname was a really common one – Jones, she said – and she couldn't remember the city he said he had come from and it was too hard to even start looking for him. I guess after that I gave up. When I'd told Simon I didn't know who my father was, he said I should get an ancestry DNA test from one of those family history sites. I could find relatives online and take it from there. It could lead to finding him. I said I'd consider it, yet something held me back.

At home in the evening after my disastrous day, I put the previous night's leftover potato gratin in the microwave and poured myself a glass of Shiraz. I remembered then the volcano on the North Island. I'd been doing a science project on volcanoes at school and Aoife had looked over my shoulder and said she'd lived beneath the slopes of a volcano. It had erupted thousands of years before, throwing tons of huge rocks around the fields. At the time she told me this, our home was in a flat arid part of Australia, so the idea of living beneath a dangerous mountain which could explode any minute had intrigued me.

The volcano was easy to find online. Taranaki, that was the name I'd had a vague idea of. I went to Google and searched 'stolen calves on Taranaki farm'. It took only a few seconds before a recent news article from a local newspaper came up, written by one of its reporters, Shelley Ward. Michael Flynn was right about a woman interviewing the man he thought was my grandfather. The article said police were investigating what was thought to be an intended cattle rustling in a place called Wexford. The owner, an elderly man, believed the would-be thieves had been disturbed and made their escape before the cattle – two young bull calves – could be loaded onto a vehicle. The calves had later been found at the other end of the road from their owner's farm. He was the right age for a grandfather. I also observed there was no name given for the elderly man, which didn't prove anything, really. I tried the White Pages next but found no one by the name of Jack Maguire in a place called Wexford in Taranaki.

I did a search for Wexford itself. There was nothing much to it. It had an old pub built more than a century ago, a garage with a sign advertising car repairs and a fish and chip shop. All the other places in the area had Māori names but when I googled a Wikipedia page on Wexford, I saw that it had originally had a long Māori name, Ohinemaia. The local iwi still used it, the article said.

Sidebars on the webpage led me to a series of articles on the history of the region. Acquisitions of vast acres of land, taken from the indigenous people by the government of the time, had begun in the 1840s and continued much later. This had led to many bloody conflicts and wars between government troops and Māori throughout the country and in Taranaki. In recent times there had been reparations and apologies in person from government ministers.

I was aware similar redress had happened with the Aboriginal people in Australia but the history of this part of New Zealand was unknown to me. I glanced quickly at the information on screen but with so many dates and difficult-to-pronounce names of people and places I would need more time to take it all in.

For now, though, I needed to concentrate on finding contact details for the man who might possibly be my grandfather. I checked the name Maguire on the online White Pages but there were none listed for Wexford.

The one person I knew in New Zealand was Rebecca, a friend I'd gone to journalism school with in Melbourne. She'd moved over to Wellington and now worked on a newspaper there which, when I looked it up, turned out to be part of the same group as the newspaper in Taranaki.

Rebecca had done well, and her LinkedIn profile listed awards she had won for her journalism. In her occasional emails, she'd urge me to come over to visit and she had been supportive when I wrote to her about the issues I was having with my new boss. I still couldn't work out why Gavin, the newly appointed chief reporter – he'd come from a Sydney newspaper, was in his late 30s, aggressively ambitious and determined to make his mark – had taken what came across as an instant dislike to me. From the beginning, he made a point of disparaging my ideas for stories, usually in front of the rest of the team. Maybe he was merely cynical and like that with everyone but, when he did it, the focus was on me. My work. I couldn't figure out where I had gone wrong.

My previous boss, Barry, had encouraged us to come up with story ideas and matters for investigation. He'd been such a mentor to me, describing me as a 'real trooper and a tenacious reporter' when I worked overtime on a story. Gavin was the opposite. He seemed to dislike me on first sight. Zoe reckoned he thought I was a threat to him because I'd got a newspaper award for an investigative article I'd written during the journalism course. Also, she suggested, it could've been that Barry had spoken well of me in their handover meeting and set him against me. Rebecca, on the other hand, declared he was an arrogant git who liked to patronise me to make himself look better. Whatever the reason, he would constantly project his own toxic behaviour onto me as though I was the one doing it. He might say, 'you have a tendency to misinterpret things' when all I had done was ask him to clarify a comment he had made.

I knew Rebecca thought I should have stood up to Gavin but when you're in a meeting with your colleagues and the managing editor of the newspaper and your new boss is gaslighting you, telling you in front of them you were wrong about something he'd told you to do, it's hard to defend yourself. Okay, I guess I should've told him what I thought of his sneaky putdowns when he first started them, but that was easier said than done.

I'd proposed an investigative report or even a series I wanted to take on. It would focus on a group of slum landlords who used their henchmen to threaten the tenants in mould-infected, leaky buildings and employed thugs to collect the rent in cash. One girl was even told she could live rent free if she did a couple of nights at one of their strip clubs. I had already traced the actual owners – the silent partners as it were – through a web of companies back to three men. Three very wealthy men. It'd be a great story to investigate, and one a tenacious reporter would enjoy chasing.

Gavin leaned back in his chair. 'First of all, as I'm sure you know, we don't have the budget for long investigations. There's no money in it anymore. And word to the wise,' he gave me a benevolent smile, like an elderly uncle might to a child, 'you can bet these guys will be well known to any of the old brigade here. They can probably tell you plenty of past stories about them. The fact is, nowadays these three will be pretty much untouchable. They move in the top circles. They've built up a respectable veneer around themselves and their companies.

'You might think it's one of their companies behind these

properties but when it comes to it, they're as slippery as eels. You won't be able to tie the illegal stuff back to them. If you'd been in the game for as long as I have, you'd know how they protect themselves.'

I thought this over. 'But …' That was as far as I got before Gavin interrupted me by picking up a copy of the day's newspaper and waving it at me.

'Who do you think likely paid for these full-page ads? For a new property development with its own lake in the centre?'

And was I aware, he added sarcastically, that these men had recently been given mayoral awards? 'They'll be at the same breakfast business seminars as the editor,' he said, as if I were a complete idiot. 'Moving right along, there's that council meeting tomorrow about inner-city transport problems in the eastern suburbs I mentioned yesterday. Get on to it. Do some background research.' He actually snapped his fingers.

I wasn't going anywhere in this job, not with Gavin in charge. After I ranted even further to Rebecca during one long phone call, she suggested I apply for a job on a New Zealand newspaper. Wellington was a great place to live, she said, and wasn't unlike Melbourne. In the end, I had decided to join Zoe in the new publishing venture. Publishing non-fiction with a focus on educational and academic books might not have the same thrill as chasing stories, but I didn't have to face bloody Gavin each morning. When I met Simon, I thought I could put it all behind me. Life was good.

I checked the time. Melbourne was two hours behind Wellington. Perfect. I picked up my phone and rang Rebecca. It didn't take too long to explain. I fudged the details of how I had learned about my supposed grandfather, saying I had come across him by chance in a local newspaper article I'd read online. I mentioned the name of the reporter. 'Is it okay to use your name when I call this Shelley Ward to ask for the contact details? I doubt she'll give me an address or phone number otherwise.'

'I don't recognise that name. She may be new to the job but she'll possibly know mine.' She said it in a self-deprecating tone, but it reminded me there had been another award recently. There seemed to be no stopping Rebecca.

'Thanks so much,' I said. 'I'll try to get to Wellington in the near future and we can celebrate your award then.'

My call to Shelley couldn't have gone more smoothly. She knew who Rebecca was and was also interested to learn that I'd previously worked on a well-known daily Melbourne paper. Thankfully, she didn't ask why I had moved on. Shelley was more interested in the media world in general in Melbourne and told me she was thinking of making a move over there. She asked me several questions about the possibility of finding jobs in Melbourne and I responded with some brief answers.

I moved on to the real reason for my call. 'So, I'm taking a trip to New Zealand. Partly on holiday but I'm hoping to write a freelance article with a focus on re-connecting with distant family in New Zealand.' Hopefully, she wouldn't find out this was a straight lie.

'Sure. How can I help?'

'I saw your recent article on cattle rustling and your interview with an elderly man. I thought he could be a distant relative of mine. My mother lived in Taranaki as a child. At Wexford.'

'He's got the same surname as you all right. What are the chances Jack could be family?'

'I know,' I said. 'Unreal.' I guess that's New Zealand for you, I nearly said, more sheep than people.

'He was pretty gutted but he didn't want to comment. Not at all. And what he did say couldn't be printed in a family newspaper.'

I laughed. 'He sounds fun. Is his farm easy to find?'

She assured me it was easy enough. All I had to do was head from New Plymouth around the coast to a town called Ōkato and after that veer left towards the mountain. This seemed to be the gist of it. 'Look out for a house with an orange roof and his is the next house along, down a track. Or ask a local to point you in the right direction.'

'Thanks. Have the police got any further investigating what happened?'

'Not that I know of.' Shelley lowered her voice. 'It was horrible. A calf panicked and got its head stuck in the narrow bars of the gate. It was trapped there all night. It was pretty distressing, especially for Jack. The thing is Jack's an old man.' She paused, thinking. 'Not that good on detail. He was convinced the gate had been shut after he put them in the paddock, but … there wasn't much to go on. I've covered the rural beat for a while now but country people here can be quite tight-lipped around reporters even if they know you.'

I heard a voice in the background on Shelley's end, someone reminding her of a meeting. 'It's a small place. Everyone knows everyone else. In fact, my grandpa worked in the cattle industry as a stock agent and later as an agricultural equipment sales rep. He would have known most of the farmers around the coast. He moved out there to the beach on his retirement. He's in a home for the elderly now. He doesn't get out as much but he'd be bound to remember Jack from those times.'

I could feel the excitement rise – someone who knew the man who could be my grandfather. I already had tickets to New Zealand, so I could look into it, what did I have to lose? I might find out more about my mother's family and be able to help an old man in trouble.

In the morning when I told Zoe my plans, she accepted my

vague, invented lost-and-found grandfather story without too much question and was immediately encouraging. When she also heard about my disastrous date with Simon – henceforth called 'the rat', she helpfully added – and my plan to fast forward the New Zealand holiday, she was even more enthusiastic. I told her I had a couple of pressing projects but I'd take my laptop and work from there.

'Don't worry too much about work,' she said straight away. 'Not when your grandfather's wellbeing is at stake, and especially if he doesn't have anyone he can rely on. That's what's important. No, you must go. And frankly, it will be better than hanging around here mooching over what's happened with Simon.'

It was obvious that this latest action of Simon's had confirmed her initial impression of him but right now, I didn't want to hear his name in any form.

'And when you think about it,' Zoe went on, 'family is what matters, isn't it?'

Was it? There'd been Aoife and me, no one else, and a lot of the time we barely kept in touch. Unlike Zoe, who could easily spend half an hour some mornings on the phone to her mother arranging a shopping trip. I nodded. Simon had put his boys first, hadn't he? So family meant a lot to him too, meant he was prepared to go back to his wife, acting all sorry and humble when he'd actually been happy with me all the time they'd been separated, or appeared to be. Now I wasn't so sure. Had he been merely killing time with me till he could get back into her good books?

As for me, I might learn more about a member of my family I hadn't known, a man who my mother had cut out of her life. It struck me – if my mother had lied, telling me my grandfather was dead, what else was there to uncover?

MICHAEL

Victoria, Australia 1864

The man was Irish. I knew as soon as I heard his voice and why wouldn't he be? Except for the Italians and the Chinese every second man here at the goldfields was Irish. It was near the end of the day and a few of us were sitting outside our huts in the settlement, our arms up to our elbows streaked in mud. When we breathed in, we breathed mud.

'Have ye found any?' he asked me, standing at my shoulder.

I knew he meant gold. 'Mebbe.'

'Enough to take you back home a rich man?'

He knew that I hadn't but I would not dignify the man with a response. By the time the company had taken its cut we were no richer than before. The best of times had gone long before we arrived here and I'd been here two years already.

He chewed on some tobacco. 'Lad,' he said. 'I can get ye back to Ireland soon enough. And with money aplenty.'

I couldn't keep my mouth shut now. 'How?'

He came even closer. 'I'm looking for men to sign up to the army, lad,' he said. 'Across the water in New Zealand. They're keeping those bloodthirsty natives there in order and they need more men. Good pay, regular food in ye belly, a uniform, and a passage back to Ireland when it's sorted. A fit youngster like yeself is exactly what we're looking for.'

I eyed him up and down. Denis, the lad who'd befriended me at the port in Ireland, came over and asked if the man was troubling me. I said he wasn't but Denis still looked him in the eye and told him to scram before he thumped him.

The newcomer laughed. 'Listen, boyo, if ye know what's good for ye. Ye know where to find me. But I won't be here long. Just long enough.'

After he left, I filled Denis in on what the man had said. He took a breath and whistled for several seconds. He shook his head, his curly hair bobbing as he did so. 'Ye are bloody mad, fella. We're here now. We could have a goldmine at our feet.'

'Could,' I said, looking around half-heartedly. I stamped my foot. My boots squelched in the mud. 'Could. We've barely seen a dozen flakes of the stuff this past few months. What makes ye think we are going to make our fortunes here? At least in New Zealand we will get a passage back to England once we have dealt with these natives. That's what your man has been saying. He says the fighting there will be all over soon.'

Denis looked at me. 'But why would ye want to go home, man? There's nothing for us, ye must know that. The famine years might be over but there's nought back there. My family has nothin' but a patch of ground a chicken wouldn't even scratch on and they can't afford to pay the bailiff even for that, most months. There's no work except cutting peat at the bogs.'

I could hear what he was saying, though my family had done better than that. The Big House where I'd worked in the stables was situated on the best land in North Kerry. The cottage my family lived in might be small and overcrowded but it was nowhere near the bogs. I didn't want to belittle him so I said nothing in reply.

Denis grabbed my arm roughly and held me by my elbow.

'I was pleased to be out of the place and I sure as hell won't be racing back there. If ye had any brains nor would ye.'

I had never known him so angry. We both stood still, glaring at each other.

Denis let me go. He rubbed a mud-encrusted hand on his shirt, which was equally dirty – so dirty you couldn't see the colour of the material. 'What is it ye want to go back to?' He seemed curious now, not so angry. 'Sure, it's not some girlie, is it?'

Some girlie? What did he mean? He couldn't know about Eliza. I didn't want any mention of Eliza and me getting back to Ireland. Denis came from South Kerry but who knew who he might tell? He didn't strike me as someone who might be able to pen a letter but, then again, people had an odd way of hiding things about themselves. I kicked at a pile of mud before walking away. He didn't call after me.

I would need to get away from here if I were to keep things quiet. I decided to take up the auld fellow's offer. Later I went and found the man, and almost before I knew it, a small gang of us, swags on our backs, were marching away from the huts of the goldfields in the dead of night.

We had not gone far when a familiar voice shouted at me to wait.

'Denis,' I said when he caught up. 'Changed ye mind, eh?'

He swore at me and spittle landed on my cheek. 'Ye never said they were offering land out there at the end of your time of service. The fella told me.' He gestured towards our leader. 'Ye kept that to yeself.'

'He never said,' I told him. 'Only that the Government would pay for me to go back to Ireland.'

'Maybe because he told ye what ye wanted to hear,' Denis said grimly, 'but I'm happy to shoot a few native fellas if I get to live like a landlord at the end of it all. With a bunch of strong lads like us, it shouldn't take long to get the better of them.'

'Ye wish,' I said. Denis made me want to laugh. He was so sure of himself. Me, all I wanted was to do my job and get on that ship sailing back across the oceans to everything that mattered most to me.

Our new leader was calling out for us to get a move on and we hoisted our gear and headed for the docks. Bound for a place I'd never heard of called New Plymouth.

Our journey took us across heavy seas by sailing ship to a place called Nelson in the South Island of the country. My relief at being on dry land again after days at sea was short lived. Very soon after our arrival, we were led on to a steamer, the *Phoebe*, bound for the North Island. From there, we disembarked at the bustling port of New Plymouth. A magnificent snow-capped mountain loomed in the distance. Egmont, someone said it was called. As soon as we were off the steamer, three officers marched our motley group to the army camp on the edge of the town. There they kitted us out with blue serge jackets, trousers, work boots and heavy coats, which we had to carry neatly rolled and slung over our chests, as well as haversacks and water bottles.

'Where's our guns, man?' Denis muttered in my ear in Irish. I saw a corporal look in our direction and told him to shut up. We'd be in trouble before we had even begun.

Captain Henry Wright, our new commander, greeted us with scorn as we lined up in front of him. 'I asked for soldiers and get you lot instead. Riff raff.'

He'd got us all right, some of the men being penniless and drifting, found at ports around Australia. Others like Denis and me had tried their hand at goldmining without success. None of us were really cut out for battle, not in any organised way, at any rate.

The captain led us away from the township to a settlement called Omata, the trail through thick vegetation taking us almost half a day. He set us making repairs to a redoubt and barricades that had been damaged not long before in an attack by the natives. 'You'll be building plenty of these soon,' he told us as we marched back to camp in the evening.

At night, a few men took off to the town to get drunk or find women, or both. 'Plenty of them hanging around the places the lads go to,' Denis assured me. 'Why don't ye come out with us?'

I refused his offer at first but I finally gave in one night and allowed the gang to drag me off to a pub in a deserted part of the town. The army men were welcome – and given a place to hide out back should any military police come looking for drunk soldiers. Any who were found would face a court martial and be confined to barracks for up to seven days.

'Get yeself a nice girl,' Denis urged.

I pretended to like one of the girls he pointed out to me. 'Aye, she's a great lass,' I told him but when he headed over to another, who seemed to recognise him straight away, I took myself to the back of the bar and hid there.

A middle-aged man with a weathered face, who was sitting on a stool in the corner, took it on himself to buy me a pint. 'Franklin Taylor is the name,' he said, reaching out to shake my hand. 'Me and the missus and the children are staying at the stockade here till our house is built. We've got some land allocated out that way. Near the coast.'

'Michael Flynn,' I said. 'Pleased to meet you.'

'I can see you're a soldier and all,' he said. 'Youse chaps do good work for us. Keeping us settlers and our women and children safe while we break in the land.'

I found myself ordering another after that. And another. When I wandered back outside there was no sign of Denis and I was now drunk. I lurched towards a bench to prop myself against when a man, a giant red-faced hulk, came at me out of nowhere.

'You been staring at my woman,' he bellowed.

I glanced behind me but couldn't see a soul. 'No, it was not me, sir,' I responded carefully. It was time to make a move. I headed towards a step and was suddenly being propelled downwards. An angry face peered at me, inches from mine. 'Listen here, young pipsqueak,' the ruffian said, grabbing my shoulders.

He was a great big fellow. I was too drunk to fend him off so I closed my eyes, waiting for the punch, wondering if he had a knife on him. I thought about fighting back and how I could do so but all my energy was gone. The man was pulled off me, his body thrust into a corner, and a punch delivered to his soft flabby belly. He let out a moan but didn't get up. I looked up to see who had rescued me.

'Thanks, Denis,' I said weakly. 'You know, I was well and good. I was all set to handle it.' Another lad standing beside Denis laughed. 'Sure, you were,' he said.

Denis pulled me up so I was standing. 'What happened to the girlie?' he asked. 'Did ye steal the big bastard's wee woman?'

I didn't answer him.

Denis flung his arm around my shoulder. 'Back to camp for us.'

We sang Irish ditties all the way there. I wanted to thank Denis properly for saving my life but the words didn't come out. I owed him one. Denis stopped mid-song and belched. Another time, I thought. He was an odd kind of lad but a good sort.

The very next day the captain announced he had given up waiting for properly trained reinforcements from Wellington.

'You're a bunch of idiots but you will have to do,' he shouted at us as we lined up before him on the grass that morning. 'There's fighting to be done.'

He led our now-armed unit away from the camp and the town with its little wooden houses and buildings. We passed by empty patches of earth where trees had been cut down to make way for even more buildings.

As the hours passed, the countryside around us changed greatly. The further we ventured through dense forest, the more fear prickled my skin. We waded through small icy streams, our boots becoming wet and swollen. The thickets of trees and damp, hanging foliage made it difficult to see more than a couple of feet in front of us as we climbed uphill in single file on the narrow tracks. Flashes of lightning were closely followed by a rumble of thunder. Torrents of water forced their way through the thick canopy of trees onto us and soon we were soaking wet, our uniforms hanging heavily on us. Huge flax bushes scratched our faces as we forced our way through them. I felt chilled to the bone.

'Watch yeself, lad,' Denis warned as a knotty root protruding from the ground nearly caused me to trip.

On we trudged, the armed and uniformed men marching or riding in front. Behind them at the rear were those less fit for the job, the newcomers and the overweight men, tagging along in front of the pack horses.

We continued in this manner until we reached a spot where we set up camp and erected tents. As we ate a meal that night prepared by the camp cooks, we learned from our compatriots what tricks our opposition might use against our mighty gun power. One of the more experienced men, an Englishman with a high-handed manner who had fought up north, warned us, 'They're determined and strong fighters, these men, and they won't let anyone stand in their way. They'll not give in easily. You paddies mustn't let your guard down or they'll have you beat.'

'We're hardly likely to,' Denis said with great bravado. 'Mick here and I know what we're doing, don't we lad?'

'We do,' I said, hoping to sound convincing.

'Don't listen to a word the rascal says,' Denis muttered to me in Irish, nudging my elbow. 'He's trying to unnerve ye.'

'Sure,' I said back. 'I know that.'

Others also had stories of war to scare us with but most of the time was dull enough and we spent it building stockades and bridges in places we visited. The few hardened soldiers among us liked to mutter about the waste of their energy and training. They were eager to go out to fight the Māori and being put to 'menial' tasks like these was frustrating. Even Denis had begun to say the same.

One evening when we stopped to build camp, Captain Wright told us he'd received word the local tribe in this area had appropriated gunpowder and firearms. 'They've been stealing horses from the new settlers,' he said. The settlers, desperate to stay on their recently acquired land, were frightened and demanding protection. 'We'll show these thieves,' Captain Wright told us, before ordering us to get some rest and be prepared to be woken after a few hours of sleep.

At three a.m., we set off, single file again, keeping our voices down, marching by the light of fire sticks and sometimes the moon. We headed towards one of the villages the horse thieves had come from. We crept up to the edges and surrounded the area. I anticipated sudden movement and yelling and warriors with muskets and bayonets; my heart flooded with both fear and a readiness to attack but a warning must have gone out ahead of time. There was no one there. The captain shouted an order and the men at the front surged forward, using their bayonets to destroy the vegetable gardens and palisades at the front of the pā.

Others from our troop tossed lit sticks towards the thatched roofs of the dwellings within and we watched until the huts themselves caught fire in a blaze of red. A cheer went up at their total destruction. The order to turn back came and we marched in single file and a strange silence towards our camp.

Back at the camp, the cooks provided us with a substantial breakfast. Despite it being near morning, as we sat around the campfire there was a singsong – rowdy Irish ballads – and a portion of booze for each man. The captain shut us down after a time and told us to get some sleep while we could. Tomorrow was another day and we didn't know what that would bring.

'Do ye think the people whose village we destroyed might seek retaliation?' I asked Denis as we headed back to our tents.

He nodded grimly. 'Aye, likely as but even so, we'll beat 'em at their own game. Surprise 'em every time. We're soldiers now, you and me. We must push on. This is what we're here for.' He tossed a few logs onto the fire near the tents where, being damp, it merely spluttered. He might have thought I was cowardly and afraid, because he then added, awkwardly, 'I've got ye back, lad.'

It struck me he said this because he was a few years older than me – and likely thought he was more experienced in the way of the world but we'd both come from small, isolated villages, and besides that, I didn't want his pity. 'This is our job now,' I said stiffly. 'Protecting the settlers on their land and making damn sure the natives stay in line.'

'Damn right,' Denis said. 'Good man.'

When he headed into his tent, I remained outside, looking up to the lightening sky for a sign of the star I'd seen previously. Ruru, an old Māori man, had pointed it out to me when he saw me outside the tent one morning before dawn at the camp in New Plymouth. The old man was a fixture at the camp, bringing basketloads of a native vegetable, kūmara, to trade for cash.

Whenever I saw him after that, as long as there was no one around I plied him with questions about his life and that of his people before the settlers and army men like me had arrived. His responses set me thinking but I knew it would be unwise to mention this to any of the men I shared the camp with. This morning, however, there was no sign of the star.

A few days later Denis was subdued and not himself. As we marched close together I could see the steam rise off his uniform. I wondered if he had got into the ale the previous night and was hungover but after we had progressed some distance he spoke to me in Irish, his voice low so the others couldn't hear.

'I've been talking to Frank,' he began. Frank was one of the lads, a tough character from a place called Lancashire in England, who had already fought up north with the army. 'He's been telling me some stories about what these warriors could do to us that would make your blood curdle. A year back, further round this same mountain, men from another troop were ambushed. Two were killed and their hearts cut out. Some kind of new religious belief in that tribe.'

'I've not heard this.' I was sick to my stomach by his words. 'Do ye believe him? Maybe he was just trying to put the fear into ye, making himself look a big man experienced in fighting these rebels. Boasting to show he's not afraid like he thinks we will be.'

Denis shrugged. 'Think what you want but that's what he said.'

I thought this over. 'Even so, all the more reason for us to defeat them first.' I couldn't let him know that all I wanted was to get through this campaign. Once it was over I'd get myself back to the port and bribe a sailor to let me stow away on a ship heading for England. I could only do that if I made sure I didn't get badly injured in these skirmishes with these bloody natives.

When he had moved forward, I let my fingers wander around in my jacket pocket feeling for the gold necklace Eliza had given me. Back at the goldfields, I had taken it to Joe the Chinaman in his little hut. I had asked Joe to fix the broken chain on it. He didn't speak much English but just in case I gave him an extra coin to keep this to himself. I had made sure, after he fixed it, to hide the necklace in the hem of my trouser leg. When we got given our uniforms at the camp I had shifted it to the top pocket of my jacket. It was less safe but with the pocket buttoned, it was close to my heart. Like Eliza.

IMOGEN
Taranaki 2018

The route to my grandfather's farm was along a coastal road. It was raining and I couldn't see any sign of the mountain. The windscreen wipers were making a screeching noise, nearly deafening me.

I had promised myself, as I started the engine of the small red rental car, I wouldn't waste my energy during this trip on my now ex-boyfriend. Instead I would focus on what I could say when I met my grandfather for the first time. My mind, however, refused to obey this instruction. Instead, it kept returning to the confrontation with Simon.

A black Jeep shot past me in a cloud of diesel fumes. Slowing, I pulled to the left to let a milk tanker go by. Its big wheels sloshed water on my little car as it thundered past, scaring me. It ploughed ahead and sped through a couple of small settlements. I followed in its wake.

A steep slope down a hill led into a small township where a sign for a café caught my attention. I stopped my car and parked on the side of the road. At the café counter, I ordered a coffee and a big breakfast and went to a covered area outside to sit at a table. A couple of outdoor heaters warmed the open space. The only other customer was a burly man in his fifties with a pockmarked face and a tattoo on the side of his neck of a single scrolled word. I tried to make out what it said but the letters ran down into the top of his black tee-shirt. The man lifted his head and met my eyes. His expression hardened.

Avoiding his gaze, I picked up the newspaper and scanned it for news articles by Shelley, the reporter I had spoken to. A small one reported on the prices cattle had fetched at an auction in a place called Stratford – hardly earth-shattering – no wonder she had been so interested in what it was like working in the media in Melbourne.

At the end of the road opposite the cafe, grey wild sea and white waves filled the narrow viewpoint. The beach was popular when it was warm, the waitress told me as she delivered my order. She was from Germany, on a working holiday. 'They say this coast is a great place for surfing as it's "wet, wild and wicked". Not many places where you can climb a mountain and then swim at the beach on the same day. Of course, now we are in winter …'

The waitress went across to the other table. 'Are you staying around here?' she asked the man.

He looked up from his newspaper. He didn't smile. 'No. Further around the coast,' he said gesturing towards the direction. He looked back down in a deliberate fashion.

'Have you climbed the mountain yet?' she asked, seemingly unaware of his signal the conversation had ended.

'Not yet,' he said. 'The weather's been too bad. I'll save it for a good day.'

He stood up, said a curt goodbye to her and headed out of the café and down the sloped entrance. As he walked past me he pulled out his mobile and spoke into it. A few minutes later a motorcycle engine roared into life, releasing a raw metallic smell into the air, then it was gone and there was just me and the waitress.

She picked up the cup and empty plate from his table. 'I get bored, so, I chat to the customers. They don't all like it.' She nodded towards where the man had sat.

I smiled at her, she seemed friendly and kind. 'It must get isolated in this little place in the winter. Not many customers.'

Shortly after, I returned to the rental car. I drove through another town before turning off towards the lower ranges of the mountain. I would've expected to see more of the mountain but it seemed to be skulking behind an impenetrable shroud. Dense, dark-green rainforest covered the hills, giving off a foreboding air. I wondered what my mother had thought when she arrived here; she would've been only a child.

A sign for a bridge loomed up ahead and I pulled over to get out. Though a long way down and not remarkably high, the river below had a strong current and was strewn with rocks. The name on the sign was fitting – Boulder River. Someone must have died near the bridge as there was a makeshift memorial with a bunch of red plastic roses placed on it. Whoever the unknown person was, I hoped they were now at peace.

I got back in the car and continued driving. Further along, I passed the entrance to a smaller road on the right-hand side and then shortly after that caught sight of the orange roof Shelley had mentioned. I pulled into the next gateway. The gate was open and a hand-painted sign at the front of the property said, 'Keep Out'. I got out of the car and went closer to read the scrawled writing beneath it: 'Owner has gun and is not afraid to use it.'

I smelt smoke and saw black fumes unfurling in the distance across the fields. My leather boots squelched on the muddy track. My body froze. It was as if I had been here before and knew this place, its moods. It wasn't a good place. A heavy vehicle had left big tyre marks on a track leading to the rear of the farm. I was tempted to turn the car around and drive back the way I had come but, instead, I made myself get in and drive along the track.

A dilapidated house standing partway along the track didn't make me feel any better. It had faded paint on the outside walls and several missing weatherboards at one end. A veranda wrapped around the side and extended to where the front of the house faced the road.

Through another open gateway was a paddock with two fire trucks parked beside each other. I got out of the car and began to walk towards a group of people in protective gear gathered around an old man who was emitting a series of hacking coughs. He was a big man with broad shoulders. He wore a bush shirt and had a reddish, weather-beaten face and white hair, uncombed and unruly.

As I approached, I could hear someone urging the old man to go and get checked out by a doctor. 'All that smoke. Did your hands get burnt?'

'Go to hell,' the old man responded, coughing some more. 'I'm fine.'

A silence followed. The men stared at me and after a time, one of them spoke. 'From the newspaper, are you? That was quick.' He looked around at the others. 'Okay, so who phoned them?'

'You can all get the hell out of here.' The old man seemed to direct his comment at me as well as the others. 'Get off my property.'

The fire crew chief shook his head. 'Not till we're sure the fire is out and I mean it about getting checked out at the medical centre.'

'That's madness,' the old man spluttered. 'I'm not leaving here till you find out who did it.'

'That's up to the police,' the fire chief said. 'You can talk to them.'

'I've told you,' the old man said. 'Someone came in here and set my hedges on fire. And that stand of trees over there. They would've had to use an accelerant.' I saw trees looming on the other side of the paddock, most of them now blackened.

'No sign of arson, no petrol containers and no smell of petrol,' the fire chief said. 'Our concern is the embers. We don't want them to reignite. We need to keep it damped down.' He looked beyond me and waved at someone who was approaching.

The someone had a woolly beanie pulled down over their ears, their hair hidden. They wore oversized gumboots and a man's heavy plaid jacket and stomped through the mud in the paddock towards us, breathing heavily. In a woman's voice the someone said, 'Jack. What's happening? What have you done?' The word 'now' might have remained unsaid, but it was implicit.

His breathing still ragged and rasping, the old man roared, 'It was NOT me, Molly. Would you look at the damage? Why would I do such a thing?' and started to cough again. He said 'thing' like 'ting'. The Irish way.

The woman sighed. 'You're a law unto yourself. Was it that you wanted that pile of gorse gone, and you've gone and done it yourself?'

He stamped his foot and mud splashed outwards. He was surprisingly agile for an old man. 'No. It will be the same bastards as terrorised my calves. The same ones, I bet. They should be strung up, and they would be if the law round here wasn't such an ass. And you can report that, too, in that rag of yours,' he said to me.

'Look.' I'd found my voice after all this time. 'I'm not from the newspaper.'

Now I had the attention of all the men and of Molly, the

woman in the gumboots. A drop of rain splashed onto my hair, another stronger one on my face.

'Then who are you?' the fire chief asked. 'Just out of interest.'

'I think I'm his granddaughter.' It came out louder than intended. Another raindrop landed on my cheek.

'Right,' Molly said, eyeing me up and down carefully. 'His granddaughter, eh? First I've heard of you.'

'Same here,' the old man said. 'You couldn't make it up. The hedge on fire, and now this.'

I looked at the man who I realised, was my grandfather, though 'Jack' seemed a more appropriate way to address him. He squinted at me, head tilted to one side, as if framing me within a photograph, marking off a mental checklist as to what he might be looking for.

'Who's your mother?'

I told him.

'And where did she come from?'

I named the village in Ireland I'd seen on my mother's passport when I sneaked a look in her box of papers one time.

Jack listened carefully. 'Aye,' he said to Molly. 'Could be she's right enough.'

Molly kicked a stone with her boot, frowning. Jack raised an eyebrow as if to check what she believed.

'All right, look,' I said, pulling my phone from the pocket of my jacket. I showed him the scanned photo of the inside page of my passport with my name on it.

'Maguire,' Jack mused. 'You don't have your father's name?'

'I don't know it,' I said coldly. I hadn't meant to say it like that. When I had imagined asking him about my father, it had been very different, not this angry response.

The old man's harsh expression relented briefly. 'Aye, that sounds like Aoife right enough. Probably said mind your business if you asked her.' He cleared his throat as if he were going to hack a wad of disgusting mucus at my feet and shot me another icy stare. 'You don't much have the look of her though, I'll say that,' he said, doubt again in his voice.

Another emotion pulled at me. Disappointment at his lack of welcome?

He frowned. 'You'll be after something, I suppose.' He made that noise with his throat again and this time twisted his head and spat on the ground. I tried not to look but too late, I had seen a shot of yellow mucus. 'So, go on then.'

The words startled me before I realised he meant me to tell him what I was after. 'I thought you might need some assistance,' I said, thinking how formal it sounded. Had I taken the words directly from that man Michael Flynn himself? Maybe I should have hugged the old man instead, but it was too late now.

Molly made a movement towards me. 'We haven't been properly introduced. I'm Molly Hall. I live next door, with my son.' She jerked her thumb in the direction I'd come from on the road. Presumably, she meant the house with the orange roof. 'Best get you all back to the house before the rain starts. We'll make our own way back. No point us getting cow muck inside your flash car.' She reached out for the old man. 'Come on now, Jack. We'll have a cup of tea.'

All the steam had gone out of him. Around me the rest of the fire crew muttered among themselves, trying to decide if the sprinkle of rain would be enough to dampen the remains of the fire, weighing up the risks of walking away and then having it flare up again. Should they leave one truck on the site with a crew for a little longer?

'You've done a great job, guys,' Molly called out over her shoulder.

Jack set off at a quick stride. He even beat me back to his

house and stood outside on the side veranda beneath the sagging roof waiting for me. 'Well, then,' he said. He put his two fingers in his mouth and whistled. I looked at him questioningly and then a large black and white dog came from somewhere around the back.

Jack bellowed a command and the dog paused, watching us both. Jack said another word or two, in an offhand aside to the dog which stayed there, waiting at a distance, still watching me. Jack called out, 'Good lad, Bandit,' and tossed a bone. The dog grabbed it and disappeared around the back of an old shed, presumably to its kennel.

Jack beckoned for me to follow him further to a door at the front of the house. He opened the door, which was unlocked, and walked ahead of me down a long hallway and into a kitchen at the rear. Stopping suddenly, he looked hard at me as if trying to work out who I was.

'I'm Imogen,' I prompted him. 'Your granddaughter.'

Jack frowned. 'Yes, yes, I know, you said that. What do you take me for? Stupid? Well,' he gestured towards an electric kettle on the bench. 'Make yourself useful. You can make a bloody cup of tea, can't you? Or didn't your mother teach you anything?'

I felt a rush of heat go to my face. No wonder my mother disowned you, I almost said, but Molly came in the door then. It stopped me blurting out words I might have regretted.

Molly was followed by a boy of seventeen or so. 'I had to pick up a part for the truck,' he said to Jack. 'Missed all the fun, eh?'

Molly took off her beanie and looked younger than I first thought, possibly in her forties. 'This is my son, Daniel. You've come all this way from Australia to see your grandfather?' She appeared to emphasise the last word for Daniel's benefit.

'Never asked her to,' Jack said. 'Never even knew she existed but what the hell, she's here now.'

I cleared my throat to respond and decided against it. I really should have booked a room at the motel I'd seen near the café where I had stopped off. That would have been the sensible thing to do.

'She's come all this way to visit you, Jack,' Molly said again. She tapped Jack on his arm as if reprimanding a child. She went over to the kitchen counter and switched the kettle on, took several cups and saucers from the cupboard and placed them on the table, before returning for a packet of gingernut biscuits, which she tipped onto a plate. 'Tea will be a minute.'

Daniel sat down and took a biscuit. It made a loud crunching noise as he ate it. His gaze was direct, almost rude. 'So, what brought you over here? Now, I mean?' I guessed he meant after all this time. I looked back at him.

'Daniel.' Molly's tone was even sterner. 'None of your business.'

'Okay, okay. Just asking.' Daniel continued to stare at me. 'I'll need to get my stuff from the living room.'

Molly must have seen my look of surprise. 'Daniel stayed the last couple of nights here with Jack.'

The kettle boiled and switched itself off. Molly went over to the counter and poured the boiling water into a teapot. She returned to the table with it.

'Jack thought there had been people marching across the paddocks at night,' Daniel said to me. He was in no hurry to leave.

His mother glowered at him, glanced towards Jack again.

'Like men to battle,' the old man said, now suddenly paying attention to the conversation. He reached across the table for a packet of tobacco and papers to roll himself a cigarette. 'Swags of them. Passing through.'

'And did you see anything?' I asked Daniel, hoping I didn't sound too sceptical.

'Nope. Nothing.'

Molly poured a cup of tea and handed it to Jack. He took a large swig. 'Not enough milk,' he said ungraciously. 'What's so difficult about making a cup of tea right?'

Molly picked up the jug and splashed a little more into the cup. I was tempted to roll my eyes at her. She passed me the teapot so I could pour my own. She and I sipped our tea.

Daniel broke the silence. 'But I did fall asleep on the couch. Not to say they weren't out there. Might've put the buggers off though, them knowing I was here.' It could've been Jack talking.

Was he serious? He was just a boy. He wouldn't scare anyone.

Molly turned towards me, away from Jack, then lowered her voice. 'We think it's just some school kids. Holiday time, they get bored.' She sipped her tea again.

'Have you spoken to the police?' I asked.

Jack scowled. 'Police. Useless buggers. They couldn't hunt down the bastards who stole my calves so why would I trust them? And as for that local cop, the new one. He's really a city boy.'

'Right,' Daniel said offhandedly. He took another biscuit and bit into it.

Jack placed the cigarette he'd rolled between two fingers, and stood up. He grabbed the newspaper and his cup of tea from the table. 'Well then,' he said, leaving the room.

'Time for us to get going. Grab your stuff, Daniel,' Molly said, turning to me. 'I'll put my number in your phone for you. If you need to know anything, we live close by. I work at the vet's in the afternoons but otherwise I'm around.'

While we exchanged numbers, I heard Jack heading along the hallway towards the front door. 'Daniel,' he called over his shoulder. 'Make sure that bloody rifle is near the back door. For when those bastards come back. And they will.'

Molly handed me back my phone and we exchanged a glance. I hoped she couldn't read my thoughts. What the hell was I doing here, intending to spend my days and nights with some crusty old guy in a neglected house far out in the countryside? A curmudgeon with a gun and a grudge? Would it have been any better when my mother lived here as a child? Was it any wonder my mother now chose to live thousands of kilometres away in the red centre of Australia, as far from this place as she could be?

AOIFE
Taranaki 1976

Aoife's granny used to say that Aoife was an old soul; that she had lived before. That she knew things she couldn't have known. That she saw people she shouldn't have – like the time when she was four and described an old woman she'd seen in the hallway at Granny's house. Granny declared it was Aoife's great-grand-mother who had died long ago. 'Coming back to check on us,' Granny said.

Aoife wasn't so sure about all this stuff. Not at all. Surely, if she had known so much, she wouldn't have let Mam and Da bring her to this strange new country last year. A place where Christmas Day was hot as hell, as Mam said, and boys went barefoot to school. Neither would she have wanted to come here two weeks before her tenth birthday.

The first day she went to the new school in the new country, Mam had gripped her elbow firmly as she got out of the car. 'Don't forget. Your name is Aoife and you come from Ireland. No need to say where. No one will care.'

When Aoife went to open her mouth to reply, Mam cut her short. 'No one will have heard of our wee village and sure, haven't they themselves got the strangest sounding place names here, anyway? No, Ireland will do fine.' She frowned and looked hard at Aoife. 'Even that might be too much.'

Aoife looked back at her mother. She had no idea what she meant.

In the end, when Aoife got to her classroom she didn't need to say much because the teacher, Miss Anderson, said it for her. 'This is Aoife, and she comes from Ireland.' Just like that. She even said her name right – Ee-fuh.

They'd come by boat from Cork to Liverpool in England and from there on an even bigger ship to New Zealand. After six weeks on the ship, they had arrived at the wharf in Wellington at the beginning of winter. They went by bus to New Plymouth and it took a long time.

Mr Murphy, who was somehow distantly related to Da, met them and drove them around the coast road to Wexford where Da was to help look after the farm for him. When they arrived at the farm, Mr Murphy drove the car through a gateway and along a muddy track, stopping the car outside an old farmhouse. He said it was his house but he'd moved to the farm cottage along the road a little.

'No, no. We can't have you being inconvenienced by us,' Mam said at once. She looked at Da to back her up. He didn't say anything but after Mr Murphy had gone, Da told Mam Mr Murphy didn't want to live in his old house any longer. When they had stopped to fill up with petrol, he'd told Da there were too many ghosts.

'You're joking,' Mam said. She was casting her gaze around the kitchen as she spoke. The lino floor looked as if it hadn't been scrubbed down in a long time.

'I asked him if he was. He said no.'

'Dear God. Ye bring us all this way only to make us live in a house with a bad legacy. Are ye mad? Or just some of the time?' She sighed. 'Right. Do I ask the priest to come in and bless it then? Have him sprinkle the old holy water around?'

'No,' Da said firmly. 'None of that old claptrap. We're not in Ireland now. They won't be up for doing such a thing here. Keep your mouth shut, woman. I'm of the opinion Murphy has had too much drink taken. It has befuddled his mind, that's all. No wonder them back home said he needed help.'

'The house is cold enough,' Mam said, pulling her coat tight. 'It would chill you to the bone. It's all these draughty timber boards. The wind is fair rattling through the window frames and that fireplace will do no good. I want my old stone house in Ireland.'

A week later, Mr Murphy told Mam and Da he was off on a trip around the South Island. He called it a tiki tour although he was actually going to be taking buses with a bunch of strangers but he sounded pleased to be leaving. Thinking he might say more about the bad things that had gone on in the house, Aoife followed him back outside. She was sorry to find he didn't have any further comments to make.

The farm was at the foot of a mountain range. It was the highest mountain Aoife had ever seen. Mr Murphy had said at this time of the year it was often covered in snow, right down to the fields. The wooden farmhouse stood in the path of icy cold blasts of wind which raced down the mountain and across the pastures to the sea in the far distance.

When Aoife woke in the night, the eerie howl of the wind or the heavy beat of the rain on the iron roof kept her awake. Like a banshee crying out, Mam said to Da one morning when they were having breakfast. Da had crammed crispy bacon slices into his mouth and didn't speak. Mam had made porridge as well. She shivered and pulled the sleeves of her woollen jersey down over her knuckles. She really hated being here in this strange country with the mountain looming over them. Aoife wanted to cry too, but what was the use?

'I wish we could go back,' Mam said, handing Da another slice of buttered toast.

Aoife was silent, pretending she wasn't there. If she agreed with Mam then it might make Da feel bad. The worst part was they had left in the middle of the night to go to the port and now she didn't know what her best friends Lucy and Emer would think of her for not telling them she was going away. How could she when she herself hadn't known?

Da said they'd be mad to go back; there was nothing at home for them. 'Look out now at what we've got here.' He swept a hand towards the window. Out in the paddock young steers were munching on green grass. He didn't seem to see the mud and runny cattle muck on the track that Aoife had to avoid each morning on her way to catch the bus.

Mam said nothing. She poked her fingers out through the sleeves of her jersey and studied her short fingernails as if fascinated by them.

'And anyway,' Da said. 'You know we can't go back, so.' He took a breath as if he were going to add a further comment. Then he caught Aoife's eye and clenched his lips shut. The uneven pink scar above the thickness of Da's left eyebrow stood out. He'd got into a fight a long time ago; someone bad had hit him with a broken beer bottle.

They had not been long at the farm when Mam took Aoife for a walk through the fields. Aoife knew to keep her distance from the big boxthorn hedges that bordered most of the paddocks on the farm. The huge hedges didn't bow in the strong salty winds. They were spiky, some of them with red berries, and had long nasty thorns that could cut into you if you went too close. There were also bits of rock that littered the paddocks and would stub your toe – stones that had crept their way up to the surface of the paddock from deep in the soil. From the eruptions long ago, Mam said.

That day Mam had been determined to make it to the back of the farm. Aoife dragged behind her reluctantly as Mam hurried them on. Across the paddocks to the side of the farm Aoife could see a swamp set in a gully and she fixed her gaze on it. From where she stood the swamp looked thick and dense as if toads lived in its murky water. She was sure she could hear their croaking. The swamp had big flax bushes and trees surrounding it that must have been there forever. Mam said it was dangerous and she wasn't to play there. As if she would. She followed Mam across a small wooden bridge that rattled as they walked over the stream.

They came to the end of the farm where there was a steep incline with ridges on the side. Mam said the Māori people used to grow their vegetable crops here, long ago. The man who ran the village shop had said it was mainly kūmara when Mam asked. Mam climbed over the wire fence first and went ahead of Aoife, breathing heavily with each step. From the top they looked out to a wild grey sea way down in the distance.

'Look,' Mam said. 'If you stare hard enough, in a straight line, there's the shores of Ireland out there.'

While Aoife was at school Mam must have sneaked away to this spot to stare longingly out to sea. Aoife had never done much geography at school, even so, she wasn't sure Dingle Bay really was where Mam imagined it to be.

As she lay in bed at night, Aoife often thought if they'd stayed in Ireland, things might not have been so bad. Back home, she had Lucy and Emer whom she had known from nursery school, and their mams had been friends. Lucy and Emer had mams like hers and fathers who were like Da. Da could be very funny when he was with his friends – the boyos, he called them – but then sometimes he drank too much beer or found the hard stuff that Mam usually hid around the house and he would start getting angry over a thing that had happened and would begin to shout. Back in Ireland, her friends all talked the same and understood each other but here in Wexford, there was Suzie Barker and her gang of tittering friends to worry about.

Suzie Barker lived further up the road. Da had told Mam that three or four Barker brothers owned a big sprawling farm under the mountain ranges – acre upon acre, he said – and they all had their own houses spread out on it. Like a stronghold. Like those big estates back in Ireland that the English landlords owned all those years ago. Them with their ill-begotten wealth. Mam shushed him and said to not get himself over-excited about things beyond his control.

On Aoife's first day at school, Suzie Barker and a bunch of other girls had walked up to her, all staring curiously. Suzie asked her if she thought Miss Anderson was pretty. When Aoife said, 'Yes,' because what else could she say, Suzie put on an Irish-sounding voice and said, 'Oh, do you tink so?' and 'We tink so, too,' and laughed. The other girls joined in.

When they were sitting outside on the benches for lunch a few days later Suzie spoke up in her strong voice which carried across the schoolyard in the bitter wind. Aoife heard the words 'ginger' and hair that looked 'dirty'. 'They call them tinkers over there, my nana says.' The other girls laughed, though not so much that they'd draw attention to themselves.

Suzie took a breath and added, again loud enough for Aoife to hear her, 'And they've come over here to squat on Murphy's land like the tinkers do in Ireland and Murphy's too drunk to know what's going on.'

So that was how it was going to go. Somehow the Barkers had already decided her family were travellers like those people in a tatty old Enid Blyton book in the bookcase at the back of the classroom. She'd sat and read it during quiet reading time.

Their teacher Miss Anderson was in her first year out of training college. She wore short skirts and smart shoes. Miss Anderson's heels clattered around the wooden floor of the classroom as she stuck up posters and took down others. After school she always had one of the boys put a big pile of exercise books and old cardboard and her collection of felt tips in a bin in the back seat of her little red Mini. The principal, Mr Kirton, stayed till the buses arrived and then left quickly. He never took anything home.

One afternoon there was a maths test. Matiu Henry, who sat across from Aoife, picked up his pencil, licked the end of it, and began to write, then he slid sideways, knocking the girl next to him before falling on the floor. He trembled and went all sweaty and Miss Anderson ran across the room and pushed the girl he'd bumped into out of the way, shoving away the chair with her on it, bent down to Matiu and touched his arm. He was shivering and flailing but when she touched him, he went quiet. Miss Anderson told a boy to run and get the principal.

When Mr Kirton came, he got two boys to help him lay Matiu on his side. After a time, Matiu woke up again and gave an embarrassed smile. Mr Kirton told two of the boys to take him to the sick bay for a rest. Miss Anderson went pink and trembled as well, rather like Matiu had. Mr Kirton gave Miss Anderson a cross look and said he'd send the school secretary to mind the class. 'Go to the staffroom and have a cup of tea,' he said. As she turned away, he added, 'He fits sometimes.' As if this was the most normal thing in the world, Aoife thought.

One Friday, Miss Anderson placed a box of books from the

National Library on a spare desk and began telling the class about the early settlers of their district and the nearby town. She pulled out one of the books and held up a page showing a stern-looking man and woman, and several children in old-fashioned clothes, outside a small timber house with smoke curling up from the chimney.

'Next week, you'll read these books and then write about the obstacles these pioneers faced making a home in their new land,' Miss Anderson said.

Suzie was the first to put up her hand, waving her arm about, her long blonde plaits swinging as she did so. 'Our family were pioneers,' she said. 'My great-great-great …' Suzie held out her hand and stretched her fingers as if she were counting. 'I can't remember but it's a long way back, maybe six generations. Dad says when they came the land was nothing but scrub. All bush. They had to live in a camp with the soldiers to protect them and go out each day to burn off the scrub and turn it into paddocks. Grandpa has photographs on the wall at his house.'

She took a breath and looked around at the rest of the class. 'And the park by the cemetery, that's called Barker Park, after Dad's great-great …' She stretched out her hand again. 'Lots anyway. And the Barkers became the first doctors and lawyers here, and one was a member of Parliament …' She took another breath. She could almost have added, 'So there.' She had a triumphant-sounding voice. 'They were the first settlers around here.'

'Well, thank you, Suzie,' Miss Anderson said quickly. She looked around the room. 'Anyone else?'

Matiu coughed loudly then lifted the lid of his desk and let it slam down. 'Not the first.'

Before Miss Anderson could say a word, Suzie was in full swing again, oblivious of the teacher frowning at her. 'Anyway,' she narrowed her eyes and glared at Matiu, 'my dad said he'd take his three-oh-three to anyone who even thinks of trespassing on our land. Anyone. He says, let them try.'

'That's enough, Suzie. Let's listen to someone else now.'

The outside bell rang.

'Interval,' Miss Anderson said, in her high-fluted voice. She gave a small sigh. 'Aoife, would you mind setting out these books?' Her shoes clicked as she headed down the corridor to the staffroom.

Aoife unpacked the box of books, taking a good look at each before arranging them on the table, and went outside to the playground, passing Matiu who was sitting on the steps by himself eating a sandwich.

'It's not theirs,' he said, the sound muffled by the bread. 'I can go where I want.'

Aoife pretended she hadn't heard him. She thought about going over to join a group of girls from the younger class who were playing hopscotch. Before she took a step, one of the group clustered around Suzie said in a jokey voice, 'Here comes the ginger-haired witch.'

Suzie looked up and the others laughed, glancing across at Aoife. Suzie had a secret to share – she always had a secret – and the girls turned away again and leaned in close. Aoife pretended she couldn't see them.

After school on Friday it was Aoife's turn for blackboard-cleaning duty. She looked up to see Matiu's grandfather in the doorway. He was a tall thin man holding a carved walking stick. Aoife had seen him before. He lived in a white house with a blue-painted roof next door to the marae at the end of town. Not many people lived there but when an event or meeting was going on, there would be lots of cars parked outside.

Once when Da had been driving her home from school, they saw people standing and sitting on the front porch of the main building. As Da slowed down, Aoife caught a glimpse through an open door of a coffin surrounded by a group of women wearing black. On the road outside the marae a tourist on a bicycle got off so he could take a photograph. Someone came out to the entrance and waved him away. The tourist got back on his bike. Da crossed himself before they drove off.

Outside the classroom door, Mr Henry bent down – it seemed to take him a long time – and took off his boots. He wore thick grey work socks like Da's. Miss Anderson, who was marking their books and sighing from time to time, must have seen his shadow. She made a little startled sound like a baby bird surprised in a nest.

'Mr Henry. How nice to see you again.' Her voice wavered.

She looked over and saw Aoife and their eyes met. It was as if Miss Anderson didn't want Aoife to leave. She wanted her to stay, to be right there scrubbing at the board where all the ancient chalk marks had made it faded and hard to write on. Miss Anderson smiled brightly, sat up straighter in her chair and indicated the visitor's chair beside the desk. Mr Henry sat down. The stick made a thumping noise.

Miss Anderson said to Aoife. 'How about you give the dusters a banging outside on the concrete?'

As Aoife went outside and banged the dusters, she heard Mr Henry clear his throat, though she couldn't hear what he was saying because his voice was low. Now and then, he banged the floor with his stick, occasionally raising his voice like Da did when he was angry. Aoife stopped what she was doing to hear him better.

'These children need to acknowledge the history of the land they live on. They can't do that if they don't know it.'

There was a pause, then Miss Anderson said in a squeaky voice, 'I appreciate what you are saying.' She paused for breath.

'I'll need to check the syllabus. It may be covered next year. I'm new to teaching. This is my first year.'

'You could teach them the correct name for this place, for a start,' Mr Henry said. He uttered a long rhythmic-sounding word, before banging the stick on the floor again.

Aoife's hand slipped and the duster fell into the bushes outside. White chalk dust floated up. Mr Henry came through the open door and sat down on the outside veranda to put his boots back on.

He looked up at her and said in his soft voice, 'You're new around here. Matiu has told me your father is the big Irishman.'

Aoife nodded.

'Well,' he said. 'If anyone should know about who has the rights, he should. You ask him. The people he comes from know well enough. They fought for their land to be returned.'

She wasn't sure how to answer and instead watched as the old man walked proudly to the school picket fence. Aoife had no idea what she was supposed to ask her father.

IMOGEN
Taranaki 2018

Jack had fallen asleep in an armchair out on the veranda. I checked the kitchen cupboard, thinking about dinner but it didn't reveal much of interest unless I was fond of baked beans and tomatoes in cans. I decided to head out to the small supermarket I'd noticed on my way to the farm and get some provisions.

I hadn't driven far down the winding road away from the mountain ranges when a large black Jeep, like the one that had passed me earlier in the day, appeared in my rearview mirror. It stayed there, following closely. Too closely.

I peered through the mirror at my blurry back windscreen. It had copped the worst of the mist and the mud on the way to Jack's and I hadn't thought to clean it before driving off. There was no one else on the road. I was suddenly anxious and my heart began to pound.

I put my foot down and sped up and the person behind me did the same. I imagined the big outsized Jeep rear-ending my little red car – I'd end up with a wrecked rental. My hands shook on the steering wheel as the car veered towards the edge of the road. Finally, a wider berm appeared and I pulled over.

The Jeep slowed as it passed me and I saw the driver – a man with big shoulders in a black jacket – turn and stare at me. Was he checking to see if I was okay? I wasn't sure. I realised he was scowling at me. I waited, my heart beating fast, till the Jeep disappeared around a corner leaving behind a burst of diesel smoke. I found a packet of tissues in my bag and got out to wipe the back window. Afterwards, I drove carefully, checking the rearview mirror from time to time.

Somewhere I must have taken a wrong turning at one of the crossroads and found myself at a place I hadn't driven through on my way to Jack's. A rough-looking garage had a sign advertising car repairs next door to a fish and chip shop. On the other side of the road was a cream two-storey wooden building. I recognised the buildings from the images that had come up when I googled Wexford back in Melbourne. An old-style hotel, its name was emblazoned on the front: The Empire.

A number of cars and utes were parked in the yard. A coffee might calm my nerves, I thought, parking the car. As I crossed the road, from their vantage point at an outside bench three grizzled old men, two in black singlets, eyed me.

'Thirsty?' one of the men said, blowing out smoke from a cigarette as I approached.

Giving them a nod, I pushed open the bar door and was confronted by a hubbub of voices and the shrill clatter of glasses and beer jugs.

The patrons were mostly men. Several sat at the bar on high stools, with jugs of amber beer and glasses before them. There was another group over at a pool table. A sudden hush greeted me, as if a stranger had walked in. I realised the stranger was me and they were staring, either suspiciously or with interest. Deciding to ignore them, I went up to the bar.

The man behind it – a big man with a handlebar moustache, white to match his long full beard – regarded me with the same interest as if he thought I was going to order a weird girly cocktail he had never heard of. Were women even allowed in public bars in rural New Zealand?

'Do you serve coffee?' I asked. I might've downed a stronger drink if I wasn't driving.

The bartender merely nodded.

'A flat white, please,' I said, 'and a glass of water.'

'Passing through?'

'More or less,' I said, taciturn in return. I had thought my grandfather was close-lipped. Were all the men around here like this? I turned away to look for somewhere to sit.

The door to the pub swung open and I recognised at once the man who came in. This was the man who had driven so badly on that back road he could've killed me. I poured myself a glass of water from the jug the bartender had passed me. The man came closer, heading towards the bar.

'A Steinlager, Fred,' Jeep Man said.

I opened my mouth to speak, without any idea of what I might say, but my barely uttered 'Excuse me,' came out at the same time a large woman with a white apron tied around her waist bounded out from a room on the other side of the bar. 'Tamati,' she called. 'Thought I heard your voice. How long are you home for this time?' She flung her arms around him before he could reply.

'Hey,' I said, interrupting their cosy reunion. It came out louder than intended. 'Hey, you.'

The man pulled away from the hug. 'Yes?' he said offhandedly.

'That was you in the Jeep. Somebody tailgated me a little while ago and nearly forced me off the road.'

The man slowly looked me up and down and shrugged. 'And you weren't driving so slowly you could cause an accident?'

A smart aleck. I detested him already. 'That's not the point. First of all, I wasn't driving too slowly. And second, I had as much right as you to be on the road.'

The big woman who had been hugging Tamati reached towards me as if she were going to separate us with her strong arms. 'Not much traffic on the back roads around here. You don't expect to see another car and anyway, Tamati drives like that no matter where.' She had a big smile on her face as she looked at him. 'I bet you get a few tickets in the city.'

'We don't drive at a crawl around here,' Tamati said to me, as if she hadn't said a word. 'You'd never get anywhere.'

'That's right,' a man in the pub could be heard responding. 'Fair enough, too, with all these back roads.'

I glared at Tamati. 'It was hardly a crawl. Have you never heard of good road manners?'

'Look, sorry if it bothered you,' he said, his tone still off-hand. 'We'll have to agree to differ.'

I didn't want to let it go. 'You mean because no one uses a road, you have a right to drive like a madman?'

'Hey,' he said. 'I think you're exaggerating things a bit here, aren't you?'

A young woman came out from behind the bar, bringing my coffee. She glanced at me, checking where to place it so I gestured to a nearby table. Tamati began to make his way over to some other men. 'Enjoy the rest of your holiday.' He thought I was a tourist. I had forgotten I had an accent that would identify me.

'Got lost, did you?' the woman said to me. 'Looking to find a way up the mountain? Not that you can see it today.'

I was thinking of my reply when Tamati turned back, as if a thought had suddenly occurred to him. 'You drove out of old Jack Maguire's farm.'

It sounded like an accusation. I didn't know why but the tone of his voice reminded me of Gavin, my former boss – the way he could add a few words to a conversation in a meeting I thought was finished, a little final message that somehow got one over me; having the last word and making me look foolish in front of other colleagues. Gaslighting me. When I had finally put my former boss and his behaviour behind me, my boyfriend had then taken me for a fool and cheated on me and right here in front of me this guy, whoever he thought he was, was acting as if he hadn't tried to run me off the road. I reminded myself I didn't know these people. Why should I tell them my business?

'I needed a place to turn around,' I lied. 'I stopped to ask a woman who was checking a mailbox along the side of the road. She came out from the house with the orange roof. She had a woolly hat on her head. Told me to turn in at the next gateway.'

The room went quiet for a while. I breathed a sigh of relief. Then someone spoke up from another table. 'There was a bit of commotion at old Jack's, eh? Boxthorn on fire. Fire engines there and all.' The man spoke slowly, a kind of rural accent that went up at the end of a sentence.

Some of the customers turned to look at him and back to me, eager to see what would happen. The man took a swig of his beer, wiped his hand across his lips. 'And there was a granddaughter turned up. An Aussie. Right out of the blue, eh?' He sounded triumphant.

Tamati shot me a look. 'Interesting, well, what do you know?' As if he had caught me out in a lie. Which he had. 'You reckon? A granddaughter, eh?' He looked as if he were musing this over. 'He hasn't mentioned you.'

What was it to him? I opened my mouth to ask him this when a tall man with curly brown hair materialised in front of me.

'Everything okay?' He looked down at me. Green-grey eyes held my gaze. His hair was closely cropped at the sides. He wore a cotton shirt that was soft and faded as if it had been washed often. I took in all these details in one long assessment like a good reporter would. His tone, I also noticed, was neutral. 'Hi there, Tamati,' he said, giving what seemed like a curt nod.

'Nathan.' Tamati also nodded and looked away. He turned back to the group of men. The din had ceased. The other men in the bar settled back to the positions they were in before but were still watching closely. The exchange had provided entertainment in an otherwise uneventful day.

'You okay?' Nathan asked again.

'I'm fine,' I said. 'What is it with this place? Questions. Questions.' I sounded snarky but I didn't care. I picked up my coffee from the table.

'You'll be Imogen.' His response wasn't what I expected, and despite myself I was curious how he knew. I sipped at my flat white. It wasn't too bad. 'I called in to see if Jack was all right after I heard about the fire. I saw young Daniel on the road and he told me you had come over from Australia to visit Jack. When I saw a rental car outside I guessed you might have ended up here, looking for directions. Easy to get lost on these roads.'

'I wasn't lost. I had a crazy driver chasing me along a narrow road.'

His alert green-grey eyes surveyed my face. 'You've got off to a bad start. People around here are generally friendly enough.' He glanced over at Tamati. Except for some, he might have been saying.

He was good-looking. He had a nice face but somehow I found myself reacting. I didn't want anyone talking down to me, mansplaining. I bristled. 'Antagonistic to anyone they think might be an outsider though.'

In the background, Tamati muttered some words to a man who had approached him, and they both laughed. 'Yeah, regular chip off the old block, eh?' the other man responded.

Nathan ignored them. 'Well. If there's anything you need …'

'Thanks, but I can manage perfectly well without help,' I interrupted because, handsome as he was, and as far as I could tell he was friendly enough, I really didn't care what he was going to offer. I didn't care how he fitted in. I wanted rid of this room full of men and their arrogance. None of them were my former boss, and I didn't have to kowtow to any of them. The thought occurred to me then that if I had stood up to Gavin when he first took over the job, maybe I wouldn't have got to a point where I felt the only thing I could do was leave. Which, in fact, I was doing again.

The noise in the pub resumed, blasting around me, as I marched towards the door. The old men in the dirty, sweaty singlets were still on the outside benches. One of them raised his eyebrow at me. 'See you around, Miss.'

'Not likely.' My body shook, probably with tiredness from the journey. I should've had that strong drink, a whisky even. I crossed the road and opened the car door.

A voice called out to me. Nathan was striding to catch up with me. I wound the window down. 'Sorry,' he said, leaning down, 'I should've introduced myself properly. I'm Nathan Campbell. I'm the police officer around here.'

The man Jack had said was useless? We looked at each other, his tanned arm resting on the window ledge. There was enough time to notice his grey-green eyes again and a lock of curly hair which flopped down from his forehead before he pushed it away from his face.

'Are you based here?' I wasn't even sure why I asked. To keep him talking?

'Sometimes, but I'm mainly at New Plymouth. There's a lot going on there right now and we're short-staffed.'

'A lot going on, like what?' Maybe it was the reporter in me wanting to follow a story.

'An influx of gang members looking for recruits. Dealing meth. Break-ins, drive-by shootings and gang initiations where they king-hit a kid with a baseball bat on a city street. That kind of thing. Like Australia, especially after your government started sending crims back because they were born here.' He smiled. Was he teasing?

'Do you know who set Jack's hedge on fire?' I asked, changing the subject.

'Ah, well. I spoke to the chief of the fire service earlier before I called in to Jack's. He told me there was no sign of any arson. So that's a good thing.'

'But he already had the problem with the cattle being turned out onto the road,' I persisted. 'Do you think somebody has got it in for him?'

Nathan looked away. 'Well, it's like this. He's made a few complaints already but the thing is, Jack has a bit of form with hedge fires.' He pushed the same lock of hair off his eyes in a habitual kind of way. It probably drove his girlfriends wild. 'The fire chief mentioned an old report he'd seen. Apparently, that time he'd set fire to a big pile of boxthorn he'd cut down. Didn't tell anyone his plans and didn't get any help. The boxthorn was dry as a bone. A westerly came up and he damn near set the whole farm and district on fire. He's not a man to get permission to do things, if you get my drift.'

'But …' I tried to think, 'just because something has gone wrong in the past doesn't mean it's his fault this time.'

He tugged at his shirt collar. 'No, that's true. Look, anyone will tell you Jack's a good guy, genuine as they come, but it's possible he's not up to looking after the farm on his own any-more. He's getting on a bit.' His response was measured as if he thought I might bite his head off. 'Maybe you could keep an eye on him, note how good his memory is, that kind of thing.'

'Don't you think it's wrong to write people off just because they're elderly?' I was angry and here I was defending an equally angry old man who I had just discovered was my grandfather.

'Well …' Whatever Nathan was going to say was interrupted by his mobile beeping. He pulled it from his pocket to check the screen and frowned as he read the message, then looked at me. 'You're here now. It'd be a good idea to keep an eye on him. See if he's getting forgetful. Look, I've got to get going. You could have a chat to Molly about Jack. She'll have a better idea if anything's changed in his behaviour recently.'

That was the last thing I was going to do. I barely knew the woman and would rather observe Jack myself. I returned Nathan's wave with an equally brisk one, letting him know I, too, had things to do.

That evening, by the time Jack took himself off to bed, I still hadn't quizzed him on the hedge fire or the calves. He watched television without talking, drifting off from time to time. He hadn't asked me anything relating to myself or Aoife. It was as if he didn't care about our lives in Australia, and it seemed pointless to even mention my father. I sensed he would have no idea who he was or where he might be. On the other hand, I hadn't passed on any details of my encounters with Tamati and Nathan either. Keeping information to ourselves, we had that in common.

With Jack gone to bed, I used the icy cold bathroom along the hallway. The room featured an old bathtub with a rusted base and a toilet with discoloured enamel which probably hadn't seen bleach in a long while. The poky shower box in the corner had soap scum on the glass door. I dismissed the bath but was equally reluctant to use the shower. Would the water even be warm? I thought longingly of my comfortable apartment in Melbourne and gave a sigh – I was here now. In the end, I made do with brushing my teeth and splashing chilly water on my face before going along to the bedroom.

I stood in the doorway to my mother's old bedroom, in my arms a pair of sheets and a pillowcase I had found in a cupboard in the hallway. The room was small and narrow and had an equally narrow bed with hard-looking pillows and a striped green and brown cover. One shelf of a small bookcase held Nancy Drew mystery books. A small cross made of rushes woven together in a crisscross pattern hung on one wall while a plaster statue of the Virgin Mary in painted blue and white robes perched on a side table.

Fumbling through my suitcase with icy fingers, I found my pyjamas to change into, quickly made up the bed, then turned the light switch off. The sheets were cold, the pillows thin, and I tried to ignore the musty damp smell. It was going to be difficult to get to sleep and yet that was what I needed most.

I must've fallen asleep, after all. I woke at dawn, sweating, my whole body damp, and tried to recall what had happened during the night. Thumping noises outside the window had woken me. Some kind of animal? A banging tree? I'd sat up in the narrow bed and automatically checked the time on my phone – it was three a.m. – and pushed aside the meagre curtain. I remembered doing this, even in my dream.

Outside, a procession was making its way across the paddock. A straggling group of six or seven people, wearing what looked like cloaks, two of them holding children by their hands. As I watched, they stopped and formed a semi-circle.

A man held up some kind of weapon. He looked uncannily like Tamati – Jeep Man. Then his gaze met mine through the glass in sorrowful anger, and I shivered. A woman carrying a swaddled baby began to sob, and even though it shouldn't have been possible from that distance, I could hear the mournful sounds she made. I wanted to shout to the group to stop, that it was dangerous, to not go any further – even though I didn't know in what way it was perilous. They turned their backs on me to continue on their way across the paddock, leaving me shell-shocked. I wanted to call out to someone to help these people even though the group had moved from sight.

Now I was awake and the day was beginning, and I knew what I thought I'd seen wasn't possible. There was no visible moon before I went to bed, and it would've been impossible to see anything at all outside in the dark. I lay in bed and thought about what could have happened. Was I so exhausted from my stressful journey and meeting the strange angry man who was my grandfather that I'd had the most vivid nightmare I'd ever experienced? Had I let this scary, dilapidated house with its rattling roof and windows frighten me so much I'd had a night-time hallucination, a vision of things and people that weren't real?

And yet, what I'd seen passing before my eyes in the night had been so real, I could've sworn I had experienced it – the tears on my face were evidence of that.

Now, I looked at the thin curtain and saw it was still drawn across the window, hiding what was outside. I lay back, turned on my side, pulled the bedcover around me and willed myself back to sleep.

The sound of voices woke me a couple of hours later. Molly and Daniel were in the kitchen at Jack's and I could hear Jack speaking in a low rumble as he joined in the conversation. It sounded as if they were talking about the weather, a favourite topic among farmers in Australia and no doubt the same here. I pulled on jeans and a wool sweater, glanced in my compact mirror at my hair, which was tousled from my nightmare, and gave it a quick brush.

'I brought fresh muffins for breakfast,' Molly said when I joined them. 'I thought you might like to come with me to New Plymouth today when I go to work. There's an exhibition at the Govett-Brewster that's supposed to be really good. Besides, you won't want to hang around here all day. There's not much to do, is there Daniel?'

Daniel bit into a muffin. 'Not much,' he said, his voice muffled. 'Except I've got to check the oil on Jack's truck and then move those steers to the back paddocks.'

I looked over at Jack, who stared back at me impassively. I had barely arrived here and already they were trying to palm me off on a tourist outing. Daniel's mention of taking the steers to the back paddocks had me interested in seeing the farm. Could there be any clues as to why someone was so keen to frighten Jack off it?

'I've spent time on a couple of cattle farms in the outback in Australia,' I said to Daniel. 'Though in a lot of places we lived it was mainly crops. If you want a hand moving them, I can help.'

Daniel shrugged.

'Well, if you're sure,' Molly smiled, 'but the city's a lovely place to explore. The walk along the seafront goes for kilometres and it's highly rated. There's always people walking it.' She wasn't giving up. 'Tourists love it.'

'It sounds wonderful. I'm a little tired though after the long day yesterday. A stroll through the paddocks here will be enough for me. I might get to see the mountain.'

'If you're lucky,' Daniel said.

I waited till she had gone and Daniel had headed off to the shed before I asked Jack a question that had been on my mind. Did he know a man called Michael Flynn? 'A man with black hair and a beard, an Irish accent, baggy old clothes?' I had been half expecting him to have shown up already, to have filled me in further on what had been going on. He was the one who had been so desperate for me to come here.

Jack sat up in his chair a little straighter, suddenly interested. 'Flynn? Was he the bastard I had building a haystack? The cheeky sod had just come out of prison and I did him a favour the one time. He did a useless job and I told him so. He didn't like it. Thought he could scare me.'

It didn't sound anything like the same man but at least my taciturn grandfather was talking to me.

'I picked up a big shovel and that shut the bastard down. He tore off down the track.'

Surely he wouldn't have intended to actually hit the man? Imagine the trouble if he had. I wanted to ask him but I also didn't want to interrupt him if he had more to say. It was the most I had heard him speak. Jack clearly enjoyed regaling me with the story and he probably had loads more lined up. It could be that listening to his stories was the secret to getting on with him and gaining his trust – like Molly and Daniel had, it would seem. Still, at least we were communicating, I told myself. I'd need to look further afield to find out any clues of any real value.

I changed the subject. 'I saw the photographs of the bulls on the walls.'

Jack shot up out of his chair, surprisingly agile for an old man. He beckoned for me to follow him into the hallway. We stood in front of the line of framed photos of bulls, all of them sporting pastel sashes.

'Yep. They're Angus. Reared them myself. They've been worth a pretty penny,' he said. 'At one time, half the herds around this part of Taranaki would have been mated with my bulls but there's only the one now. Champion. He's descended from this one – Duke was his name, a wonderful beast.' He pointed to a black and white photo of a stocky black bull with a ferocious expression on its face.

He pointed to another photograph in colour. 'Champion's three years old and in his prime. I'd say he's as good as Duke, his forefather. He's in the paddock over the bridge at the back of the farm.'

The beast seemed to glare at me and I'd make sure to avoid that paddock. I was keen to see the rest of the farm, though. When Daniel came back to the house from the shed I was ready, gumboots on. It was quiet around the back of the house. I pointed to the back of the shed. 'Do you take Bandit to move the steers?'

'Nah, leave him to sleep. He gets too excited with the young ones. Tries to show them who's boss. I dunno why Jack puts up with him. He's an old dog. He's seen his best days.'

Like Jack, I thought, but I kept this to myself. Two of a kind.

I followed him around to where the steers were. Their paddock came right up to the window of the bedroom I'd slept in, Aoife's old room. The noises I had heard in the night could have been them thumping against the wall. All was quiet now and in the paddock nothing but a small herd of steers, grazing.

Daniel strode behind the group, which had gathered to look at him, as if they were curious. He let out a yell that sounded a bit like 'hey ya' and a hiss, and the cattle turned towards the gate, following a well-used path. We came behind.

Daniel continued to herd the steers along the track until it came to a stream which ran through a paddock, separating it into two. A simple bridge made of timber allowed access to the paddock on the other side and was gated. A wire fence at the rear of the other paddock signified the back boundary of the farm, with the rest of the land sloping upwards towards the base of the mountain ranges. I could see the heavy green ranges, the trees dark and foreboding, snow peeking through the mist rising off the slopes of the mountain.

A black creature in the field across the bridge let out a bellowing sound as the young steers moved forward. He stamped his feet, looking ferocious. I stopped mid-step, my heart beating a bit faster. 'Jack's pedigree bull?'

'Yep. That's Champion all right,' Daniel said. He stopped too and looked across the bridge and then back at me. 'Don't worry. We're not going into his paddock. The steers go into this one over here.' He made another 'suss suss' sound and the young steers moved in a body towards an open gate nearby, still on this side of the bridge. Daniel waited until the last of the steers had gone through the gate and then closed and latched it.

I felt the tension leach out of me.

'Jack's done a lot of breeding from him. He's been offered big money for Champion from some AI outfit but he's always said no.'

Artificial insemination. 'I saw the photos. He's won a lot of awards.' I tried to keep my voice calm but our proximity to the bull was scaring me even if he were behind a gate.

'Yeah,' Daniel said without much interest. 'Jack takes him over the bridge a few times a week, so he's got all the grass to himself.'

'You wouldn't want to come across him on your own in a paddock. Not on a dark night.' I meant it.

'Yep. Doesn't have any horns but he's still one tough dude all right.'

Across the paddock the steers were heading towards another boundary, a tall hedge that ran along the left-hand side of the farm. This would be the road where I had driven on to Jack's place. It must veer around to the right. The top of a large yellow machine – a piece of earth-moving equipment – peeked over the hedge. In the distance the noise of heavy machinery broke the silence.

Daniel saw the direction of my gaze. 'That's the Barkers.' He sounded dismissive, even angry and obviously didn't like them, whoever they were.

I waited for him to go on.

'They own the farm at the other end of that road over there. They've got access through that road and one on the other side of their farm. They're running a road through their farm so their trucks can use either entrance, drive through from one side to the other. They've got farms on the other side road over there, too.' He waved his arm towards a boundary hedge on the right of Jack's property. 'They're always up to something. More money than sense, Jack says. They've been using that big machine to crush metal from the stream bed and spreading it on the track. It's the same stream that comes through here. All these little streams off the mountain end up flowing into the river further down.'

The river I'd seen that first day in Taranaki. The stream meandered towards what looked like trees and a swamp closer to the hedge on the right side of the farm. 'Are they allowed to? I thought rivers and streams came under resource laws now?' I had read about this in the newspaper at Jack's.

Daniel shrugged his shoulders. 'Yeah. Well. That's the Barkers for you.'

Powerful players then? 'It sounds like a big operation.'

'It's big all right. When farms come up for sale around here the Barkers buy them. A couple of the big milking sheds on those farms can milk a thousand cows each day, centralising everything.'

'That's a lot of work.'

'Yeah. They've brought in a bunch of guys from the Philippines.'

Jack's farm was a much smaller enterprise and likely right in the way of the Barkers' development plans. 'Do you think they might be looking to expand further?'

'Dunno. Wouldn't put anything past them.' Daniel turned and began to walk back in the direction we had come. I followed, thinking. I could picture a road going through the middle of Champion's paddock at the back of Jack's land, opening onto the side lane to the right of the farm. It could link up all the Barker farms on either side so trucks could take the shortcut between their other farms. Or if they had even more land – like all of Jack's farm – it could be part of any further expansion programme they had in mind.

'Would Jack sell to them?'

'Not likely.' This time it was easy to detect the grim tone. 'Can't stand them. There's always been bad blood between them.'

Jack mightn't want to sell to the Barkers. Without any evidence – and I didn't have any right now – what lengths would they go to get the land? One of the stories I had researched during my journalism course back home in Australia had focused on the dirty tactics some big businesses had used to push rural people off their land. It had been Aoife who had suggested the story. She'd introduced me to the farmer she worked for and he had found me others to interview about the aggressive illegal tactics the companies were using. I had promised I would protect my informants' anonymity when I wrote the article. It might have been for a student paper but none of them wanted their names out there. Nor, for that matter, did my mother.

Right now, though, I didn't have that much to go on, and I didn't intend to tell Daniel what I was thinking about the Barkers. Was I letting my imagination take over?

Instead, I changed the subject. 'Have you and Molly been living in the cottage for long?'

'A few years now. Since I started high school.'

Saying nothing, I used an old journalist trick of simply waiting in the hope that he'd fill the silence by talking.

'We had an old campervan when we first came. It was a shit winter that year. Cold as hell.' Daniel said this with such fervour, as if the bitterness of the place with its bleak winds sheeting off the mountain had left an indelible memory.

'We were parked up near the bridge, and Jack came by and asked if we were lost. Mum said she was looking for casual work but there wasn't much around. Jack said it was too cold to sleep in the van and we could stay in the cottage on his farm in exchange for Mum doing odd jobs around here and later on, I helped too, after school.' It was the most I'd heard Daniel say.

Without noticing, I'd walked through a pile of manure from the steers. It squelched under the gumboots. I lifted my feet quickly away, trying to rub the mess off the bottom of the boots onto wet grass. It would be easy to begin to hate this dark damp place; like Aoife had.

'And then she got the job at the vet's?'

'Yeah.' He looked down at my gumboots. 'Jack's been really good to us,' Daniel added. The way he said it, he could have trotted this statement out on more than a few occasions.

Pausing to pull up his sleeves, he plunged his arms into a water trough that serviced a paddock and the cattle race. He played around with a piece of steel at the bottom, checking the trough was filling up. He was engrossed in how the mechanism worked.

'And you like farm work?'

He shrugged and looked up from the trough. 'It's okay. I'm doing a farming course in New Plymouth. Animal husbandry.

Learning all the practices. Mum wants me to go in for young farm cadet of the year. She reckons with all the farms around the coast there's plenty of jobs out there if I do well on the course.'

A distinct lack of enthusiasm – probably his mother's dream for him. 'But you're not as keen?'

Again, a shrug.

'What would you really like to do?'

Daniel's face immediately brightened. 'Learn a trade like car mechanics. Or fixing and maintaining motorbikes. As a job, I mean. My dad's going to help me find a motorbike.' He closed his mouth firmly as if he had said too much.

So there was a father nearby. 'Does your father live around here?'

This time Daniel definitely clenched his teeth. 'Nope, not here.'

A subject better left alone.

He headed off, stopping to open a gate into another paddock. He pointed to a shed next to an old barn. 'Jack used to milk cows here. There's nothing much there now but we can take a look if you want.'

I nodded. I was keen to see everything on the farm and since Daniel had decided to take on the role of tour guide, I was pleased to accept his offer without appearing too nosy.

When we reached the shed, I followed him across broken concrete. This was where the dairy cows would have milled around while waiting to be milked. At the other end was a room with a three-quarter wall and a ladder propped up against it. I peered in. The room was full of rusted dairy machinery – nothing to see really.

I followed Daniel again as he began to head back towards the house. I saw the Jeep parked on the track first, then Tamati and Jack. Jack was bent over, patting Bandit. When we got closer I saw the old dog was panting heavily as he lapped up water from a bowl on the ground.

Jack turned to look at us. Tamati said nothing.

'What's up?' Daniel said. 'Bandit looks like shit.'

'Look at him,' Jack said urgently. 'Tamati's just brought him back. He says he found him way down the road at the Barkers. About to have a go at some lambs with their mothers. I thought he was down the back with you.'

'Yeah, well, he rarks the steers up too much, so I left him behind. Anyway, he was fast asleep.'

'Did you actually see him?'

'No. He was quiet like when he sleeps in his kennel.' Daniel sounded surly. 'And he sure sleeps a lot these days.'

Jack snorted and clutched at the dog's mangy fur. 'So you never checked. He's likely to have been out all night. I'll be hearing about it if he has done anything to the animals, I can tell you. If Tamati hadn't found him, I dunno what he could've done.' He spat on the ground. 'If he'd got into those lambs and mangled them … it doesn't bear thinking about.'

'Yep. If any of those Barkers saw him even sniffing at their lambs from over the fence, it would've been bang bang, one dead Bandit,' Daniel said. 'Old man Barker generally has his three-oh-three on standby in his truck.'

I shuddered. Bandit wasn't the most attractive of dogs but I'd never wish this ending on him.

'Lucky he let you catch him,' Daniel said to Tamati. 'He can be cantankerous, the old bugger.'

This was no doubt why Daniel wasn't keen to take the dog to the back of the farm with him. No love lost there.

Tamati shrugged. 'Well, lucky he knows me then. All's well though, eh Jack? Caught him in time. No harm done.'

'But how did he get down there? He never goes out on the

road. And even if he did he'd never have belted it all the way down there. He knows to hang around home.'

'Bit of a mystery,' said Tamati, shrugging again.

'No bloody mystery,' Jack said grimly. 'Someone took him. Someone did it on purpose.'

There was silence. I wondered what the other two were thinking.

'I'll take him back to his kennel,' Jack said. 'Tie him up. He'll need a good sleep.'

'I'll leave you to it,' said Tamati. 'I got somewhere I need to be.' The three of us watched him walk over to his Jeep. I suspected I knew the conclusion the other two had reached. That Jack was getting old and he was losing it. A bit like Bandit.

MICHAEL
Ireland 1862

'Twas the horses that brought us together, Eliza and me.

My da knew horses. I had learned much about them from helping him in the yard of the Big House while Mr Griffiths, the English owner's land agent, was out collecting rents and arrears from the tenants. Sometimes he might go by horse and trap to Listowel, the nearest town, on business and be away most of the day.

My two cousins and I also practised our skills on a wild pony their da had caught in the woods and kept tethered on a small patch of scrubby land behind their cottage. The pony was a sturdy white colt with a nasty temper, though I was sorry when my cousins and their da were gone one morning along with it. People said they fled in the night with their rent unpaid, taking the pony with them. At any rate, when the bailiffs came, the cottage was empty. Gone to America, it was said.

I was just turned eighteen and waiting outside Maggie Foley's pub the evening the news spread that the Beecham family were returning from England to the Big House. We always called the Beecham's Irish home by this name. It was as close as could be to a fortress, with its tree-lined entrance and long carriageway up to the front of the sprawling three-storey grey slate house.

My mam had sent me to fetch my grandfather and my uncles, who were among those in the smoky public house, and I could hear the hubbub of voices coming from inside. You could hear the excitement even among the younger ones because there'd be work again for housemaids, footmen and labourers – and regular money.

The Great Famine, or the Bad Times, as we called it, cast a long shadow in Ireland. We still blamed the English for what had happened to our country and people. I had been born into the famine. I grew up in the aftermath of it. When it continued over the years that followed and there was no sign of it abating, Mr Beecham, who was also our landlord, returned to England taking his family away in fear of them being attacked. He left everything in the care of his fellow Englishman and employee, Mr Griffiths. During those long years, Mr Griffiths was in a powerful position at the Big House. As well as collecting the rents he was responsible for the day-to-day management of the estate.

Mr Griffiths kept my da on to look after the few horses that remained on the estate. In the worst of the famine times these were locked away each night for fear of starving people stealing them to sell or to eat, even though in our Gaelic lore eating horse meat was frowned upon.

When our country lost the potato crops to infection and its inhabitants began to starve to death, large numbers of hungry and desperate men and women arrived at the big houses, breaking down gates or storming the stone walls, crying out for food, knocking on the windows and terrifying those inside.

As I waited for my uncles to come out of the pub that evening, two musicians – Old Patsy and his friend Jeremiah – were talking quietly about Griffiths as they sat on the bench outside. Soon they would go inside and play with the other musicians. They had with them a bodhrán, Uilleann pipes, a fiddle, and a flute. Mr Griffiths, Old Patsy said, had no intention of letting the poor and starving of the parish take advantage. He vowed to set his three big hound dogs on anyone approaching the property. He'd told people he would let them attack first and worry about who the person was later.

When he spoke of this, an old man sitting nearby looked around stealthily. 'Your man once shot a fellow who had come by with his family on their way to the docks to try to catch a boat to America,' he said, his voice lowered. 'The family had been evicted and the poor man was only asking for a handful of bread scraps to keep them going on the road, like, food for the journey. 'Twas heinous, I tell ye.'

A few days after we heard the news about the Beechams, Da came home at dinnertime and said he had good news. 'Excellent news,' he added in Mam's direction. He tapped me on the shoulder as Mam placed pieces of black pudding made of pig's blood, barley and seasoning in our bowls and we passed the sliced soda bread around the table. 'Mr Griffiths will give ye a job. He needs extra hands now they'll be purchasing more horses. Ye'll be working at the stables.'

'Riding?' I could hardly believe it. How did he know I could ride?

'No, ye'll be fixing bridles and oiling harnesses in the tack room.'

My grandpa patted me on the back with his bony hand. I could tell he was pleased. My two uncles got by on what they could grow on the few acres of land we rented, and odd bits of work they did for the landowners outside our neighbourhood. They might walk the ten miles or more there or hitch a ride on a donkey and cart from its driver. There were whole days with little work. Grandpa was not a man for talking and he'd been mostly silent since my grandmother died. It was how he grieved, our mam said, leave him be, she would say.

Now Mam gave a little yelp of joy. 'Thank you, Jesus, and your dear mother Mary,' she said, putting down the frypan of black pudding and raising her hands towards heaven. 'The good Lord has answered a poor woman's prayers. And, Lord knows, we can do with the money.' She glanced shyly at Da and I could see she wanted to say more. 'Mind you, behave for them at the Big House.'

Da grimaced. 'In particular, watch how you behave around Mr Griffiths.'

I thought of what I had heard about him a few days ago. Now Mam was so excited for me to be going to work for the man, and yet how could this be? Maybe she had never heard those same stories. I was quiet then, my mind occupied with how I could soon be riding the horses at the Big House.

In the beginning, Mr Griffiths kept me so busy I'd no time to even sneak a peek at the Beecham children. Occasionally I heard high voices, children chasing each other around the enclosed walled gardens, and once I spotted a blonde-haired child in one of the paddocks closest to the house. I didn't have an opportunity to spy anything much, since I spent most of my days in the stables forking hay and straw, washing down the hard floors and trying to avoid being given a sharp nip or a backwards kick by one of the meaner horses. I kept my mouth shut like Da had warned me.

Mr Griffiths generally spoke to me using some badly spoken Irish words peppered here and there among his English. I was well-versed in English. The only way to get on in our country was to learn the language of the invaders. However, when I came across the other lads and lasses who worked in the Big House or out on the farm, I spoke in Irish. Mr Griffiths had no idea how much of his mother tongue I understood and I wanted to keep it that way.

One day, raised voices close by the stables drew my attention. I turned back from sloshing down the yard with a bucket of water and a straw broom. Two girls – one about my age, the other a few years younger – were with a little boy of seven or so. Two bigger lads, both of whom walked with swaggers, accompanied them. Young lords of the manor.

I avoided being caught staring at the group – I knew my place – Da had emphasised this to me more than once. You didn't act to be seen. You kept to your place. Invisible. You mustn't give anyone any reason to become angry or annoyed. People had been sacked for less. Saliva had built up in my mouth and I wanted to spit it out onto the muck on the ground though I knew not to.

Mr Griffiths came around from the little nook he some-times used at the back of the stables where he would check the accounts and how much the horses were costing the estate, as he referred to it. I had already worked out for myself he went around there to take a nap in the cot under the eaves. It meant he was well away from the prying eyes of any of the servants at the Big House, or Mr Beecham himself.

'You'll be wanting to ride this afternoon, Miss Eliza,' he said in English to the girl who looked about my age. 'Your father told me earlier to find a good 'un for you.'

The girl frowned. 'Ah, Mr Griffiths, no, not today, only my cousins will ride.' She indicated the smaller lad. 'Henry,' and turned to the other, 'and George.' So that was who these strangers were.

The one called George strode forward, cocky in his step. He wore tall boots and carried a whip.

He stared at Mr Griffiths in a brazen way. 'What have you got? I like a big horse. A strong fellow.' He cracked the whip smartly against the bottom of the fence.

Mr Griffiths gave a half smile. His tone was deferential enough though there was a gleam in his eye. He indicated the horse Mr Beecham had recently acquired from another English landowner in Galway. The colt had been stamping and pawing at the ground in the yard although he appeared quiet now. 'Of course, sir. Magic Mountain here is the biggest in the stables, but he'll not be easy.'

I shifted my gaze downwards towards the hard ground and kept it there. Magic Mountain was a devil of a beast. The black colt had huge haunches and a fierce mouth when he bared his teeth. I knew to get out of his way quickly when he was in a mood. He was hardly a pony to take out for an afternoon's amble.

The boy called Henry muttered under his breath to the other. It sounded to me he may have asked, 'Are you sure?'

George ignored him and said loftily to Mr Griffiths, 'Can you saddle him up, auld fellow.'

Mr Griffiths winced at the rude manner of address, yet said nothing. He turned to me instead and spoke in his badly pronounced Irish, perhaps to show them I was an underling. 'Mikey, lad, go and get the saddle for this one. Move along, lad.'

I knew to do as I was told and sharpish. I went into the harness room which smelt of leather and saddle soap and took down Magic Mountain's saddle. It was made of strong leather and heavy. I carried it back around to the yard.

Behind me, I sensed Mr Griffiths watching as I saddled Magic. I kept a watchful eye on the young colt. I knew he could be excitable and I wanted nothing to go wrong.

'Will you be riding, young sir?' Mr Griffiths now asked the smaller boy.

Henry scuffed his boots on the ground. I had caught how he looked at Magic, how he sized him up and down, but he wouldn't want to confess to any fear of this powerful creature in front of his female cousin.

'What else you got?' he asked, surly enough. As if it was no matter to him. Would Mr Griffiths get me to fetch the one we called Pudding? Meaning he was a sweet and placid animal when in fact he was exactly the opposite. I wouldn't put it past the wily manager. Mr Griffiths merely nodded peaceably and said he would send the boy – he meant me – for a mare we called Biddy.

'She's a good ride, sir,' he said. 'Got the makings of a brood mare.'

I went back to the stables and led the mare out, carefully avoiding the dribble from her mouth as she nuzzled my hand.

We helped the lads mount, led them out of the stables and watched them as they headed in the direction of the woods beyond. Eliza, her sister and younger brother gaily followed them on foot.

I walked back to the stables with Mr Griffiths. 'I think, laddie, we will give them time to get them horses used to them,' he said slowly as if his mind was on something else, like a nice draught of beer. I wasn't sure that was what he really meant, as he was chewing on a thin piece of straw and I could not tell for sure. 'I have a job or two to do in the office first.'

It was a while before we set off, on foot, after them. We took a route through the beech trees. It was dark in there and you couldn't see too far ahead. Overhead in the trees, birds chirped. There was no sign of the riders or the Beecham children. We continued, silence surrounding us, then we saw a little posse of people gathered around a figure on the ground. We walked closer, Mr Griffiths maintaining the same steady pace.

George was clutching his leg. Magic Mountain was nowhere to be seen. 'The bastard tossed me,' he said angrily. 'He hasn't been trained properly. I went to pull him up and he reared. He's done a runner.'

Mr Griffiths looked concerned. 'I am sorry to hear that, sir.' He turned to me. 'Help the young gentleman to get on his feet.'

I moved towards the fellow.

George lifted his arm, warding me off. 'I can get up by myself.'

'You might have hurt yourself,' Eliza exclaimed. 'Don't try to get up on your own.'

She looked at Henry who handed Biddy's reins to me and went to help. George still protested but must have realised he was better to be aided.

'That animal needs to learn its lesson,' he said. 'Eliza, I will be speaking to your father about his bad behaviour. He's poorly trained.'

Mr Griffiths smiled. 'When you do speak with him, I'm sure Mr Beecham will inform you of Mountain's successes with the previous owner in Galway. I've heard a stud in the Curragh is hoping to have one of their thoroughbred mares mate with him. Mountain's reputation is well known but of course, you must have a word with Mr Beecham about him. He will be interested to hear your opinion on the colt's training.'

George shot me a look of malice. 'Very well, your lad can bring him back in, can't he?' He took the reins for Biddy from me. 'I'll ride this one back. Help me up.'

Magic was standing placidly beside a tree at the end of the woods. I took him by the reins and spoke quiet words of comfort to him. It was then I noticed the blackthorn stuck in his shoulder. He had been ridden too closely to the hedges and it was no wonder he had thrown the useless bastard. I wondered what Mr Griffiths would say, or Mr Beecham if he knew this oik had damaged one of his prime horses. It would not be up to me. My job was to be invisible, keep my mouth shut and get on with what I had to do. I began to walk Magic slowly back to the yard. I'd find some pinchers there to take the thorn out.

Several days later, Da became mad ill with a cough that bothered him all through the night. I had been kept awake hearing him. Our cottage was small, and it took nothing for us to catch a sickness off each other.

'Will ye go up to the Big House?' Mam asked. She wrung her hands on her apron, twisting the waistband nervously.

'Aye,' Da said. 'Ye know Mr Griffiths. He won't allow a man to be sick.'

When we got to the stables and Mr Griffiths saw Da bent over the little hedge nearby, coughing up all manner of green stuff, he called me over.

'Your father can muck out the hay barn,' he said. 'You, lad, come with me.'

To my surprise, he led me to Magic. 'This one cannot go a morning without a ride. You will have to take him out. I've seen you with the horses. Time for you to take your turn. He needs a good run.' He gestured for me to saddle him up.

The colt was pawing the ground, saliva running from the sides of his mouth. I moved quickly out of the way of his hooves. The horse shuddered and glared down at me, his nostrils flaring. I persevered and placed the cumbersome saddle over his heaving body.

Mr Griffiths led him to the side rail and held my knee clasped in his hands so I could swing myself up onto the horse. When I climbed on, the colt's body relaxed beneath me. He was looking forward to being ridden and his escape to freedom.

I was nervous enough myself but once I gripped the reins and started to walk out of the yard towards the lane to the forest,

I knew I was in the right place. I turned and looked back to the stables. Mr Griffiths was nowhere to be seen. I thought he might have saddled up another horse and accompanied me but he was obviously expecting me to ride this massive creature on my own. Was it a test of my ability?

We entered the entrance to the dark woods and Magic, recognising the place, whinnied. He champed at the bit, keen to race ahead to freedom. I gripped the reins hard in case he might toss me like he had the cousin. George was a much bigger lad than I, and yet the colt had managed to unseat him. I would take care to stay on.

We trotted steadily beneath the tall dark trees, the light coming thin through the green canopy above. I had no need to grip the reins so fiercely and found myself relaxing into the saddle, my movements in tune with his, so let him move into a canter. Even so, I could tell that Magic wanted to pick up the pace. Faster, faster, he seemed to be saying. We were coming to the end of the woods and up ahead was an area with few trees.

Magic gave a wee buck and broke into a gallop. He hurtled forward like he was in a race yet there was no one ahead and no one behind. I crouched behind his ears, hanging on with my knees, and let him go. My heart was pounding as I too experienced the sense of freedom he was so obviously demanding.

We raced around that field as if it were a circular track. Magic began to sweat under me. He was having a brilliant workout and I was urging him on. I realised I wanted that sense of liberty as well. I never wanted to get off. I never wanted the rushing wind in my hair to cease. If I could, I would have taken Magic and headed away far into the distance.

It was then I heard the barking of dogs. It was Mr Griffiths with his hounds, here to stop me in my tracks.

I slowed Magic to a walk as Mr Griffiths beckoned me towards him. He had tied one of the gentler mares to a tree and it struck me that he was not as proficient around big horses as he liked to pretend. I guessed it would have been Da who always rode Magic. I thought of the danger Da would have been subjected to in the past and wondered about the times some of these horses here at the Big House might have thrown him till he had learned how to tame them.

I rode back over the paddock to Mr Griffiths, holding the reins tightly so that Magic would settle into a quiet trot.

'Very good, lad,' was all Mr Griffiths said to me. He looked Magic over, casting his eye, no doubt, over the sweat on the colt's flanks and body. 'A good workout by the look of it. We might have you riding at the Curragh at this rate.'

I didn't know whether or not he was joking. It would be beyond my wildest dreams to go to one of the famous race meetings I'd heard Da talk about. 'Thank you,' was all I could say.

In the days that followed, Mr Griffiths gave me the same old jobs I had always done. No riding. Had I imagined his words? Was he backtracking from the promise he'd made? Or had I heard it wrong?

So I was surprised when Miss Eliza, in a long skirt wrapped around her body like an apron my mam might wear, came down to the stables on her own. She told Mr Griffiths she would like to ride one of the ponies. He nodded to me and said, 'The laddie here can assist you.'

I wasn't sure how experienced a rider she was. So far I had never seen her on one of the horses, nor even showing any interest in the stables.

'Get the side saddle from the tack room for Miss Eliza,' Mr Griffiths said to me. 'Put it on the little mare.'

I went to the back of the stables, did what I had been told and led Biddy out of the stall.

I thought about helping Eliza up onto the saddle but Mr Griffiths took over. Once Eliza was seated sidesaddle, he directed me to walk with her around the yard till she was used to Biddy's gait. 'Out of the yard and into the lane,' he told me, 'no further.'

I grimaced, wondering if I'd ever again get to have the same freedom I had experienced riding Magic through the fields on the other side of the woods.

Eliza said nothing to me as I walked beside her. It was difficult to tell how secure she was on the mare. She had a way of looking down at me and curling her lip that I found to be insulting and snobbish. I reminded myself who she was and where we were. I was a servant and that was all I was. I saw she had shortened her reins as if she intended Biddy to take off along the lane.

I looked back at Mr Griffiths for an indication of what to do next.

He came over to us. 'Miss Eliza, are you ready to ride in the paddock on the other side of the stables?'

Eliza nodded.

Mr Griffiths told me to get one of the other mares and go with her.

Once I'd saddled up, we headed along the lane to the paddock and I took my cue from Eliza. She was a neat rider with a good seat. She had been taught well. Something must have happened one time to make her nervous, hence the reluctance in her manner when she had come into the yard to talk to Mr Griffiths. Now she seemed to have regained her confidence. She urged the mare into a trot and set off ahead of me. I followed, keeping behind her, knowing my place.

We spent the next half hour riding in the field. Eliza didn't speak to me, and I didn't speak to her. At the end, however, she appeared happier, she even said 'Thank you' as she dismounted.

After that day, I saw George and Henry in the grounds from

time to time though they never acknowledged me. They were likely staying the summer and I would be pleased when they were gone.

One day, Eliza surprised me by coming down to the stables and addressing me. 'You're from the cottages near the village. Your family didn't leave when all the others did.' She said this with an air of detachment, stating a fact. Who would she have asked to find this out?

I thought of my grandpa, too old and weak to make the journey to the port. We had stayed because of him. I wasn't going to say that was why the nine of us – my grandfather, my uncles and my da, Mam and my sisters and I all crowded together into our small cottage on the edge of the village. There was a time when we and our relatives filled two cottages, side by side, but that was before the forced evictions and the other families leaving for the port.

'Aye,' I said, continuing to scrape out Magic's hooves. I thought about how that horrible cousin George could have caused such harm to this proud animal and yet received no retribution.

'You're good with the horses,' she said. 'Even my father says so.'

I didn't know what to say.

'You had better not be too good. Lest my father sacks your father and keeps you on in his place.'

I shot her an upward glance. Would that be likely to happen?

Eliza reached up to touch the big colt. Magic whinnied and stamped a hoof and she withdrew her arm quickly, twirled around and was gone. I didn't know what to make of her. She was no older than me, yet she had the confidence only the daughter of a rich man could have. I didn't much warm to her. I was determined to keep out of the way of the young masters and mistresses. My life and my job were worth more than that.

The next time I walked two of the horses down to the river

to soak their legs, Eliza was there, sitting on the bank reading a book. She looked up but didn't seem disturbed by my presence.

'I didn't know ye were here, miss,' I said. 'I'll take the horses someplace else.'

'No, you can stay.' Her tone was imperious and again it rankled but there was nothing I could do.

I nodded and kept my distance. She was a long way from the Big House and the river was not the place for a young lass on her own. After a time, she laid the book down on the side of the riverbank. 'When you are finished here, can you accompany me back to the house?' she asked.

The request surprised me. She had struck me as more independent than that. 'Certainly, miss,' I said. I turned to the second horse who was pawing the water and splashed him back. He reared a little and skittered but it was nothing to worry about. I led the pair onto the riverbank and waited for her to come over to me.

She looked about her, scanning the area around us. 'Have you seen my cousins? Have they been at the stables?'

'They headed off on foot to the village sometime after the midday meal.'

Her shoulders fell, as if some tension had left her. 'And you haven't seen them come back?'

'No,' I said.

They would have gone to the illicit drinking room at Mrs Harris's wee shelter among the abandoned shacks on the edge of the village, a place you wouldn't notice unless you knew where to look. It was a rough dwelling, and these lads would feel they were real men if they went in and drank some of the hard stuff Mrs Harris and her brothers brewed, or even demanded food, no matter they had this aplenty at the Big House.

I didn't say anything about any of this. We walked in silence, an amicable quiet between us. I was surprised when we got back to the stables and she thanked me for my trouble. I nodded and left her to walk to the house through the park, while I returned the horses to their quarters.

After that I would see Eliza here and there around the grounds. She would give a slight inclination of her head to let me know she had seen me. Sometimes she was with her two cousins, in which case she would ignore me.

Mr Griffiths had finally allowed me to exercise most of his precious horses and I was in the far field one day doing so, working with a pair of them one by one, with the other tied to a post, when Eliza came along. She watched as I brought one of them over to the water trough.

'Can I help?' she asked, indicating the young horse. 'I can hold him for you while you fetch the other.'

'He's strong. Are ye sure?'

She nodded. I went to get the other, Magic. We stood side by side at the trough, holding each horse by its bridle.

'They're grand, aren't they?' she said. 'The ones back home are meek and mild compared to these.'

'Are you missing your home?'

'Yes. England is so different. Our land is laid out in neat fields and even the rivers seem tamer. Here it is so wild. There's a grimness about the place. Dark and damp.' She shuddered.

I thought about it. The mist and the wild hedgerows, untamed fields and forest were all I knew. The mountains remained in the distance. There was the sea, too, but that was a long way from our land here with its burnt-out remnants of cottages and huts.

'In England, I knew where I was,' she said quietly. 'We lived on our estate outside the village. The locals knew us and waved to us and greeted us when they saw us in the village. Here the people are wild and scurrying. They scuttle away when they see you.'

I smiled at the description.

'And,' she drew breath, 'they don't like us because we are English. If my mama were here, people would like her. They would say how kind she was to them.'

There was little I could say to that. I had heard her mother had died in England. It might have been why the family was here now. She sniffed. Was she crying? I didn't know what to do. In the end, I reached out and lightly touched her shoulder. I wondered if she would reprimand me for such an action. I was a stablehand and should not do such a thing but she did not react at all.

'They don't like us,' she said again. 'Because of the potato shortage.'

I nodded. What could I say? There was more to it than that. I knew the long history that went back hundreds of years.

'I have been reading old Irish newspapers in the library at the house,' she said. 'So much happened that we know nothing of in England.'

Magic had stopped drinking. He shook his head and sprayed us both with water.

'Goodness. That is one way to stop me from speaking.' She smiled, wiping a couple of tears from beneath her eyes. 'Can I walk this one back to the stables for you?'

I thought about what old Mr Griffiths might think but then I decided to risk it. If he said anything, I would tell him Miss Eliza asked. He knew I was not allowed to be rude to the English owners of the property.

To this day I am not sure how it happened but soon me and Eliza started to meet regularly. She timed her daily walks with my outings with the horses. No one at the stables said anything and I decided they didn't notice anything amiss. Mr Griffiths was usually taking a nap or drinking tea and eating soda bread in his back room. We began to talk on all kinds of subjects.

At home in my little cot at night I would think of our conversations, of how her hand sometimes almost touched my wrist, of her smell of violets, and the way her breath caught in her throat when she was talking passionately about a subject she was interested in. She wanted to alleviate the plight of poor women and children. She had great plans to go out among the people in the nearby townlands to talk with them, to see how she could help. I wasn't sure if I should warn her this would not always be well received.

After Da got the illness, Mam caught it from him. My sisters had it, too and it was only me that kept going. What went on at the ruined cottages was, I imagined, of no interest to the people in the Big House, yet Eliza must have heard my family were ill. She came to the stables with a basket of scones. 'For your mother,' she said.

That evening when I took the scones home to Mam, she regarded me with suspicion. 'Where did ye get these from? You didn't steal them from the kitchen, now, because if ye did, your da's life won't be worth living. Nor yours.'

'Miss Eliza brought them to the stables,' I told her. 'She said they were for ye.'

Now it was the scones that Mam was regarding with suspicion. 'And why would the cailín do that? She doesn't even know me.'

Even so, she gave a resigned nod and took them from me. 'We'll have them with our tea.' She put her hand to her mouth to cover a cough. 'It will save me baking soda bread. But don't ye be telling them at the Big House that I am ill. Any excuse to evict us and that Mr Griffiths wouldn't hesitate.'

I wanted to say that they weren't that bad but I stayed silent. I couldn't tell Mam the feelings I had for Eliza. I knew she wouldn't be happy to hear me say such a thing. She would want me to know my place, to keep my distance from the English family and, at any rate, Mam didn't like to be argued with, especially when Da was not around.

Dusk had come in early that evening as I was busy watering the horses and feeding them hay. The birds in the hedges were making a fair racket, though the noise I began to hear now was different – a high-pitched sound that swept up above the land to the sky. I thought it was the cry of a bird which had become stuck or broken a wing. Or was it not a bird but an animal of some kind? A rabbit a fox had attacked? A squirrel? The sound was too sensitive, too finely tuned for that. I looked around to see where it might have come from, then started walking towards the entrance to the dark forest. It came again, still in the distance but now piercing the air.

I walked carefully so my boots wouldn't make a noise on the hard ground. I heard the sound again. It was more like a cry – the cry of a lamb that had lost its mother. It was a guess, I had no idea, though I was determined to rescue the poor creature, no matter what.

A sudden gust of wind blowing through the woods and setting the trees and branches to sway and rustle sent me off the scent. I heard it again. Not an animal, not a stray woodland creature. A human.

I began to run. I needed a weapon to defend myself with but saw nothing except for a fallen branch. I carried on, thinking hard as I ran. A rock? I looked to the right and left of me until I spotted a stone lying on the side of the track. I hefted it up and continued on.

A flash of colour caught my eye when I rounded a corner. A

piece of white cloth. Like a truce sign held aloft in a battle. It was an item of clothing. A shawl? I ran harder then, off the path and through the black tree stumps following a trail only I could imagine. Dead branches cracked beneath my feet. I no longer cared, desperate to find the female crying out in the midst of the woods. Not likely to be a fairy tale banshee.

Two figures were wrestling on a piece of flat ground. From behind I could make out a man, his bulk covering a smaller person who must be a female. I ran towards the man, hitting his head with the rock. I dropped the stone to one side and hauled him away. My gaze fell on a young female face frozen in utter fear: Miss Eliza.

Her skirt was thrust up to her waist and her red under-petticoat had been ripped. Her blouse was torn open. 'Help me,' she whispered.

By now the villain – I knew at once he was her older cousin George – had spun himself around. He gripped me around the throat. Acting fast, I raised my leg and kneed him, surprising him. I went for the advantage. His hands fell off my throat and I launched myself at him, pummeling him in the face. Blood spouted from his nose. I picked up the rock and hit him again, this time in the stomach. As he lay on the ground groaning, I dropped the rock and kicked him in the head, knocking him out.

'Michael.' It was Eliza, her voice high yet strong. 'Stop. Stop. That is enough.'

I couldn't stop. Utter hatred for the ugly brute coursed right through me. I went to kick him again.

Eliza pushed me to one side, bent down and listened to his chest. I watched her, adrenaline causing my heart to beat wildly. 'He's still breathing.' Her expression was grim, anxious as she raised her arm and pushed me with a shaking hand. 'You will be in terrible trouble. You need to run.'

'I can't leave ye here,' I said. 'He's a great danger to ye.'

'More likely it's you who will be in great danger if he recalls what happened when he comes to. Michael, I will be forever grateful to you but you are now in grave danger. Please go.' Her breathing was fast and her voice broke.

'I will not.' I was surprised how strong my voice sounded. 'I will see ye back to safety.'

She exhaled slowly. 'Only to the edge of the woods. We mustn't be found together.'

When we reached the end of the woods, she stopped and pulled at my arm. 'I will go home and then raise the alarm a little later. Give you time to get away. You must have never been here. I will say George and I went for a walk, and he went off ahead through the trees chasing after a deer and I lost him. I will say he must have tripped on roots in the woods and fallen. That he could have got concussion. I will think of what to say. Please, go. You will be in terrible trouble if he remembers you fighting him.' She looked so stern. So sad. 'My father will have you arrested.'

'He was trying to attack ye,' I said.

'I know,' she said. 'I know what he would have done if you hadn't come along but he is a liar and a bully, and he will tell the story a different way. He might say it was you attacked me and he was trying to fend you off. I know him only too well.'

I caught my breath.

'For my sake, please,' she said. She came towards me and reached up to hug me. 'I will never forget what you have done. Please go back a different way. Go home and ask your father to help you flee.'

I breathed in her violet scent, did as she asked and turned to walk away.

'Michael?' she called out.

I spun around.

'Take this,' she said.

I looked at what she held out to me. It was a gold heart on a thin gold chain she had retrieved from around her neck. 'He's broken it. Like our friendship but, please, keep it till we meet again.'

She leaned towards me and indicated how the locket could be opened. On one side was a coloured sketch of a woman with blonde hair. The other side of the locket contained a likeness of a little girl who I recognised as a young Eliza.

'My mother gave this to me back home in Kent not long before she passed. It's my greatest treasure.' Tears sprang to her eyes. 'She said for me to think of her when I prayed at night and I would be protected from harm. I want you to take it because you have risked so much to protect me. It will keep you safe. God help us, you will need protection, surely.'

I didn't know what to do. If I were caught with the gold necklace I'd be branded a thief and I was already a near murderer. Once this bully regained consciousness, I was a marked man. My life was finished. I knew I had to run. I reached out and clutched Eliza's arm and took one last look at her before I turned away.

The darkness of the night began to creep down as I ran all the way home. I got to the cottage, my lungs nearly bursting with the strain. Grandpa was the only one there. He breathed fast listening to my story. I could barely get the words out. While I was telling it to him, Uncle Bart came in with a bucket of milk from the cow.

When he heard my account, Uncle Bart exhaled heavily. 'Jaysus. They'll string you up.'

'Divil they will,' I said strongly, though I could feel the fear rise up to my throat.

'Shut your mouth, ye senseless eejit.' Uncle Bart's breath whistled through the gap where a tooth was missing. 'Always too big a man for your own feckin boots.'

Grandpa, hearing footsteps, looked to the door with fear. It opened and my other uncle, Con, came in. After Uncle Bart told him what had happened, Uncle Con took hold of me, pulled my arms tightly behind my back and shoved me into a corner near the open fire. He ordered Uncle Bart to run to the man at the end of the village who owned a cart.

'Ye will leave here tonight, or ye will be dead by the morning,' Uncle Con said. His breath was strong, stinking of alcohol, probably the poteen from the cottage down the road. 'Mr Griffiths will see to it.'

When the door opened again it was Mam carrying a basket of eggs. Hearing what had happened, her body shook and she began to keen loudly. Uncle Con, however, told her to hush lest the noise reach the neighbour. If anyone knew what had happened, we would be in great trouble. He ordered her to fill a small bag for me and another for him. 'We'll need a little sustenance for the journey and a coat and round up whatever money you can.'

There was no sign of Da. He had likely stopped on the way home for an ale at the bar as he sometimes did. After a long while the wheels of a cart rattled in the distance. Uncle Con hauled me out to the roadside where we waited. The night sky was black. Mam had followed us out from the cottage, crying silently. When she saw the cart halt outside the cottage and Uncle Bart get off it, she clutched hold of me. I was reluctant to cast her off but Uncle Con took me by the arms and pressed me onto the back of the cart. Before I could fight him off, he reached up and held a powerfully smelling cloth to my face.

When I came to we had arrived at a small town called

Castleisland and Uncle Con was handing some money to the man with the trap. The man thrust his cap down on his head and turned the horse to hasten back the way we'd come. Uncle Con put his arm around my shoulder and told me he had travelled this route many times, seeking work in Cork. We were standing at the beginning of Butter Road which led to the Butter Exchange in Cork. 'From where butter is exported to America,' he said, nudging me to start walking beside him. 'Keep your wits about ye, lad.'

The only light was that of the moon appearing fitfully now and then from behind the fast-moving clouds. We trudged onwards. When the sound of horse hooves and a rattling trap could be heard coming up behind us, Uncle Con stepped us to the side of the road and called out, asking was there room for the two of us. The driver stopped his horse and we clambered onto the trap, sharing it with two barrels of butter. Uncle Con made conversation with the man, who seemed eager to pass the time this way, but I found myself falling to sleep and every so often coming to with a start.

Night became day. I had no idea where we were until eventually we arrived at Cork and the man stopped his horse, pointing us in the direction of the port at Queenstown. I could smell the fresh sea air. From there I would get a ship to England, Uncle Con said. That was where Eliza came from and I knew the family would be returning there. I would have to find where her family lived in the place called Kent. In the meantime, I'd find work in the area – and wait for Eliza to return. None of this I said to Uncle Con.

When we arrived at the port, Uncle Con led me to a bench. 'Here. Ye look groggy, lad. Put ye head down a bit. I'll see if I can find some water for ye.'

When I next looked up, Uncle Con was near the front of

a small queue at the ticket office, speaking urgently to a big strong-looking lad a little older than me. I saw him point in my direction, and the lad nodded. Uncle Con shook his hand and patted him on the back. He returned to me. 'Ye man says there's a pump around the back of here, son. Come with me.'

Once we had drunk our fill of water, Uncle Con handed me a ticket. He took a deep breath. 'Ye must move fast, as old man Griffiths will have set the police to look for you already. Take care of yeself lad.' His voice was rough and I thought I heard him sob, but he coughed and spat on the ground, shook my hand and gave me a push towards a ship docked on the wharf.

When I walked up the gangway to the ship, a cheerful voice behind me said, 'Stick with me, laddo. We'll be travelling together, that we will.' It was the man I had seen Uncle Con talking with but I had no idea who he was and I said so.

'Denis, that's my name,' he said. He told me he was from a small village in the south of Kerry, near Castleisland, where Uncle Con and I had begun our walk on the Butter Road. 'So, we are both Kerry men and that's the truth.' He patted my arm. 'Not like these bleeding Cork men I saw lined up down there. We'll keep our distance, so we will.'

The boat set off shortly afterwards. The Irish Sea was fierce. The ship rocked wildly on the journey, and many staggered and fell down. I joined Denis in leaning over the side of the deck and was sick till my innards finally tossed up what little was left in there.

'We're a right pair,' Denis said grimly when both of us were no longer vomiting.

When we arrived at Liverpool, I was ready to make my farewells to my friendly companion, now I would make enquiries how to get to Kent but Denis had my arm in a strong hold. 'This way,' he said, leading me towards a sad queue of men ahead of us. When I went to pull away from him, he grabbed me even harder. I tried to protest but he persisted, adding sternly, 'I have instructions from your uncle.'

'I want to go to Kent,' I said, but a man came selling tickets and Denis bought two. I asked him where the ship was going and he said, 'You'll see.'

We were at sea an entire day before I learned I was going to Australia. I cursed my uncle. I cried in my sleep. There was nothing I could do. I listened to the men in the sleeping quarters talking among themselves. They were heading for the goldfields. There was money to be made there, one said. He saw me listening. 'Aye, you can come with us, young Mick,' he said. He spoke English like Mr Griffiths but his manner of speech was rougher. 'But you'll need to get through this journey first. Six weeks at sea will make you a man. None of that snivelling. I aim to be extraordinarily rich.'

Denis, near me on a bench, laughed loudly. 'We all will be, by God.' It hadn't taken me long to work out Denis was a talker and much of what he said was bluff to make himself sound tougher than he was.

If he had anything further to say, it was silenced by a bout of coughing. I leaned back away from him. I had seen too much of this with my da and I wasn't keen to pick up any illness from this man who had tricked me at the port in England. I realised Uncle Con had paid this fellow to trick me and the only thing in this lad's defence was he did what he was asked. It was just not to my benefit.

The men turned to playing cards, putting money in the middle, but I didn't join in. I watched them as they played and worked out the rules of the game. I was sure if I had a chance and any money, I'd win. The ticket on the boat would have wiped my uncles and parents out of what little money they had but I was not grateful, not at all. Already I was thinking how I might find gold and become wealthy and board a ship bound for England, where I would propose to Eliza.

After this, we were stuck down below. With the wind strong and wild, we could not go up on deck. I stayed low on the ship, kept my nose out of trouble, and didn't get into fights with the drinkers.

AOIFE
Taranaki 1977

After school each day Aoife took the bus home. The bus dropped her off at a bobby calf shelter on the side of the road, not far from the farm. Suzie, who had sat sniggering at her with a bunch of girls, got off further down the road.

Sometimes Suzie would ask girls to her house to play, or to see the new puppy, or her redecorated bedroom. Mrs Barker would pick them up after school on those days. What Suzie had to show was endless. Aoife could see the chosen ones staring at her from Mrs Barker's car some afternoons as she lined up for the bus, laughing at her. Nothing had changed since she got here.

Suzie wasn't on the bus today but the two new girls were. They were twins, big tall girls and tough-looking. Their father had come to work on the Barker family's farm. They'd be gone at the end of the season. For now they were here and there was Suzie whispering to them at their first playtime and passing out chocolate biscuits from her lunch box. Later Aoife noticed one of the girls eyeing her up and down in a considering kind of way. She was sure Suzie had said something to them about her.

This afternoon, the twins got off the bus at the same stop as Aoife instead of staying on till Suzie's stop. They crossed the road after Aoife did and then walked behind her, almost standing on the back of her ankles. Even though Mr Murphy's farm was not far ahead, she couldn't avoid the sense of menace that came from them. She had done nothing to them, nothing. She didn't know what to do. Should she turn and confront them?

Up ahead, she saw a big man in his heavy work jacket and gumboots. Da must've been trimming the boxthorn hedge on the side of the road. Now he stood and watched from a distance. One of the twins, Clemmie, crossed the road to the other side again, and the other girl followed. The three walked in silence until they reached the farm. Da gave a hard stare at the two girls, as if he had got the measure of them already.

Aoife and Da had started walking up the cattle race that ran along the paddock to the house, when Da turned to look carefully at her. 'Those girls,' he began.

Aoife looked back at him, wide-eyed.

'What did they do to ye?'

'Nothing.' It was true. How could you describe the terror two big girls could cause by almost treading on the back of your shoes? And their heavy breathing, she remembered that sound. You'd know they were behind you, all right. Clemmie had muttered a word quietly before she crossed the road. It sounded like, 'Later.' Aoife had an idea what that might mean. Later in the week. Another time.

'If they do anything,' Da said. 'I'll sort them.'

Aoife shook her head. That was why they were in New Zealand, in this godforsaken place as Mam called it, because that was Da. He might react in anger without thinking of consequences and the people who would get hurt would be Mam and her. He was like that. Mam called it being like 'a bull at a gate'.

By now, Aoife had an idea of what had happened in Ireland. She'd lain in bed many times piecing together snippets of information she remembered from when a man knocked at their door in the village late at night. He had waited outside on the porch while Da and Mam argued and argued. She had half-hid behind her bedroom door, listening. She heard how his cousins from up north had sent instructions for Da.

She tried to picture the scene they were arguing about. A stolen green Ford Cortina, its engine idling, waited on the street outside the bank when it opened on a quiet Tuesday morning in Tralee.

She imagined a man in a suit behind a desk to one side, two women in bank teller uniforms behind a counter awaiting customers and the bank manager in a back office. A big commotion as two men in masks, holding pistols, stormed in and demanded cash from the tills. They told the tellers to put whatever they had in the bags they'd brought with them. The manager, a big man, coming from out the back, confronting the two masked men and telling the staff to get down. One of the masked men pointing his handgun at him and firing it. The manager falling to the wooden floor, bleeding. The robbers filling what bags they could and hightailing it out of there.

A lad skiving off school, who happened to be passing by, had later reported seeing the men race to the green car that had its licence plates covered, the doors swinging wide open. Could Da have been at the wheel? Or was he one of the men inside the bank? Afterwards this man brought orders from up north. Da, Mam and she had to leave. They were driven to the port and were soon away on the boat.

Here in their new country, Da was already causing trouble. He'd boasted to Mam that he managed to get one across a Barker brother at the saleyards. It was to do with bull calves this Barker brother wanted. People in the district tended to stand back if one of the Barkers wanted anything, Da said. Not Da.

Da ran the bidding up, on purpose almost, and he had enjoyed it. The Barkers might have money but it didn't mean they got to run the show, he said.

In the kitchen, Mam had wrung a tea towel in her hands as she listened to Da. Her face darkened and she opened and shut her mouth. In the end, all she said was, 'Oh, Jack, mind how ye go, so.' And 'Was that wise?'

'Stole them right under the bastard's nose,' Da said triumphantly, as if she hadn't said anything at all. 'He didn't like it all right.'

Da had a plan for going ahead. He would buy up heifers in calf. When they calved, he was going to break the cows in at Mr Murphy's unused milking shed. He had the gift with cattle, he said. His own da had the knack as well. He had talked to a number of the younger farmers from around the coast, some had just started farming. They'd borrowed the money or inherited a farm from their fathers but knew bugger all about farming. Others had the cash laying around to be used – under their beds most like.

Mam picked up a plate and began to wipe it. She frowned. 'And the money for all this?'

'Well,' said Da expansively, 'I've got that sorted. Pretty much. Murphy says he'll loan me money to get started. Just till the money comes in from overseas.'

He had been in touch with his cousin, Barry, the one in America. 'I heard he has a good business out there leasing limousines to rich people. He's done well. He and his brother (up north, Aoife almost added for him) owe me. Seeing as it was me that had to go into hiding, not his brother. Not him nor the other bastards. They did me in. If it weren't for that wee fella skiving off school and spotting the car …' He glanced shiftily at Aoife as if suddenly registering she was there.

Was that why they couldn't go back? Now if Da did anything to these big girls, he'd really be in trouble. They were already living at the end of the world. They would have nowhere to run.

'Barry's been talking to people. Sympathisers. People loyal to the … ah … the cause, like a lot of Yanks are, them with their Irish ancestry,' Da was saying loftily as if he was giving a speech. 'They have the cash. It will be grand.'

Mam turned away. 'What about Mr Murphy? Ye can't be taking over his farm for your own business. He might hide away in his cottage most of the time but this is still his farm, not yours. He won't like ye taking over like this.'

'Don't ye worry about him,' Da said. 'You know I can sweet talk anyone. Your man's onside with the scheme. So long as someone else is doing all the work but he gets a cut, he's happy enough. He's pretty much lost interest in the farm, as far as I can see. He gave up on the dairy cows a while back. He'd rather head down to that South Island again. He's got a mate down there as it happens. Looked him up while on his tiki tour. He'll cause no trouble, none whatsoever.'

'I wish ye had never …' Mam began. She looked at Aoife and seemed to change her mind. 'Ye weren't a kid, ye were a grown man. Everyone else had moved on from all this malarkey long since, got on with everyday life. But oh no, ye and your cousins, them with their talk of the big cause, a United Ireland, ye had to be big men. And there was not even any money in it. How mad could you be, damn it. For God's sake, ye had your own child to think about.'

They had had arguments like this before. Each time, it went nowhere and soon Mam would either be in tears or heading to the bedroom and slamming the door. Aoife took out her homework and tried to concentrate on that instead.

IMOGEN
Taranaki 2018

After days of drizzling rain, the dull skies cleared a little. I had spent most of the time in the house with Jack, working on my editing files. Jack was often asleep in front of the television (on at high volume) and we didn't have much to say to each other. I was pleased to escape the dreary atmosphere and head off to meet Shelley Ward at the beach at Ōakura. I had texted her two days ago and we had arranged to meet up. I recalled her friendly voice from our previous phone conversation and was looking forward to seeing her in person.

Shelley was as optimistic as I had recalled. My gloom lifted as we walked from one end to the other and back on iron sands under a still grey sky, Shelley asking me another bunch of questions. She was definitely keen to make a move to a newspaper or perhaps television or radio in Australia. Should she go over there first to check the place out? How about accommodation? Would it be easy to make friends? I realised she was currently living and working in a small, mainly rural part of New Zealand where things were very different, so I did my best to answer.

As I followed her to the same café on the main road with the same German waitress, she asked me another, very different, question and one that was harder to answer. 'What made you go from a newspaper to book publishing? I'm curious.'

Curious was exactly the right word to describe her, I thought as I pondered my response. I could see how her open, friendly manner made her seem more innocent about the world than she was and could be a real plus for her in journalism. She knew how to ask leading questions. As for me, I needed to probe her knowledge concerning Jack and the people in the local area. At the same time, I didn't want to bring the conversation down to the despondent feeling I had had earlier.

The German waitress recognised me as we approached the counter and greeted me with a smile. 'Back again,' she looked around before pointing to the outside area, 'and our friend is back. He must like my coffee.'

I followed her gaze. The motorcycle man was at one of the tables reading a newspaper. As if he sensed my interest, he turned and caught my eye. I thought he intended to stare me out, like that game we played as children where the first to blink lost the game. I wasn't going to play that one. Instead, I lifted my arm and gave him a little wave. 'Nicer weather today,' I called cheerfully before walking over to a table far away from the man. Shelley raised her eyebrows.

'Met him here on my first day, small place.' I smiled at her as we sat down. 'About leaving the paper. My news editor and I had a difference of opinion. More than one.' I sighed as I recalled what had happened back then. With a bit of luck, she wouldn't probe any further.

Shelley grimaced. 'So, it's not always wonderful on these big newspapers?'

I didn't want to put her off. 'It was just him, really. A personality conflict. My bad luck, I guess. I could have applied for other jobs in the media but my friend Zoe had been looking at starting up a niche publishing company and asked if I'd like to come on board. I thought about it. What did I have to lose? I could always return to newspaper work later. So I handed in my notice and joined her.'

I realised I didn't want to talk about it any further because it made me even more aware I still missed my life as a reporter, the frantic pace at times, the excitement of the unknown. If it hadn't been for Gavin, I would still be on the newspaper, maybe even winning awards like Rebecca. I also didn't want to dampen Shelley's obvious enthusiasm for her career. The waitress brought our order over and we sat in silence for a while as we tucked into our chicken and cranberry sandwiches. I took a sip of coffee. It was my turn to ask the questions. 'I remember you said your grandfather might know Jack?'

'Yes, that's right. I called him yesterday and asked what he remembered about Jack. He said he'd known him for a long while. Says he was a real wildcard back in the day and there'd been all kinds of stories about him in that time. Had a few stoushes with people here and there, and I think even run-ins with the law.'

I thought of Jack's story about the man building the haystack. Jack had taken to him with a shovel. There were bound to be more stories, and likely more people with grudges against him but wouldn't most of them be elderly like Jack? Or even dead by now? If he had had a few brushes with the law like Shelley was suggesting, there might have been some incidents that had seen him end up in a police station.

'If there were court cases or anything like that, then there might be old newspaper reports,' I said, thinking aloud.

'It's possible, though I'm not sure how many of the old newspapers will have been put on microfiche. It's likely not far enough back in history for that. I can ask the librarian at work.' Shelley didn't sound too enthusiastic. Maybe library research wasn't her thing. Shelley leaned forward, suddenly much more engaged,

'Also, my grandpa said Jack was a good sort despite the stories and it was a bloody shame bad things were happening to him.'

'That's good to know.' It also meant her grandfather could be a useful source of information. 'What's your grandfather's name?'

'Hayden Ward.'

I nodded. 'I must ask Jack if he remembers him. Speaking of names of people, I met someone called Tamati. We exchanged words in the pub on my first day. Not very nicely. I think we took an instant dislike to each other. He said he knew Jack. Seemed surprised that he'd never mentioned a granddaughter.'

'Sounds like Tamati Rangihau. Talk about nosy. Comes up here from Wellington from time to time. Some people say he's seeing someone here and his role on the marae rebuild committee is just an excuse to come back. And, of course, she's married to someone else.' She grinned. 'Coastal people like to gossip. Makes life more interesting. He's good looking and can be a charmer, I'll say that much for him.'

I ignored this. I didn't care how good looking he was. That was not the point. 'He was at Jack's as well after he found Jack's dog, which had gone walkabout up the road. Said he'd rescued him from attacking some lambs on the Barker property?' Very convenient, I wanted to add but kept silent.

Shelley nodded. 'People help each other out around here and Tamati grew up in the valley so he will have known Jack for a long time. He'd recognise his dog and know he was a long way from home.' It was clearly no big deal as far as she was concerned. Her phone sounded, indicating a text. 'How about Molly?'

'How do you mean?'

Shelley was distracted by the screen. 'Well, she helps on the farm, doesn't she? She might have noticed things that weren't right. Or if anything unusual has happened. Mind you, she and her son haven't always lived here.'

Before I could reply, there was another beep. 'Damn. Sorry, I've got to go. We'll have to do this again. We could get some sightseeing in, take a trip to the mountain. I know someone who knows the mountain well and could go with us.'

It was time to leave. I waved goodbye to the waitress as we left. The cafe was now empty of customers. I didn't envy her the job.

When I returned to Jack's, he was sorting through mail at the kitchen table. He opened one envelope and took out its contents. He held the piece of paper closer to read the words, glaring at it.

'Something wrong?'

'No.' He crunched the paper. 'Junk mail, that's all.'

He stood up quickly, for an old man, and tossed the scrunched-up paper onto the fire. I thought I caught a glimpse of words typed on it in black letters before the fire devoured it. He gave a satisfied nod. 'Junk mail. Bloody rubbish. Dunno how they get my address.' He glared at me as if I might be going to ask him a question.

He was lying to me. For now, though, I could only pretend I hadn't noticed anything was up. 'Fancy a cuppa?' I said, heading across to the tap. I filled the jug and put it on to boil.

MICHAEL

Taranaki 1864

Our troop pressed on through the forest, trudging wearily. There were more Māori settlements to vanquish, our captain told us. The enemy had been destroying settler farmland and now a number of the farmers and their families had fled back to New Plymouth. It was our duty to quell the rebellion by the Māori opposition and reinstate the settlers.

I didn't much like the captain. He had an impetuous way about him that made me distrustful of him, including his choice of three a.m. forays. Sometimes we set up camp for days on end. Nothing untoward happened and all was quiet. The captain seemed determined to have us march through the whole of this part of this bloody godforsaken country, as I sometimes thought of it, and conquer every pā we came across, even though the inhabitants had done nothing to provoke the locals. I suspected Captain Wright wanted his name to shine in any future records of the war. I didn't voice my suspicions to Denis because I was still not sure I could trust him. 'Trust no one' was now my motto in these dangerous times.

As we moved further away from the safety of the camp at New Plymouth, we'd sometimes load our guns and fire at what would turn out to be nothing more than a fern-covered hill where a slight movement had been detected. It was clear the Māori were more astute than we'd been informed. At times, they would allocate parties of scouts who moved silently and stealthily and were often one step ahead of us. More than once, I got a sense of a group of warriors watching us from the darkness of the flax and fern of the forest. When I went to look again or nudged Denis to silence, they would be gone, leaving me wondering if I imagined them. Was I going mad out here in this wilderness?

We were getting even more jittery, day by day. At night around the campfire people muttered terrifying tales to each other about the tactics of the Māori warriors we could be facing. One older man told us about a campaign he'd been in up north. It became known that some of the Māori warriors had made a habit of disguising themselves in pigs' skins before creeping up to a camp and tomahawking the sentries.

An Irish lad was on lonely sentry duty when he heard a rustle in the bush a few yards away. Instead of reporting the incident to the sergeant as he was meant to do, the lad panicked. He fired a shot, waking the camp and putting everyone on high alert for an invading war party. A search party was sent out only to find the slain body of a sow, killed by a bullet to her heart. When I heard this, I was pleased enough not to be that Irishman finding he was now a laughing stock.

Day after day our troop kept marching. One morning we rounded a corner and came face to face with a flooded river. The captain stood by the bank and ordered us to wade across, holding our rifles up high so they wouldn't get wet and our packs against our chests so we could float if we had to. We set off, Denis and I together not far behind a couple of lads and another big one, a red-haired Scotsman with a ready joke or two whom I had spoken with once or twice around the campfire in the evenings. I looked down at the fast-moving water and the rocks sticking out of it in places and felt as if I were going to be sick.

Up ahead, halfway across the river, the Scotsman, perhaps concentrating on holding his rifle aloft, lost his balance. He fell sideways into the rock-filled surging water, half his body slipping under. A red stain began to spread across the surface.

I heard Denis curse beside me. 'Oh, my God, sweet mother Mary, Jaysus, the man's hit his head on those rocks.'

Hearing this, I bent over and vomited into the river.

'O'Reilly, you and Wolfe stay behind and get the man out. The rest of you keep going,' the captain shouted.

I tried to look again but Denis thumped me lightly on the back and we moved on. Neither he nor I said anything further about what had happened. Not even that night when we could have spoken of this in private.

IMOGEN
Taranaki 2018

The woman I had seen greeting Tamati in the pub on my first day in Wexford came around to Jack's one afternoon. She was selling tickets to a fundraiser for the primary school. 'We've got a great bunch of volunteers putting it on,' she said. She told me the entire district usually turned out for it, and Jack always bought a ticket (but never went, as he told me with some satisfaction when she had gone.)

'You go with Molly and Daniel,' he said.

I pretended indifference but, in fact, I was excited. This would be the ideal opportunity to check out possible suspects – the person or people who had tried to make Jack's life hell.

Early in the evening on the Saturday night, I pulled from my suitcase the one dress I'd packed, put it on, stepped into a pair of heels, and added make-up and bright red lipstick to complete my look. It seemed 'party' enough for Wexford, where I'd quickly observed that the locals favoured gumboots as their preferred footwear.

When I came out to the kitchen, Jack was seated at the kitchen table, a cup of tea in his hand. I did a little twirl, feeling a bit silly when Jack glanced at me but didn't say anything.

'Will you be all right, Jack?'

'Fine. As fine as ever.'

No surprise. He'd prefer staying put with his newspaper and usual evening glass of whisky. I might have liked to stay home too but I had a job to do.

On the way to the event, I asked Daniel to tell me what usually happened. 'They'll have music, a band, and acts and skits and things. Usually there's an auction – or a silent auction – and performances. If it's like in past years.' His tone didn't contain much excitement. More like studied irony, suited to a teenager.

'Sounds fun,' I said equally drily. I made sure to hide my interest. I didn't want Molly and Daniel to know I wasn't going for the performances. What I was interested in was watching how the people in this secretive district acted in each other's company.

Utes and cars were already parked outside when we got there. Molly and Daniel stopped to say hello to someone they knew. I walked ahead and paused to look up at the night sky wondering if I could make out the Southern Cross and be reminded of home. Tonight the sky was too cloudy to see anything. I caught a glimpse of a man on a motorbike under the trees opposite the hall's well-lit entrance. I was fairly sure he was the same man I'd seen twice now at the café in Ōakura. He must have been checking out what was happening at the hall.

Molly and Daniel caught up with me and as we traipsed inside, I heard the roar of the motorbike starting up. You couldn't stay long in this district without seeing each inhabitant at least twice, I decided and now I was about to see the rest of them, some for the first time. A small group of Filipino men – farm workers most likely – standing together by the door moved apart to let us through.

Inside, the hall was already crowded with locals. Daniel went over to greet a group of young guys I assumed were his mates. I checked out the room, recognising several faces, a couple of the fire service men and the guy with the deep voice who had told the entire room at The Empire who I was.

In a corner, Tamati harangued a tall man who appeared to be listening intently. After a time, two other men joined in the conversation. The older man must have made a joke because Tamati and the others burst out laughing and Tamati tapped the older man on the shoulder. He caught sight of me and nodded before turning back to the conversation. I turned away. I had no desire to renew our acquaintance tonight.

As the five-piece band at one end of the room started playing the Bob Marley and the Wailers song 'No Woman No Cry,' Shelley walked in with Nathan. He spoke to her, leaning closer. She took off her coat and handed it to him in an easy way that surprised me. With all her questions about working in Australia, I wouldn't have expected her to have a boyfriend. Or maybe just not Nathan.

Molly offered to introduce me to some of the other people, and we made our way towards a group. Their keen expressions told me some had already heard about the granddaughter arriving out of the blue but before Molly could introduce me, an elderly woman came towards me and grabbed both my arms in a hug so tight I feared my bones might break. She wore an apron, as if she had been working in the kitchen. 'Ana. Ana. You're here.'

'I'm sorry,' I said. 'I'm not Ana. I'm Imogen.'

The old woman didn't appear to hear me. She reached up and put both her hands on my face, holding my cheeks. 'My darling girl. Where have you been?'

What should I do? Flustered, I looked around for help. Another woman, also wearing an apron, came to my rescue. 'Now, Auntie, no good running away. We need you in the kitchen.'

'But,' the elderly woman said plaintively, 'I want to talk to Ana here.'

'This young woman isn't Ana. Auntie's getting forgetful. No worries. We'll go back to the kitchen, shall we, Auntie?' The woman smiled at me, took the old woman by the hand and began to lead her away.

'Who did she mean?' I asked Molly. 'Who is Ana?'

Molly shook her head. 'I don't know.' She turned to the group of locals and introduced me. I smiled, quelling a sense of unease. The conversation returned to the provincial rugby team and how it was doing. Framed photographs of rugby jerseys lined one wall.

The conversation was interrupted by a tall woman with an imposing manner who had strolled across to us. She spoke in an over-bearing tone to Molly, telling her she should go and check what was happening in the kitchen. 'It's a shambles out there.' She waved Molly away, leaving the two of us.

'I heard you were staying with Jack,' she said, without any preamble. 'Glad I've caught you. Come to check up on him, have you?'

'Sorry?' Who was this woman? And what business was it of hers?

'You must know, the upkeep on the farm is a disgrace. All that trouble with his cattle polluting the waterways. That stream of his used to be so clear.'

'I hadn't noticed.' On the walk around the farm with Daniel, I'd observed the heavy machinery across the road, the burnt-out hedges, the paddock with Champion grazing and the partly demolished shelter. 'The stream looked fine to me.'

The woman ignored my response. 'You're a city girl, so I've heard, but honestly, your grandfather needs putting in a retirement home. He's past being able to look after a farm on his own. The sooner someone gets him to shut up shop, the better for him. And the better for the district.'

'Sorry?' I asked again, less tentatively this time.

'Honestly, the council has been patient about it up till now, but ... take this as a warning. Something needs to be done soon. The sooner the better.' She paused for breath. 'It's not merely that he's past it, which I am sorry to say he has shown countless times that he is, but ...'

'Enjoying the party?'

I recognised the voice and spun around. 'Shelley.' I was pleased to have her interrupt this one-sided conversation.

'Suzie, good to see you,' Shelley said to the other woman and turned to me. 'Jack's not with you, I take it?'

'No,' I said.

'I hope people have been looking after you.' Shelley stared hard at Suzie.

The other woman glanced around the room. 'I must make a move. People to say hello to.' She waved towards the crowd. After a short hesitation, she turned back to me and said, 'How is dear Aoife, what is she up to these days?'

Having heard her vehemence about Jack, nothing should have surprised me about this woman. Except for one thing. I always thought Aoife had left so long ago no one would remember her. 'You knew my mother?'

'Yes, indeed. That poor girl. That thick Irish accent. And, of course, Jack hasn't changed, well, not for the better. I always thought she and her mother escaped at the right time.'

I gazed at her, stunned.

'I don't think I could have coped in her place. I'm sure her own mother couldn't. The whole emigrating thing was a huge mistake, really. At least you can sort Jack out now you're here.'

'Suzie,' Shelley interrupted, indicating over her shoulder. 'I think there's someone over there wanting to talk to you.'

'Right, of course. My constituents must be heard,' she

declaimed, starting to march off towards another group, then she paused. 'Shame about what happened. Though we could all see it coming.'

What did she mean? I opened my mouth to ask, but she was gone.

'What the hell?'

'Bitch,' Shelley said succinctly and then, in case I hadn't caught her meaning the first time, 'Prize bitch. She's on the council, represents the area. Also, she's one of the Barker family from the far end of your road. The nobs. Likes to throw her weight around. She was a real estate agent before she got the council job.'

I wanted to ask what the 'bitch' had meant about Jack and what she could have meant by her other comments, but I heard the sound of a microphone being tested. Mina, the woman I had seen at the pub that day, began speaking into the mic, asking people to clear some room for the entertainment.

Shelley leaned in closer. 'What were you going to ask?'

I hesitated. Now wasn't the time, nor the place. 'An old lady thought I was someone called Ana,' I said instead. 'She was insistent. It was quite freaky. Like I was a ghost.'

'I don't know anyone called that name,' Shelley said. 'Was she one of the kuia from the marae? Wouldn't surprise me if she thought you were one of her grandchildren. There's lots of rellies we haven't seen here come from the cities when there's a tangi or big hui.'

'I guess so. She was helping the other ladies in the kitchen. She was quite insistent.' I didn't know what to add. I hadn't mistaken the icy sensation that went through the back of my neck when the old woman had persisted with her belief.

Mina called for quiet. Someone came to stand beside her and gave a reminder about the silent auction. 'Make sure you take a look at the lists on the walls over by the kitchen. As you know, part of the proceeds from this evening's entertainment will go to help our young kapa haka group take part in the national competitions in Auckland, and tonight, they'll showcase some of their work.'

A troupe of girls and boys in traditional costumes filed onto the stage area, accompanied by two guitarists. The children began their first number, a powerful dance and song routine. They performed three songs in all and the hall erupted in applause and cheers at the end.

After this came other acts, other songs. Some in Māori, others old country and western numbers. A comedian kept people laughing for a time. The locals were a varied bunch when it came to entertaining.

There was no time to talk or to ask Shelley to fill me in on who was who in the throng of people. When a girl of about sixteen, with spiky pink hair and skinny arms in a sleeveless dress, began to bellow out a rousing rendition of 'Amazing Grace', others joined in.

The accompanist was still quietly strumming his guitar at the end of the song when there was a commotion at the hall entrance. A door slammed. An angry male voice resounded down that end of the room, and there were other loud sounds as if someone was arguing with that person. I tried to make out what was being said but from the crush in the middle of the room it was impossible.

Beneath the rose-tinted lighting in the hall, a dark figure stormed his way through the crowd. The first thing I could see was the gun with a long barrel he was brandishing. A woman across the room screamed and then another. My body swayed and the floor seemed to come up to meet me. I regained my balance as two men in the path of the man reached and grappled with him, trying to restrain him. The man shook them off and charged towards us. It was Jack who stood there, a rifle in his right hand, anger filling his face with a wildness I hadn't seen before.

Could I intervene? Would he even know it was me? 'Jack,' I called out, at the same time as he again waved the rifle.

Two women in front of me grabbed their children to them. One of the kapa haka kids started to cry. His mother shushed him.

'Jack,' I said again.

He ignored me. 'Right, you bastards. Who did it this time?'

'Jack,' Mina said. 'Calm down, old fella. What's the problem?'

Jack ignored her, too. 'Go on, you can tell me, you spineless bastards.' He glared around the crowd. People began to shuffle backwards, away from him.

'What's happened? Come on, Jack, tell us.' The voice was strong and calm. I recognised it straight away. Nathan's voice.'

Jack clutched at the gun as if he planned to wave it directly at the crowd. 'Someone let six of my young steers out onto the road. They made a ruckus, woke me up as they ran down the cattle race past the house. I know someone must have been chasing them, herding them. There were lights. Torches, I think. I heard a motor.'

I could hear the accusation in his voice and another sound. Anguish? His voice broke. 'And the bull. My prize pedigree, Champion. One of you bastards did it. Go on, tell me, you lousy cowards.'

Silence.

'Not brave enough, eh? I'll tell you what you've done.' Jack's tone was deadly now. 'My prize bull ... My prize bull. Champion.' He said the bull's name again, then stopped. There was a hiss in the room as people spoke among themselves. 'The bastards must've chased him out onto the road. Probably set a dog on him. I got in the truck and went after them, but too late. The steers bolted and Champion – he got caught up in the barbed wire by the front gate, got it around his neck and front legs. He had blood all over him but he's kept going. He's dragged himself a hell of a long way down that road and onto the bridge. Lying in the middle of it.'

I remembered the bridge and the memorial to the man who had died.

'The bridge. Shit. The tanker will be coming through later tonight.' I wasn't sure who said this, but it made people gasp. I could hear women near me making weird keening noises.

I pictured the bridge, knew how narrow it was and a big milk tanker coming upon it suddenly in the dark.

'My prize bull. Beyond help. Can't move him easily. But … but he's not dead, you bastards. I went home to get my gun. But …' His voice choked. 'So, go on, you big brave idiots, you let him out on the road. Are you going to finish him off? You cowards. That bull was worth more than a thousand of you, you bastards. You know who you are. Don't think I won't get you and when I do, I'll rip your bloody throats out.' He brandished the gun.

Nathan reached out and took the gun from Jack, who surprisingly made little resistance. 'I'll go and check him, Jack. Leave it to me.' He turned to the crowd. 'Can someone fetch him a whisky? He's in shock. And get on to someone at the factory to warn the tanker driver. We'll need to get down there before any cars head that way. You stay here, Jack.'

'No, Nathan.' Jack was weary now, as if he had exhausted all his pent-up energy and anger. 'No. He's my bull. I'll come with you.'

I pushed through the people in front of me. 'Jack.' I took his arm, half expecting him to pull away, push me off, but he didn't resist. He didn't even seem to notice me. I continued to clasp his arm while we made our way slowly through the hall and out the door, Shelley close behind us. Outside Nathan indicated for us to follow him to his car. Daniel and Molly headed over to hers.

By the time we reached the cars, other people had spilled out into the road, too. Local farmers, people who would know what it was like to lose one of their prize cattle. If something needed doing, they'd be there. In Nathan's car, Jack sighed heavily from time to time, occasionally letting out a low moan. Tears stung my eyes but I didn't know what I could do or say to comfort him. The cars drove behind in a tight procession, following us towards the place where Champion had ended up.

The headlights of Nathan's car shone on the bridge in the darkness. He got out first and held the door open for Jack, motioning Shelley and me to stay back out of the way. He said quietly to me, 'The animal's in pain, he might lash out.'

A couple of young steers were grazing on one side of the road and showed little interest in us. A man from one of the other vehicles came to shine a torch on the injured creature. It was the tall man who had been talking to Tamati in the hall, but Tamati wasn't in the bunch of men.

The bull moaned as Nathan spoke softly to it. He had taken charge. No one was questioning it. He reached out and touched the side of the big animal. It didn't move or thrust him away. Instead it lay there, its leg bent and limp.

Minutes – it seemed like ages – went by. Nathan spoke quietly to Jack. 'We'll get the vet. The kindest thing will be to put him down.'

Molly came up to stand beside me. 'Richie's gone to Taupō,' she said to Nathan. 'Fishing weekend. It'll be the on-call vet, the young one and he'll take too long to get out here if he doesn't know the roads.'

Nathan turned. 'Jack? Are you okay if I take over here?'

Jack didn't reply. He shook his head and let out a stifled moan. He was crying. I wanted to go over to him, but Shelley held my arm tightly. Champion was too dangerous to get close.

'Just do it,' he said.

'All right, Jack.'

Nathan walked back to the car. He opened the boot, retrieved Jack's rifle and checked it was loaded. I wanted to scream out so many questions. What kind of person or people would do this to an old man? Who would deliberately chase a bull and these young energetic steers out onto a road in the dark? Who would have done such a thing knowing the outcome could be so terrible? Around us, the people who had followed Nathan's car to this spot were silent. Shocked. Sorrowing. It couldn't have been one of them, could it?

Nathan walked back to Champion. Behind the huge creature, the headlights from Nathan's car lit up the figure of a man in dark clothing. He was standing still, watching the bull, his hand stretched out towards it. I was sure I saw him, and that I knew him, but when the bull moaned, my gaze went to him and when I looked again there was no sign of the man. It was dark. Surely I couldn't have seen anything.

I focused on Nathan now. He stood looking down at the massive animal. A shot rang out, deafening in the still night air. It was all over. Hot salty tears flowed down my cheeks. Making my way to Jack, I put my arms around him. His body relaxed into my arms for a few seconds before he shrugged me off.

We stood in silence while the men who had driven in convoy with us conferred among themselves, deciding who would round up the steers. One said he'd fetch a front-end loader from a nearby farm, saying, 'Champion needs to be moved off the bridge as fast as possible before he causes an accident.'

Thinking of this once-wonderful beast being shunted to one side like a broken-down train carriage made me want to be sick. A sad ending for a proud animal and a tragic ending for an evening that was meant to be about celebration of community. Someone grasped my hand. It was Shelley. She stood beside me, both of us silent.

Nathan's phone rang. 'As soon as I can. On my way,' he said, moving towards his car.

I pulled my hand from Shelley's and walked over to him. 'You're leaving?'

'There's an incident at Ōakura,' he said. 'I'm the closest.'

'But shouldn't you be taking fingerprints off the gate at Jack's?' My tone was loud, belligerent, but I didn't care. 'Checking out who has been at the farm? Who did this?'

He looked down at me. 'Champion's dead. There's nothing that can be done right now. We've got an emergency over there. A more urgent emergency.'

'But you have to find out who did it.' My voice rose even higher and I clutched at his arm. 'You can't just leave.'

'Look. I've got to go.'

I stood in his way. 'No.'

'I could take fingerprints tomorrow but you know what? Likely there'll be none.' His voice had become stern.

'You mean they wore gloves? Wiped them off?' I grabbed his arm again to stop him leaving, not thinking about anything but Jack and his cherished bull and determined to stand my ground.

'No.' He moved a little as if he were going to reach out and push me away. He lowered his voice. 'What I mean is it's more than likely Jack left the gate open. Again. He probably forgot to close it. Or someone did. Look ...'

'But surely ...?'

'I've got to go. People's lives could be in danger.' This time, he strode away without looking back.

I didn't care. Unknown people whose lives were at stake weren't my concern right now. Anger boiled up in me. I turned towards Shelley but she was ignoring me, hurrying after Nathan.

'Wait,' she called. 'I'll come with you.'

I knew she'd want to cover this other incident for her paper but what about Jack and what had been done to him? I stood there, arms folded and teeth clenched. I hated the pair of them.

MICHAEL
Taranaki 1864

Days later we marched through a settlement of a few recently built settlers' cottages and one or two other buildings, and Captain Wright ordered us to put up our tents nearby. In the evening, a new order came. We were to track down a pā where a group of warriors were hiding out. The same men had ventured onto a settler's land and captured the man, his wife and two children. Other soldiers had tried to rescue them, at great cost, the man had died in the resulting battle and the warriors had kidnapped the son. Our mission was retribution, nothing less. We were to attack and kill as many of them as we could.

Our captain led us into the forest under the cover of a moonless night, where all around us was black and dense. We could barely make out each other in the darkness. We marched for two hours, the night air chilling. The lines were halted.

'Attack. Now!' our sergeant yelled.

Screams abounded as we rushed at the fenceline of a small pā. Shots were fired from our men and came back at us from behind the palisade. Three of our men fell, all heavily wounded, and others of our troops were sent in to drag their bodies away from the pā's foreground.

The black night clung to us. As the soldiers around us lit

tapers, I could see the warriors guarding the picket fence posts were young boys who couldn't have been older than twelve – certainly not real warriors. No matter how young they were, though, the ones lining the fence had weapons all right. Muskets. That made them our enemy.

I lunged forward, intending to shoot. As I did, something stabbed my shoulder and I cried out in pain. Warm blood gushed down my arm to my wrist. One of our men rushed to drag my young assailant off me, taking over and holding tight to the boy. A number of these young warriors had been hiding in the forest to the side of the village and had come out of the darkness unseen to attack us with their tomahawks and whatever weapons they had mustered.

'Watch those young scoundrels,' the sergeant shouted. 'Don't trust them.'

In the end though, it didn't take much to overpower these young boys, some of whom appeared exhausted from lack of sleep due to being on guard all night. Soon we had them lined up against the fenceline, while other soldiers turned over the food huts, scattering kūmara, other vegetables and drying meats in front of the dwellings.

Some feet ahead, Eddie, a fellow Irishman and a simple sort of lad, turned to call out to another soldier. A young prisoner he was guarding, who had been lying on the ground in either fear or exhaustion, seized the Irishman's rifle and shot him. Blood splattered as Eddie's brains scattered over the ground. 'Get the young bastard,' someone shouted. A shot rang out and the boy was dropped.

The corporal shouted for us other men to watch our prisoners. 'Tie them up if you have to.' We didn't need telling.

Another shout came. A woman and a young lad were running towards us through the palisades. One of the soldiers, I couldn't tell who, fired two shots, one after the other. The woman fell first and then the wee lad. He couldn't have been older than five. Another soldier dragged their injured bodies away. 'That'll teach 'em,' somebody shouted.

One of the troop tossed a lighted taper and fire whooshed along the fences around the pā. Screams came from the women who, with their children, were still in the pā. In a bunch they poured out towards us, terrified. The soldiers towards the front captured them easily enough. They lined them up and forced them into a long single file ready to herd them back to our camp. Other soldiers caught hold of the stray horses that were cowering in fear and excitement, harnessing them with ropes made of twisted vines. They were ours now.

It was time to leave. My arm ached with pain. I lifted it and held it under a lighted taper. The damage looked worse than I expected and I felt giddy then, as if I might keel over.

'Show it to me,' a corporal ordered as he approached.

He drew a knife to cut off part of his shirt down to the elbow and tied it tightly around my arm. I couldn't tell if it hurt because the night air was cold and my limbs were frozen.

'I'll be fine,' I said. My voice was weak.

'Would ye look at that,' Denis called out.

The fire had spread from the fences and the entire place was blowing up in bright red flames. The flax roofs crackled and the simple dwellings were burning to the ground. The captured women began to cry, producing a high-pitched weeping and wailing sound. One tried to run back towards the dwellings but was grabbed by two soldiers and tackled to the ground.

'Move them on,' the captain shouted. 'In single file.'

We did, shouting instructions to the people in a language they could not understand as we led them off to captivity.

The men in our garrison were jubilant that night as they sat drinking a portion of ale around the fires at the camp. Extra food had been dolloped onto plates. I knew I should have been happy because we had achieved our mission. We were real soldiers now but when I thought of poor Eddie, my fellow Irishman, and the awful bloody and unnecessary deeds that had been wrought due to his loss of attention, I felt sickness and dread. My limbs trembled.

'Ye all right, Mick?' a voice said in my ear. It was Denis.

The sick feeling welled up in my stomach and guts. 'I dunno. Poor Eddie. And that woman and boy. Those women in the pā.' I stopped and the tremble went through me again.

'Don't worry about a thing, lad,' Denis said as if he hadn't heard me. 'We're proper soldiers now. That shithead of a captain can't condemn us anymore. We did it. Showed him what we could do.'

I couldn't stop thinking about what I'd seen. 'What we've done is nothing short of murder plain as night is night and day is day. Surely these people are no different from our own people back home, them with their potatoes, and fish, and children and after all is said and done, isn't it their land? What right does this Government have to take it so forcibly?'

And why, I wanted to add, why in God's name are we doing their dirty work for them? The despair and anger I felt as I spoke raced through my body.

'Ruru, the old man who sells vegetables at the camp, told me the government lied to the chiefs about an agreement and that's why his people are fighting now. He said they are protecting their rightful lands, their homes and their families. It's the same as back home, no different at all. Can ye not see that? That rogue Oliver Cromwell and his army of men did exactly the same to our people, confiscating the land off the Catholics. My family and yours have suffered because of that oppressor ever since. Can't you see what's happening here is no different?'

Denis tapped me on my other arm and I felt his fingers pinch my skin. 'Listen, mate, don't you be talking like that. Are ye mad? If the captain hears he'll have ye guts for garters.' He looked pointedly towards where the captain was making his rounds of the men. He spoke quietly in my ear and his spit landed on my cheek. 'And don't even think of absconding. The trouble ye'll be in isn't worth thinking about. Not if ye are planning to go home after all this is over. I tell ye, keep those thoughts to yeself and keep ye mouth shut, if you know what's good for ye. Think on, there's a good lad.'

The captain came over then to stop by where we sat. 'Well done, lads. You did better than expected. Those Māoris are a treacherous lot, by God. There is much more work to be done.'

I thought of Eliza then. I wondered how much more of this work, as he called it, I must do before I could find a ship to take me back to go in search of her. My fingers sought out the locket she had given me, touching its outline and, in my mind, I spoke to her.

AOIFE
Taranaki 1977

The two new girls had grabbed the seats at the back of the bus where Suzie normally sat. Aoife could see the two little Lawson kids picking up their school bags and making ready to get off. It was their stop. Their mother met them in her ute if it looked like rain. Aoife waited till they were at the door to the bus, then shot out of her seat. The bus stayed motionless as she got off quickly. She waited till it had moved off before crossing the road.

That first time she and Mam had walked right to the back of the farm, she had noticed a gate leading to the small side road. The gate was partly hidden by the hedge and was called a Taranaki gate. There were others like it on the rest of the farm. It was made of wire and batten, and stretched between concrete posts, with a barbed-wire top and five plain wires. It wouldn't be all that easy to climb but she would face that problem when she got to it.

She walked along the side road, peering into any gaps in the hedge, looking for the gate. She found it after a while and climbed over it carefully, making sure the hem of her pinafore dress didn't catch in the barbed wire. A sudden gust of salty wind made her look up. Grey clouds loomed on the other side of the farm. A rumble came, a sound that could only be thunder. If she ran, she could make her way across the paddocks back to the house. As she took a step, thunder sounded again and then a sudden heavy downpour. Cold drops slid down the back of her neck. The rain became small hard balls of hail and she had nothing to cover herself with.

A small group of cows-in-calf that Da had bought at the auction had moved to stand under a big tree with overhanging branches. She was afraid of approaching them, lest one of the more skittish ones stood on her foot with its sharp hooves. One of them, and then another, had turned and were now eyeing her. What if they decided to stampede and race towards her? Looking about for a place to shelter, she spotted a sizeable gap in the boxthorn hedge in the opposite corner. She walked towards it deliberately and confidently so the heifers wouldn't chase after her.

Once there, she bent down towards the opening. The space inside was bigger than she expected. A person could stand up in there easily. It was surprising one or two of the cows hadn't found the hole and ventured inside but people always said cows could be dumb. They followed the leader, stuck with the herd.

Aoife squatted and wriggled herself inside. It was like a secret lair. A sharp acidic scent flowed up from the ground as if one of the younger, smaller heifers had crashed its way in and done a wee. Tossed in a corner was a tin cup, old-fashioned looking, like a mug a boy scout would take camping.

It looked like someone had used the shelter before. Probably Mr Murphy sheltering from the rain before checking on his cattle. Somewhere to have a smoke.

Aoife took a deep breath. That was what it was, she decided, Mr Murphy's old shelter. So now, all she needed to do was wait, safe from the cows, till the downpour stopped. When eventually it did, she ran through the paddocks and down the cattle race until, breathing heavily, she reached her house.

Once Da had started buying the heifers, he cheered up. Some evenings, he'd come into the house from the farm and get Mam to run a bath for him and fetch him a clean shirt and trousers. In the kitchen, he'd look in the mirror as he dragged a comb through his damp black hair. He was heading out with the lads for 'a few beers'.

Da had found himself some friends. It couldn't be any of the Barker brothers because he still went on about them thinking they were better than anybody else around here. He smiled and didn't reply when Mam said to him he'd been told to keep to himself, lie low and stay out of trouble. That way, they could go home when things settled.

One night Da brought home a wiry little man with a nasty face who wore a cloth cap on his head. Aoife recognised him as the man who sometimes cut back the boxthorn hedges on the sides of the roads and on the farm. His name was Harry Duncan.

Da told Mam to get out the whisky from the bottom of the china cabinet. It was saved for special occasions – not that there had been any. Mam gave a tired smile and told Aoife to come with her to the kitchen where she dished up four plates of food from the pots on the stove while the men started drinking.

Harry shovelled the food into his mouth, laughing when Da told a joke. When the little man mentioned a poker game, Mam's face set in sharp lines.

'It's clear as a bell to me, Harry,' Da said suddenly. 'I can tell what they're up to from a mile away.'

'If you say so.'

'I mean,' Da went on, 'that's how they operate. Keep a man out. If he's too bloody good for them. A man with a better eye for cattle, say. Or how to make a bob. They don't want him here, they show it. Know what I mean?' He thumped his glass down sharply on the tabletop.

'You could be right,' Harry said.

'Need to take a leak.' Da got up and slammed the door to the hallway behind him.

The little man speared a potato and said to Mam, 'Very good, missus.'

Mam inclined her head without smiling or looking at him.

'Is that greenstone?' The man squinted at the big piece of stone Mam had picked up that day on their walk through the back paddocks near the swamp. She had brought it home and put it on the fireplace. He spoke through a mouthful of potato. 'It's big enough. Looks like you could do real damage with it. Where did you come across it?'

'It was here when we came,' Mam said as if she couldn't remember.

Aoife opened her mouth to speak. She wanted to remind her they had found it near the swamp, that she remembered the day but Mam gave her a hard look and she closed her mouth.

'Oh,' the man said, raising a forkful of meat to his mouth. He chewed for a time. 'I've heard some weird stories about these old weapons being found and things going wrong after. If it were me, now, I wouldn't have that in the house.' He speared another slice of beef, frowning and sat back in his chair. Something was on his mind. 'Mind you, you must have heard the stories about this house.'

Mam shook her head. She picked up Aoife's and her own empty plates and stacked them noisily as if to remind him it was time to be going.

The little man took no notice. 'Aye,' he said, his finger picking at a bit of beef stuck in his teeth. 'Murphy, his brother and his parents were in the kitchen. They heard music coming from the sitting room but no one was in there. The piano was playing. All by itself.'

'So, of course it was, why wouldn't it be?' Mam muttered under her breath, quiet enough, but Aoife heard her.

'And some weeks after, they got a letter telling them Murphy's uncle had died. He'd been living in Sydney and got in with a bad crowd and was shot. Fairly sure the time of day they heard the piano was the exact time of his death. Or so I was told.' The little man paused dramatically. 'Not just that. There's Murphy's brother. He was only a lad. He was found dead down at that swamp. Cursed, see.'

Mam shuddered.

'Of course, Murphy himself reckons he's seen a man in full army uniform walking through the rooms at night. You ask him.'

'That's time enough for ye bed,' Mam pushed Aoife's shoulder. 'No more of this nonsense please,' she said to the little man. I heard enough of these old stories in Ireland, Mr Duncan. More than enough. They were always hocus pocus. Bogus. We won't be needing them in this new country now. Not at all thanks.'

'Tell you what,' the little man said as if she hadn't spoken. 'This place has a bad feeling to it, right enough, and it's not only the house.'

Aoife wanted to ask him what he meant but her mother gave her another push and she did as she was told and went to her bedroom. It was cold at that end of the house, very cold. She wondered if Mam would remember to bring her a hot water bottle to place her feet on under the blankets.

Much later, Aoife had no idea when, she heard shouting. It

was Da mainly and Harry was protesting or trying to apologise. After that she heard the door slam, and Da and Ma were in their bedroom, talking loudly. They were back to what they often argued about. Da was saying Mam didn't understand what he and the cousins had been fighting for and why he'd had to help the cause, that she didn't know her feckin history.

'History. Bullshit more like,' Mam shouted back this time. There was a crashing sound. 'Ye and those eejits weren't bothered about the history. And ye were old enough to have more sense.'

'Think what ye want,' Da said. 'I'm off to bed.'

Mam didn't give up. 'It was ye all over. Reckless. Not thinking. Not telling me what ye were up to behind my back. I know my history, damn it.' Aoife heard another crash.

After that, Da started to come home late at night. Once, he made such a noise opening the back door he woke Aoife. She had been dreaming about the man in uniform, the one Harry Duncan said Mr Murphy had seen. In her dream other men were chasing the uniformed man, and she could smell fire. It was the strangest dream. She must have woken up because, suddenly wide awake now, she heard voices. Her father had crashed his way to the phone and she guessed he was calling Ireland – late at night calls were cheap. He was asking about his money again.

IMOGEN
Taranaki 2018

The morning after the terrible fate Champion had suffered, Jack didn't say a word. He had gone outside to sit on an old wooden bench, staring mutely ahead at the paddock where the rescued steers were grazing. His body was motionless and he was still in shock. I watched him for a time through the open doorway before walking back into the kitchen feeling helpless. Molly was coming over soon to check on Jack, though I wasn't sure she could rouse him from his despair.

I knew I had to find out who was responsible for Champion being chased from the farm. It had to be the same person or people who had caused all the other havoc. Where to start? Shelley had made the choice to go with Nathan, so when she sent me a text apologising for rushing off and asking how Jack was, I made my own choice – I ignored her message. That meant now I was really on my own.

I was all set to join Jack in his mood of despair and was berating myself for being so useless when I remembered there was someone who might be able to help me. Not Shelley, but her grandfather. Of course, Hayden Ward had known Jack and he probably knew most of what had gone on in the district. It was possible, too, he remained well informed.

Shelley had said he lived in a retirement home. It took a single phone call to the one home in the district to find him. When Molly arrived, I asked if she could stay with Jack while I went out. There was something I needed to do, I said, and I didn't think Jack should be left on his own. She looked at me curiously but didn't ask any questions, and I wasn't prepared to let her know anything.

In the car, the news came on the local radio station and the lead story was all about a home invasion at Ōakura that had taken place the previous night. That would have been the incident Nathan had responded to. 'Terrifying for the occupants, a mother and her toddler daughter,' the reporter said. It had been serious all right. I remembered how angry I had been at Nathan.

As I drove, I wondered what Shelley's grandfather might know about Jack. Old people could be fickle in their memories, good as anything one day but not the next. Should I expect to find a frail little man dozing off in a chair in the lounge of the retirement village, surrounded by old people with dementia, and with possibly not too good a memory himself?

Yet the man who looked up when one of the caregivers showed me into the home's sunroom was playing Solitaire on an iPad. The room was empty except for him. A walking frame stood beside his chair.

'Imogen, Jack Maguire's granddaughter,' I said, extending my hand to shake his.

'Aye,' Hayden Ward said looking at me carefully and sighing heavily. 'I've heard about you. I also heard about what happened to Jack's bull last night. Terrible. I'm deeply sorry, please tell Jack that. And on top of that, a dreadful situation at Ōakura Beach. What's the world coming to, I wonder?'

'The radio had a report on it. The invasion must've been terrifying for the people in the house.'

'Yes, and for the people at the beach. The community there is very tightknit. Everyone knows everyone. I'd say it was drug related. These gangs from Auckland have been coming down this way. They think we're easy pickings. We used to be a long way from that kind of carry-on.' Hayden sat up straight in his chair. 'Now, down to business. I'm guessing you're here about what's been going on at Jack's?'

'I am,' I said. 'I've been trying to find out, but even Nathan isn't interested in what's been happening and he's the local cop.' I sounded frustrated. The accusation was there but I didn't much care. I was over Nathan. 'He thinks Jack's just lost it. You know, old age. So he's simply ignored any of Jack's complaints to him.'

Hayden smiled ruefully. 'Ah, it can be difficult to be taken seriously when you're a bit older. Especially if you can't get up and about as easily as you once could. Same around here – I can wait two hours for someone to bring me the newspaper with the crossword puzzle. Mind you, Nathan's probably just doing his job and, of course, he's from Auckland, a city cop, not so used to the ways of people here in the country. Though his mother came from New Plymouth, I believe.'

A fount of knowledge? I was tempted to ask him about Shelley and Nathan and whether anything was going on between them but decided to stay out of it.

A voice sounded in the hallway. One of the caregivers chatting loudly to another.

'Country folk keep things close to their chests,' Hayden went on, 'and they've never liked bringing law enforcement in when there's a problem. Rather do it the country way, like they've always done. Mind you, with that home invasion stuff people are going to have to change their way of thinking.'

'Yes. I guess the city isn't that far away.' I had a more pressing question. 'Shelley says you don't think Jack's been responsible for all the issues with his cattle?'

Hayden chewed his lip. 'I don't really know. Someone could want to get at him for some reason.'

'Why though? And why now?'

'He's not much of a people person and certainly not a people pleaser. He always knew how to pick a fight all right. You wouldn't want to be around him when he's in a temper. A law unto himself.'

'You've known him a long time?'

'I have. I worked as a bookkeeper in the early days, doing accounts for the auction company that ran the saleyards in Taranaki. There were a lot of those yards in different towns back in the day. I came across Jack often at the yards. One time ...' he paused, deep in thought, remembering.

'I had to walk through all the yards to take some papers and I came across Jack with one of the Barker boys. The lad was accusing Jack of running up the prices and said Jack had got a mate to do some bidding on the sly. Jack denied it, of course, but young Barker wouldn't accept this. A bit of a kerfuffle ensued. I'd never seen a man fall to the floor as heavily as the Barker lad that time and Jack, well, he had that innocent look. A tearaway, all right.'

We were both silent then, Hayden no doubt recalling what he'd seen, and me thinking of Aoife growing up as a child with the man he was describing. Short-tempered, definitely not in control of that temper and maybe a stranger to the truth when it suited him. Here I was defending him to Nathan.

Hayden cleared his throat. He looked awkward now as if he might have said too much. 'I'll say this for him, he was a master at buying and selling cattle in his day, one of the best around. Knew how to pick a beast. I have a lot of respect for the man.

What happened last night on the road was a terrible thing to happen to anyone.'

In the corridor a caregiver, calling out to another staff member, was pushing a wheelchair past the sunroom with an elderly lady in it. The old woman appeared to be sleeping. I turned back to Hayden.

'What else is on your mind?' he asked shrewdly as if he already knew.

'Before I came here I didn't know I had a grandfather. My mother implied he was dead. She might have even told me that. I found out there is this person I'm related to and he doesn't particularly care about me being here one way or another. I know almost nothing about him but it's clear he needs help, that someone's out to get him, and … well …' I shrugged. 'He is my grandfather, after all.'

The old man scratched his nose, thinking. 'He's always been touchy, easily fired up. Will have made himself a lot of enemies along the way.'

That was easy to imagine.

Hayden shifted in his chair, getting more comfortable, and didn't speak for a few minutes. 'When your grandmother disappeared suddenly with your mother all those years ago, even then, well, there were plenty of people thought he had killed them both and buried them on the farm.'

I couldn't believe what I was hearing. 'What? You're joking?'

Hayden continued to gaze at me, clearly intent on choosing his words carefully. 'Everyone was saying things. It probably got out of hand but that's the kind of idea people got about Jack. People talk. They like to spread rumours. They had heard things, I guess, or liked to imagine things. People reckoned your grandmother wasn't happy with what he was getting up to with regard to Murphy and the ownership of the farm.'

'My grandmother died in Australia years ago but my mother is very much alive. She's in Australia, not buried on the farm.' Even though I was aware Hayden had tried not to upset me, anger and disbelief rose within me. I wasn't sure why his comment – ridiculous gossip from years ago – had upset me.

'Of course,' he said softly. 'We realised that later when ... but your mother wanted you to think your grandfather was dead? Why would that be, do you think?'

I had asked for information. He was a direct-speaking man and if I didn't like what I heard in return I would have to deal with it. I thought about my reply. 'I don't know. She might have blamed him for the way he treated her and her mother, I guess. She seemed to have bad feelings about the farm. I mean, even the house itself is pretty rough and ready and it might not have been much better when she lived there.

'The other thing.' I hesitated. 'I met Tamati Rangihau at the pub when I first arrived. And he's been at Jack's talking to him. I've seen him. Jack's dog had run away and he brought him back. Or that's what he said. Why would he visit Jack?' I might sound overly suspicious but I didn't care.

'Well, Tamati.' The slow pace of Hayden's speech now struck me as buying time, mulling over what he might tell me. 'Tamati's on the local marae rebuild committee and I believe he's involved with a project to put drifting young urban Māori in contact with their roots, the tribe and iwi they come from. Help them learn their whakapapa.'

'Whakapapa?'

'It's an individual's genealogical history, you could say. It links Māori to their ancestors, the gods, their family, their marae and their ancestral land. That's how it could be defined.'

In the silence that followed his words, it hit me I wasn't unlike these young people in the cities with their lack of knowledge of where they fitted in. As for Tamati, it wasn't easy to match his apparent selflessness in being willing to help others with the man I had come to think of as Angry Jeep Guy. No matter who was the real Tamati, the question still remained: why would he be hanging around at Jack's?

Hayden seemed to read my mind or maybe remembered my original question about Tamati. 'He could be calling in to see Jack about anything, really. He'll have known him a while.

'I remember when he was just a lad. A bright kid then but wild at times like a lot of the kids around here, out in the country. Of course, he's all grown up now, into the political stuff.' He moved in his chair as if it was still uncomfortable and chuckled. 'His family's well regarded around here. He'll be having a yarn with Jack, that's all. The two are a bit alike, I would've said. Rush in without much thought.'

Had he heard about my altercation in the pub with Tamati? I decided to leave it there. Hayden had obviously dismissed Tamati as a threat. I wasn't so sure. I had to trust my instincts but I wasn't about to try to convince an old man that he was wrong.

I tried another tack. 'What about the Barkers? I met one of them last night – Suzie?'

'Right. They're an extremely wealthy family. Been in the district for years since the early settlement times when they would've got land cheap from the government of the day after the confiscations. They've amassed huge holdings. They own most of the land around there and they're expanding. You'll have seen their trucks going up and down.' He definitely spoke more readily now, on an easier subject. 'There's been some articles in the paper about ill-treatment of the cattle by their workers on one or two of the farms. I suspect they'll wangle their way out of it. Money buys you good lawyers.'

I remembered the question I had asked Daniel. 'Could they want Jack off his farm?'

Hayden shrugged. 'If they were up to something they'd be bound to keep it quiet but they've known Jack all this time and they'd know when he says no he means it. Water off a duck's back to them, I would've thought. The farm's not that big. They'd have loads of other options.'

I had another thought. Daniel had mentioned Jack seeing intruders walking across the farm. I remembered the nightmare I had had on my first night. 'Silly question, but could the farm be haunted?'

The old man chuckled, enjoying the change of tack. 'Oh, people like to talk about ghosts. It keeps them amused. And frightened. Of course, there'll be ghosts around that farm, for more than one reason.' His gaze moved around the room as if he were expecting to see an other-worldly creature. He leaned back, linking his hands behind his head.

'If you brought an exorcist in they'd be busy for months. I heard an old story about the keys on the piano playing in the sitting room in the old days when there was no one around and somebody in the family died soon after. Murphy's brother. He was found lifeless in the swamp back of the farm. Wasn't very old either.'

'Who was Murphy?'

'He owned the farm before Jack ...' Hayden seemed to stop himself mid-sentence, releasing his hands. I waited for him to go on. He sighed. 'We used to call him Mad Murphy because he always had these stories. He once said his mother told him, "We've never been alone here in the house. Not even when there's just the one of us." It made my hair curl, hearing it.'

I thought of how frightening it had been for me, too, in the house that first night.

'Odd thing is he was a bit of a loner himself, in many ways.' He stopped speaking, as if he were choosing his words carefully again. 'Mind you, any bit of land around here will have ghosts if you believe in that kind of thing. You only need to look at the history of the place. Ghosts or not, no one has clean hands if you delve far back enough. Take Parihaka.'

'Further around the coast?' I had seen a sign on the road advertising a festival to celebrate the arrival of Puanga, the bright star which, to Māori, signalled a new year. It occurred in winter, so I realised the notice was out of date; the event had taken place before I arrived.

'Yes. You might have read how last year the Crown met with descendants of Parihaka pā to offer an apology for the terrible things that happened there nearly a hundred and forty years ago? The government offered nine million dollars in restitution for the invasion of the pā. I heard that old people at the meeting spoke about their ancestors, women and children who were left behind when their men were arrested and taken away by government forces. Imogen, women were raped.' He paused, as if struggling to continue and sighed heavily. 'There were many other wrongdoings.

'Nothing is ever completely in the past. The Pākehā at the time and those who followed might have forgotten about these brutal conflicts but for the Māori these longstanding struggles continue. Things are never fully forgotten. The old people who endured this treatment may have passed on but not before giving their accounts and the history remains there forever.' He gave another long sigh, his breath emitting a small burst of air into the little room.

'That's just one place with its memories. There are others all over the region – and wider afield. These wars cast a long shadow. Of course, around here, plenty happened. Land was at the heart of the conflict then. Once you understand about the land, well … I've read some of the history.' Hayden went quiet, reflecting on this. 'Aye, there'll be ghosts all right and if you ask me, no one around here is immune from the fallout of what went on all those years ago. I have said this for a long time but sometimes Pākehā don't want to know. They'd rather forget it happened.' Clearly fatigued, he fell silent. He was an old man, worn out by such a long speech.

A noise startled me. I realised the sound was from Hayden's phone and he glanced at the screen. I guessed it was Shelley. She might not appreciate me quizzing her grandfather, but now, as I stood up to leave, I realised it was too late to ask him to keep my visit a secret from her.

MICHAEL

Taranaki 1864

Later that night after the company had scorched the village, I woke sweating and trembling. I couldn't stop thinking about what we had done. The women? The children? I couldn't remember what had happened. Had we left any of the children there, to be burned?

One thing was clear. I had to return to see if anyone had survived those frightening flames. I crept out of the tent and put on my boots and heavy jacket. Walking over to the fence where we had tied up the horses, I moved among the unsettled steeds, hastily stepping away from one which tried to nip me and another which was stamping its feet. At last, I found one who, though shivering a little, accepted my hands on his flank. I nuzzled his nose and spoke gently to him, calming him in the same way I did the horses back home.

The bridle was hanging beside him so I put that on and flung my leg over his back. I turned him out of the horse line and set him in motion. Away from the camp, I turned the horse onto the track back towards the village. I wanted to see what had happened to the place we had burned. I might be able to save any women and children who were still hiding in or near the burnt pit.

The horse whinnied quietly as we set off along a blackened trail and I reached out to pat his neck to quieten him. Above, the moon peeked out of the clouds. I hoped it would guide me. I had not gone far before hooves thundered after me. Another horse and another rider. I nudged the horse lightly, urging him to go faster. The horse behind gathered pace, too.

'Mick,' a voice called close behind and I knew who it was at once.

'Denis.'

'Stop where ye are at, man. What are ye up to?'

'Taking the horse for a ride.'

'Lad, that's no good.' Denis sounded breathless from trying to control his horse. I hadn't known him to be a rider. 'I warned ye. Ye'll be in great trouble. Absence without leave, I tell ye, they won't take that lightly. Ye'll be punished for being a deserter, man.'

I didn't care. 'I'm going to check on the women at the pā, see if I can help them.'

'It'll be too late. The men will have returned and there's but one of ye against a bunch of them. Leave it be.'

The path was narrow and Denis's horse was abreast of mine. He reached across to grab my reins. I tried to push his hand away but he held on.

'Mick, c'mon,' he said.

Our horses moved apart and I rode on. I had got some way ahead of Denis when behind me his horse gave a high-pitched nervous whinny. Pulling my mount to a halt I turned around to look. At the same time, trees were swaying noisily in the forest and Denis's horse took fright and reared up.

Denis shouted out, trying to calm him and, as I watched in horror, Denis and his horse plunged headfirst over the side of the bank. I slipped off my horse and ran over to the edge of the path. It was too dark to see Denis or his horse. There was no sound from either. 'Denis?' I called softly into the blackness. A little louder: 'Denis.' I thought I heard the name echo but there was no reply from the dark depths of the hillside.

Suddenly I heard the sound of footsteps on the track and I knew at once it was men marching steadily in my direction. A rallying cry – voices belonging to warriors – bellowed in the night air. I looked behind me but all around was black. These men would be on their way back to their village. There was some distance between us still, and the warriors were on foot, but these men were trackers and hunters, and they would know if a man or a horse had gone over the side.

As for the horse Denis was riding, if the animal were alive, he might be jumpy, skittery, his neighing alerting them to where he and his rider were. What hope had I of doing anything? I had a decision to make. Stay and look for Denis and be slaughtered by the warriors who would be gaining ground on me? Or flee for my life?

I swung my body back onto the horse and kicked him forward. I flicked the reins and he took off, racing back towards his home, the village. What might happen when these warriors got there to find their women and children gone? Or discovered burned bodies? I knew only too well. I had to escape.

Ahead of me the track divided and became two. I needed to avoid the route the warriors were going to take but I didn't know which way to choose. Saying a quick prayer for guidance I sat tight. The horse swung towards the right and we entered a tunnel-like alley of flaxes and trees that smelled damp and fetid, the ground squelching beneath the hooves.

The horse stumbled before righting himself but something like fear now passed through his body. On either side of us the branches of dripping low-lying trees reached out to cling to my mount and me like they were vines. He suddenly jumped over a stump in the path and I found myself flying over his head. Landing hard on the damp ground, the breath slapped out of me and I knew I was trapped in this bad-smelling place. Frightened, I remembered no more.

AOIFE

Taranaki 1977

Neither the twins nor Suzie were on the bus after school. Someone said the twins had gone up north with their father and they might not come back. Aoife got off with the Lawsons and waited till they had gone on ahead, before crossing the road, and walked along the side road again towards the Taranaki gate. She didn't want to go home yet. Mam might pretend to want to listen to her day but the last thing Mam wanted to hear were Aoife's problems. Most of the time Mam was fretting about missing Ireland, all the way across the sea.

When she got to the shelter, somebody was already there. She thought at first the man asleep inside the hedge might be a swagman, like the man in a story Miss Anderson had read them. Swagmen were people who used to walk around the country, long ago, visiting farms to see if they could do odd jobs in return for food and shelter. They left little collections of stones in a funny order outside the front gate to let their swagmen friends know the place was good, or in a different order to say it was no good.

Aoife was still checking out this man when he made a moaning noise and she started, ready to run across the paddocks to her house.

The man began to speak. His voice was thick, as if he had trouble getting the words out, and spoke to her in Irish. She knew enough of the language from her Granda who had grown up on Cape Clear, the island off Cork where everyone spoke Irish. He had spoken to her in Irish since she was a baby.

'Where am I?' he asked. He sounded like her Granda – the same sing-song sound and lilting voice. A lump came into her throat as she realised how much she missed him.

'You are on our farm,' Aoife replied in Irish.

The man moaned and stirred again. 'Denis, is that ye, laddie?'

'No, it's not him.'

The man closed his eyes. She stood in the entrance to the shelter trying to decide what to do. Nearby a cow noisily munched on grass.

The man opened his eyes again. He made a faint movement towards her and she flinched. She wondered if she should run away but she saw the man's arm, how he held it as if it was hurting him.

This man wore rough-looking clothing and had a beard and unkempt black hair that stuck up in spikes, but he didn't seem as old and crinkled as the picture of Swagman Bob in the book Miss Anderson had read them. She gazed at him steadily, waiting for him to say something else.

'Where am I?' the man asked again. 'I need to know where I am.'

Aoife stared into his blue eyes. She knew that tone, the way of speaking people from home had that went fast when the person got excited and had something to tell you.

'You are in a shelter. It's under a hedge,' she said hesitantly, in English this time. She spoke slowly in the hope he would understand her. 'The farm belongs to someone else, but my da is the one looking after it. My da and my mam.'

She thought the man blinked. A tear ran down his face. He stared at her and spoke in English. 'Listen, cailín, can you help me to stand up? Denis will be looking for me.'

Aoife frowned, trying to make sense of this. Who was Denis? Was this man one of the casual workers at the Barkers'? Had he lost his way? 'Have you come far? From under the mountain?'

The man looked at her helplessly. He shrugged and looked down at his arm.

Aoife caught a glimpse of dull red and brown. Blood. 'Has someone attacked you?'

The man didn't say anything.

'Do you need anything?'

Inside her school bag was a left-over jam sandwich from lunch and an apple she hadn't had time to eat in peace. That seemed so long ago now. She leaned into the shelter, towards the tin mug inside, careful to avoid getting too close to the man in case he leapt at her. She took the mug over to the cattle trough and filled it up. Returning with the mug of water, she put it down inside the opening to the shelter and pushed the apple towards the man. She left the bread in its wrapper, close enough for him to reach.

'Denis should be here,' he said again. He went quiet for a time. Aoife could hear his breathing, harsh and ragged. 'I ... Where is he?'

'I don't know.'

The man shivered, shaking his head so that his damp hair swung on the ends. She could smell the sweat off him.

'Are you cold?'

He shook his head.

What should she do? If she ran home and told Mam about the man, she'd be in trouble for not coming home the right way and she might have to explain about Suzie and the gang, and the big girls from the Barkers' farm, and Mam might get cross again and tell Da, and he might storm down to school or to the Barkers to yell at them, and that would make it worse and … she didn't know what else to think. No, better to say nothing. She could fetch a couple of blankets for this man later when no one was watching her.

'I'll come back,' she said, nudging the food a little closer. 'What's your name?'

'Michael,' the man said and closed his eyes.

'I'll come back as soon as I can then, Michael.'

She picked up her bag. Twice she looked back yet there was no movement in the hedge.

The next day Aoife got off the bus again across from the side road. She had gone part of the way along the narrow road when she heard a footfall behind her. Could it have been a lie about the twins going up north? Had they been lying here in wait for her? She didn't know whether to look around to see or to pretend she had no idea they were there. She gripped her school bag. If they tried anything she could bash them with it and run.

A sniffling noise followed. It was a sound she recognised. 'Matiu,' she said, spinning around. 'How did you get here? Were you on the bus? You're not a bus kid.'

'Trevor let me on,' he said. Trevor was the driver of the school bus. Some people said he was a hippie because he had long wavy hair. He drove fast around corners with a roll-up cigarette in one hand.

'He's not meant to.'

'Yeah, well he knows me and he did anyway. My koro is doing some work down at the Barkers'. They'll be there till late. It's a bit of an emergency, something to do with the drains and a dead cow. I dunno, wasn't really listening. What are you doing?' He seemed to say all this without taking a breath.

'Heading home.'

'Can I come? It's boring waiting till he's done.' He shot her a sideways glance and sent her a smile. 'And I'm hungry. We could eat something at your house.'

'I saw you eating Paul T's peanut-butter sandwiches. You can't be hungry.'

'I am though. My mum used to say I've got an appetite like a horse.'

'Where's your mum then?'

Matiu looked away. 'Gone. She's not here.'

'Okay. You can come but I'm not going home straight away.'

'What are you gonna do, then?'

Aoife tried to look mysterious and decided to say nothing. They marched along in silence. She thought about nasty Suzie and her gang with their little secrets. 'Can you keep a secret?'

Matiu nodded. 'I guess, nobody tells me them much but I get to hear things sometimes when I'm around the kitchen at the marae. Sometimes they tell me to go away or not to be so nosy.' He rubbed his chin with the top of his tee-shirt. 'But mostly they don't pay me any notice. I like to figure out what's going on. I hear stuff you wouldn't believe. Some of those aunties sure have stories.'

'What kind of stories?'

'I can't tell you. I don't tell anyone. I know how to keep those stories to myself.'

'Well, you need to promise or I won't tell you,' Aoife said firmly. She wanted complete agreement or it wouldn't be worth it.

Matiu spat on his hand and thrust it at her. 'Put it there.'

Aoife was tempted to push his grubby hand away. Ugh, she

wanted to say. Yet she made up her mind and spat on hers, and they shook.

'Oughta have been blood really,' Matiu said, 'but spit's as good as.'

Aoife nodded. It was done now, even if her hand felt sticky. 'There's a man living in the hedge on our farm.'

Matiu didn't seem excited. 'You mean, old Murphy? I thought he'd gone away again.'

'He's back, but it's not him. This man's a stranger.'

'Where is he?'

'Wait and you'll see.'

She and Matiu walked towards the gate. Had she done the right thing telling Matiu? It did feel better having an ally, someone with her, and now she and Matiu shared a secret, like those stupid girls.

Her pulse quickened when they neared the gate. She climbed over it, followed by Matiu. They kept up their silence. At the opening to the hole in the hedge, Aoife put her finger to her lips and went ahead first.

The man was no longer there. She stared hard at the ground inside the hedge. The tin cup was still there, still filled with water though the food had gone. She could see one of the heifers had got close to the entrance because there was a runny pie of fresh cow muck outside. It was dark and dim inside the shelter now that the sky had clouded over. Rain was on its way. Had she imagined there was a man here?

Matiu followed her inside. 'Where is he?'

'Not here, dummy. What does it look like?' Aoife was angry. She should never have said he was here. Now she looked like an eejit.

She pushed her way back outside, catching sight of a streak of blood on the ground. Did that mean he'd been here? Then she saw a splat of cow muck. Was the blood from a cow? Maybe a young steer had rough-housed a heifer? She turned back to Matiu.

'He must be around here somewhere.'

'Where?' Matiu stared around him. His gaze fell on the thicket of trees nearby. 'What's over there?'

'The swamp,' she said. 'Mam says it's dangerous.'

'We should check it out. He might be in there.' He headed in the direction of the swamp, swinging his arms. Aoife was left behind.

He got close to the swamp and stopped, listening to something. He ducked down and, with his hands, pushed through low branches, tramping through a row of tall flax bushes until he was out of sight. He was gone a long time. Should she go and look for him? Aoife heard a strange sound, like singing. She waited for Matiu to call her to join him – she was going to refuse to annoy him – though she heard nothing. She called out his name a couple of times but he didn't reply. Annoyed, she decided to start heading home. Matiu'd get a surprise when he came out to find her gone.

She was at the next gate when she heard him call her name and she waited, her foot on the wire near the post. 'Over here.'

Matiu caught up to her. His face was pale and he was breathing hard. 'She's right, your mum. What she said.'

Aoife stared at him. 'It's just an old gully in the trees. You're chicken.'

'No, I'm not. You wouldn't understand.' He turned and stared back at the swamp, at the trees moving in the wind. He was breathing hard as if he'd been winded, like the time Aoife hit her chest climbing over a low wall at the back of the house. 'You shouldn't go in there, Aoife.'

'Oh, I see, but it's all right for you then?'

Matiu frowned. 'No and yes. Anyway, it's dark in there and the water at the bottom is all murky and stagnant. It stinks.'

Aoife sighed. He was trying to be all mysterious, but it wouldn't work with her. She kicked at the ground. 'You can come to my house for afternoon tea but if you so much as breathe a word about any of this, about the man, and you going into the swamp in the gully, I will kill you.'

'Sure, sure you will.' He punched her on the arm. He was quiet on the way to the house. After a time, she heard him sniff. 'That swamp.'

'What about it?'

'I dunno. Something's strange in there. Not the stink by itself, that's just because the tree stumps are rotten. Something happens when you go in there. It clutches at you. I dunno. Like a gale dragging you in.' He shook his head, hair flopping from side to side and gazed into the distance. She could almost see his mind working. He shook his head, dismissing some idea. 'I'd have to check it out again to know for sure. There's a kēhua in that place. There must be. I bet it gets weird there after dark. Who is the fella, anyway?'

Aoife shivered. 'He said his name was Michael. He was just there and needed help. I wanted to help him.'

'Maybe not.' Matiu sounded far away. He was still trying to be mysterious.

'Don't you tell anyone.'

'Want to spit on it again?'

'Nope,' Aoife said grumpily.

She turned and walked faster. She could hear Matiu behind her, breathing noisily through his nose, gumboots squelching in the mud as he tried to catch up with her. She wondered where the man had gone. Was he okay?

IMOGEN
Taranaki 2018

The river was much higher today, sweeping swiftly over the big grey stones. I had pulled over under some weeping willows so my car wasn't too visible to passers-by and hiked from there to the bridge. It was as if the river were drawing me to it. Like the mountain and its ranges, it had been here for aeons.

A chainsaw reverberated from somewhere over a hedge. Reaching the bridge, I gazed down into the fast-moving river. Had Aoife stopped here sometimes? Had she stared down into this torrent of icy water wondering what secrets it held?

The stream that flowed down the mountain and through a corner of Jack's farm was a tributary of this same river. The river wound through land belonging to other people. They would have their own stories, their own history but, for now, I was interested in only one story – Jack's.

The flowers I'd seen on the side of the wooden bridge the first time were now limp and lifeless. As I reached to touch them, a voice behind me made me jump.

'Are you all right there?'

It was the same man Tamati had been talking to – or haranguing, as I had thought at the time – at the fundraiser that evening. An older man, someone possibly Aoife's age. Tall, as I'd noticed the other night, but clearly muscular too, his arms bare in his black wool singlet. His forehead was damp from exertion.

'I've been admiring the view,' I said. 'I'm staying with Jack. I'm his granddaughter.'

He looked at me closely. 'Yes. I saw you with him. At the fund-raiser. I'm sorry about what happened to Champion.' He held out his hand. 'I'm Matiu Henry.'

I shook it. There wasn't much to be said.

He gestured to where I had been looking. 'Our awa, our river. It flows down from the streams and swamps of the mountain, our maunga, and both are sacred to us Māori.' He paused to wipe his brow. 'Many of the Pākehā call it Boulder River, because of its boulders.'

'How very imaginative of them,' I said.

He chuckled. 'Exactly right. That's what I've always thought. I can see we'll get on well. I like your sense of humour, Imogen.'

I found myself smiling back at him. It was nice to be appreciated.

Matiu turned to face the road. 'I've been trimming some trees on the land across the way that belongs to our whānau.' He indicated with his thumb. He must've been the one using the chainsaw that was now silent.

'I heard the chainsaw, it makes quite a noise when everywhere else is quiet.' I looked down at the river again. 'Someone died here?'

'Yes. A while ago. We have deaths here from time to time, sadly. Something about this river attracts risk-takers. Kids coming here from town, jumping off the bridge, they don't see the dangers. When the awa is up, it's not apparent that it's full of stones. Sometimes there's a car crash. They take the bridge too fast. Like this one.' He gestured to the flowers. 'A nice lad, too. From around here.'

'And suicides?' I wasn't sure why I asked but I knew hearing about deaths at the river was already giving me goosebumps.

Matiu nodded, his expression suddenly serious. 'Those too. You can sense them?'

I didn't respond. I was thinking about the feeling of doom about this river. It was like it had a bad-luck curse attached to it. Could it ever be removed?

'We place a tapu here after a death,' explained Matiu as if he had read my mind. 'We hold karakia at the site, and put up a sign warning people not to go in the river or try to fish in it until the rāhui has been lifted.' Below us the river wound lazily on its way. 'But ... sometimes what has happened goes back many years into the past.'

I thought this over. Did he mean generational trauma? Somewhere in the distance came the sound of a motor or machinery, the noise making me shudder, and I reached for my necklace, touching it with my finger and thumb. It was still there. I pulled it out from its hiding place under my jumper. All safe, and yet ...

Matiu looked down, then his serious brown eyes met mine. He took a sudden breath. 'Aoife's necklace. Auē. I'm so sorry. I mean surely I would have ...' He closed his mouth firmly and turned and walked away from me towards the other end of the bridge. I thought I saw his shoulders heave. He stood there for some time before he walked back to me, his eyes glistening with tears.

I'd been shocked into silence by his dramatic response to my necklace, then I realised what he must be thinking. 'No no,' I said hurriedly, almost too late, 'no, she's not dead.'

'But you have the necklace? Not Aoife?'

Now we were both silent, each processing our thoughts. In the distance, the noise started up again. An engine, not a chainsaw.

'She gave it to me a long time ago,' I said.

I remembered the day I found the necklace in a little steel box in the top drawer of a dresser when Aoife and I were packing to leave one of the farms we had stayed at. I asked who the little girl in the locket was and she said she didn't know. It was a mystery.

'Why don't you wear it?' I had asked her.

She shrugged, seemingly uninterested in my question. I said if she didn't wear it, could I have it? I begged her to let me have it. She had a strange expression as she took it from me. 'Leave it alone now. Don't touch it, it may be cursed,' was all she said then. 'It wouldn't surprise me if it were. Too many bad spirits at the place I found it, at any rate. No good can come of it.'

Still, she hadn't got rid of it. When I was leaving to study journalism at the University of Melbourne, the first time I was going to be fully apart from her, she handed me the little steel box. 'You might as well have it,' she said. 'I shouldn't have kept it. I should've left it where I found it. It wasn't mine to keep and, if anything, it's made my life worse.'

Matiu watched me closely, as if trying to read what was going through my mind. 'Why do you think she passed it on to you?'

'She said maybe having it would be different for me, that was all.' I hadn't paid much attention. I was so excited about going to university and putting down roots, making proper friends and not always being on the move, which had been the one constant in my childhood. For most of my life, Aoife seemed to be looking over her shoulder, running from something.

Now I wished I had persevered and asked Aoife many more questions before I came to this place. I kept the necklace and Aoife hadn't asked for it back. I liked wearing it. It made me feel safe, no matter what she'd said about it being cursed. I liked picking it up and looking at the little girl and the older woman inside the locket, and wondering about their story.

The machinery noise had cut out.

'What's made you come here now?' he asked.

I stared at him. How much would I tell him when so few people here seemed trustworthy? Even someone as open and friendly as Shelley had managed to let me down. 'Curiosity, I guess. To find out for myself. To find out what's going on.'

'That's brave of you.' Matiu reached out towards the bouquet of flowers and touched one dead bud lightly. 'You came here to be with your grandfather?'

'I did. Though he doesn't seem to want to get to know me.' The bitterness in my voice jarred in the quiet air of this place. I realised how much it had shocked me to be treated so coldly when I arrived, to be unwelcome in this land where my mother had spent the middle years of her childhood. 'Sometimes he's okay to talk with. It seems to vary depending on his mood, I'd say.'

'He has a lot on his mind.' Matiu untied the knot around the flowers. He picked them up and let them fall over the side of the bridge. I watched them fly lightly down to touch the foam. They bobbed on the surface for a time before moving on with the flow. 'So you felt kind of called here, is that right?'

'Yes …' I hesitated, reluctant to tell him the real story.

'You're like your mother in that respect, having a strong spiritual side. She said her grandmother told her she had it.'

'What spiritual side?' I frowned. I didn't know why being compared – even favourably – to Aoife annoyed me so much. 'You're talking to the most sensible non-spiritual person on earth. I'm pragmatic. I operate from logical thinking. That's who I am.' I remembered then the negative energy I had felt when I first saw Jack's house and the nightmare I'd had that first night, though that hardly made me psychic.

Matiu laughed. 'You also have a fighting spirit, like your grandfather, and like Aoife. She was like that. She stood up for what she believed in. I meant a different kind of spirit, one like intuition. Your mother said sensing was a gift of the Irish.'

The last of the faded flowers had drifted away and I glanced back at Matiu. 'Like a second sight, or seeing ghosts?' I hadn't seen any, had I?

'Possibly. Seeing things you could not know. You knew Jack was in trouble.'

'But …' I stopped myself. I didn't want to mention I had learned about Jack from a homeless man on the street in Melbourne, a man called Michael Flynn who had told me my grandfather needed help. I shifted from one foot to the other, weighing up what to say.

Should I ask him about Tamati? Voice my suspicions? I remembered the evening in the bar after work when I had vented yet again to Zoe about Gavin and what he'd said in the newsroom meeting that day. She'd said I needed to move on, not allow myself to become obsessed with him – obsessed, that was the word she used. She'd said it bluntly, in that crisp way she had, and I felt mortified but also a bit annoyed because I wanted her to be on my side, not pointing out the obvious. Of course, I had become a bit obsessed. Who wouldn't? Was that happening here – me becoming obsessed with a man I hardly knew?

Matiu was observing me closely again. 'I'm sure you will have spoken to our local police officer about what's been happening to Jack. Has Nathan been any help?'

'No help at all. In fact, worse than no help.' A grim comment but it was true. Nathan had completely shut down my suspicions.

Matiu's expression changed. He frowned, serious now. 'That's not good. You need to impress on him how much it matters to you. And Jack.' He looked down the road. 'I know you feel you don't know me, and people haven't made you as welcome as they should have, but whenever you need my help, I'm here. Remember that. You're not on your own.'

He must have intended his words to be comforting, even so, a ripple of fear passed through me, chilling me. *You're not on your own.* Something about the words themselves frightened me. They reminded me of my meeting with Michael Flynn.

'Okay, thanks.' I started to walk away.

'Imogen?' Matiu called after me. 'I wondered …' he paused, awkward. 'Did Aoife ever …?'

I turned back, waited for him to complete the question.

He shook his head. 'Forget it.'

I remembered the elderly woman at the fundraiser. 'Do you know someone called Ana?'

Matiu straightened. 'Yes. The one I know died a long time ago.' He said this warily as if wondering why I would ask.

I felt conscious I had overstepped the mark. 'I'm sorry. It was just that one of the old ladies at the hall the night of the fundraiser mentioned an Ana. No one seemed to know who she was.'

'You weren't to know. She was my half-sister. She was coming down here from Gisborne to see our koro, hitch-hiking home, waiting on the side of the road, and got run over by a drunk driver. He said he didn't see her. The kuia would remember her.'

He shook his head and turned away in pain. I had never met the man and yet I had managed to upset him twice in the space of ten minutes. Saying sorry again wasn't going to help.

It had been a strange conversation. I made my way back to my car where it was parked under the thicket of trees and as I unlocked the door, I glanced down. The front tyre was flat. I squatted so I could see it better. Someone had slashed it and the tyre was deflated. The blade had left a gaping hole. I straightened up, gazing around but it took a while to register the white envelope that had been thrust beneath the window wipers. I slit it open. Large letters that looked like 24-point font filled an A4 page – strikingly similar to the one Jack had opened and thrust in the fireplace. *Go back home.*

Was this meant directly for me? I tossed it on the front passenger seat, walked around the car and kicked the tyre, not that it did any good. I looked around again but there was no sign of any culprits, naturally. They would be long since gone. I shrugged and went around to the boot of the car to find the spare tyre.

Thankfully, outback life had taught me a few practical skills and changing a tyre was one of them. I got out the jack, plonked the car up, and began work. I had the replacement tyre propped up and ready to put on when an engine sounded beside me.

A face peered at me from the driver's seat of a black Jeep. 'You all right there?'

Where had Tamati come from so suddenly? Surely I hadn't conjured him up by merely thinking about him? 'All good,' I said briskly and turned back to my task. I hoped he'd take the hint.

'Sure?' Tamati parked the Jeep and got out. He took the replacement tyre from me without asking and levered it into position. 'How did it happen?'

'I don't know. Maybe I drove over a nail.'

'Hmm.' He reached out to touch the unusable tyre lying beside him on the ground. 'It feels like it's been slashed to me.'

'Really?' I said. Briefly, I thought of showing him the note – a thought I cast aside almost immediately.

We exchanged glances. 'Anyway …' I said. Now it was my turn for questioning. 'What are you doing down this end of the road?'

A look crossed his face as if he were planning to tell me it was none of my business and he said, 'Looking for Matiu. Have you seen him?'

'Down by the bridge. Oh, and thanks for your help. I can

manage now.' I sounded ungracious but right now, after finding that threatening note, I didn't care what anyone thought of me.

'Are you sure?'

'Yes.'

'Okay then.' He nodded, got back into his vehicle, and drove off. A shiver went through me, and it wasn't from the cold draughts of wind that had sprung up while I stood under the tree. Whoever had done this meant business. They were sending me a strong message. What was it I wasn't meant to find out about?

The sound of the Jeep engine roaring off reminded me of the noise I hadn't been able to identify earlier. It had been the engine of a motorbike and it had been heading down the road towards the Barkers' farm.

After what had happened to my car tyre, I couldn't face returning straight away to Jack's house. He'd covered up so much of what had been going on and I didn't think he would reveal anything further if I told him about the tyre. I got in the car and drove, with no idea where I was heading. I had driven almost as far as the Ōkato township when my phone rang. I pulled over and picked it up.

'Imogen,' a familiar voice said. 'You haven't replied to my texts. I was worried about you.'

I breathed out again. The child within me was pleased – I had worried Shelley. Well, she was the one who had raced off after her boyfriend leaving me to cope with a bereft Jack on my own. The more mature version of myself came to the fore. 'Sorry, I ...' I didn't know what to say. 'I was so focused on Jack ...'

'Of course. Look, can you meet me at Ōakura? At the beach? We can have a walk and you can tell me what's been happening. I might be able to help.'

I waited by the carpark at the beach. In the distance loomed the Paritutu Rock, the port at New Plymouth and the Sugar Loaf islands. I was pleased there was time to inhale the sea scents and watch the wild white waves coming in to lash the sand. Maybe, maybe, I could put the interference with my car and the threatening note behind me. I turned to look for Shelley and saw her making her way towards me from her work car.

She smiled in such a friendly way I was immediately ashamed of my behaviour. I had shut her out and refused to reply to her texts. I had no real idea of what had come over me that night, anger and hurt, or both. Anger on Jack's behalf and hurt that the one person I had thought of as a new friend had abandoned me to go off with the very cop who refused to believe my grandfather needed his help. A man who ignored what he saw as useless complaints.

'Sorry to have left you in the lurch after that terrible incident. Poor Champion. Poor Jack.' She waved her hand in the air as if trying to capture what had happened. 'I was torn. I had to go with Nathan to report on the home invasion. The chief reporter would've been really pissed off if he found I'd known about it and not headed straight there. You know what it's like in the newsroom.'

I wondered if it were pleading or reasoning I could hear in her voice. If I were being rational and sensible, like the Imogen of old, of course I would understand. No question about it, that was what good reporters did. They chased a story but that night at the bridge, I had allowed my emotions to colour everything.

'Let's walk,' she said. 'It's so nice along the sand. I love to come here when I can.'

We set off, disturbing a flock of seagulls that had been gathering nearby.

Shelley picked up a stone and skimmed it into the sea. 'I ran the idea of old articles about Jack by our librarian at the paper. As I thought, the time period is too recent to be on microfiche at the library. The ones that aren't on microfiche are just piled up on the shelves in the storeroom. Without knowing which dates to look for it would be a huge task. Sorry not to be much help there.'

It sounded like a dead end. 'Thanks for asking, though. It was good of you.' I meant it.

'Have you found out anything else?'

Now was the time to be open with her. I told her about the incident with the car, the deliberate puncturing of its tyre. I hesitated when it came to mentioning the note the person had left. A little scrap of caution held me back. What if she told Nathan and he stirred up a storm, rushing in to question everyone? No, I needed to take this slowly and discover things by myself.

'Then there's definitely someone who wants you out of here and off the case,' Shelley said. 'It means Jack wasn't imagining things.' Had Shelley had reservations, too, doubted Jack's story a little, despite what she had said to me? Maybe that was her being a good reporter. I was beginning to wonder if I'd ever had what it took to be a successful journalist.

'I met a man called Michael Flynn outside the pub who said he knew Jack,' I lied. I could hardly say I had met him in Melbourne – that would be too weird. 'I think he was passing through the district. A man with a beard. Black hair. He sounded Irish. Quite handsome in an old-fashioned way. Have you come across him around the coast anywhere?'

Shelley slowed to a halt. 'Not that I know of. Though we are getting people coming through the district from other places. Could he have been a seasonal worker on one of the farms? They tend to be transient. Some of them stay at local campsites.'

'I'm not sure.' Should I tell her how we met? Again, I felt

myself hesitate, strongly conscious of a need for caution. It was strange, though, that Michael Flynn hadn't sought me out since I'd been here. Maybe he was still in Melbourne.

'I wonder if this man might be someone he met through his Irish connections. I know some of the new migrants from Ireland are helping each other settle. There's a business network, and a group called, would you believe it, Irish Mammies in New Zealand.'

We both smiled at the name. 'Like Mrs Brown,' I said, thinking of the TV comedy.

'You need to get Nathan on your side,' Shelley said, walking again. 'I'm sure he just needs a bit of persuading to see common-sense and then you can tell him all you know.'

I took a deep breath. 'Well, he's your boyfriend, isn't he? You know what he's like. If you were to speak to him that might help.'

Shelley had stepped ahead of me, picking up pace. She turned back looked bewildered. 'Boyfriend? Now why would you think that?'

Because you two were so cosy, I said in my head. The thought remained unsaid. 'I'm not sure. I thought someone said …'

'We've known each other since we were kids. He's older than me though. His mum came from New Plymouth and used to come back often. She and my mum are third cousins or some-thing like that.' She paused, looking at me as if I were a bit odd. 'He and I hung out with all the other cousins when there were funerals and family reunions.'

Big family get-togethers weren't part of my childhood. Nor were distant cousins. Nor even childhood playmates who I might still know. Yet if Aoife had stayed here I might have been part of this world too, distantly related to half the district.

'So, you need to sit down with Nathan in a non-threatening

environment and let him have all the facts. Or even just your suspicions.'

'Which don't really amount to much. Except there is some-one out there who has it in for Jack.'

'And that's a start.'

'Is it? I already told him and he's taken no notice.'

'You both need to tackle it calmly,' Shelley said helpfully. 'Have a sensible conversation.'

'Maybe,' was all I said, gritting my teeth.

AOIFE

Taranaki 1978

In the night, a wild storm blew up and woke her. It sounded like a banshee screaming the world down. The house shook and windowpanes rattled. Aoife sat up on her bed and looked through the window – outside was nothing but blackness. She pulled the woollen blanket over her head and tried to sleep again. The next time she opened her eyes it was morning and she could hear her parents talking in the kitchen. When Aoife went to join them, Mam handed her a plate with bacon rashers, egg, sausages and a slice of toast.

Da had come from the cowshed to check for any damage. 'The roofing iron on the hay barn next to it has lifted, in places it's barely hanging on by a thread.' He went to the phone and dialled a number.

'Can you come right away and give me a hand?' he said into the phone. 'The winds might come up again and if they do the whole shebang will blow.'

Aoife could hear the person at the other end of the line, a man talking excitedly, his voice going faster and faster.

'All right, all right now, see ya.' Da put the receiver back on its cradle. 'The hay will be ruined if any more rain comes,' he said to Ma. 'We'll be cursed.'

Ma wrung a tea towel in her hands. 'Can Mr Murphy not help?'

Da scoffed. 'He's been on a bender this past week and sure, he'd likely fall off the ladder as soon as ye look at him. No, Murphy's as useless as a one-legged man in an arse-kicking contest.'

Aoife wanted to chuckle but she took one look at Mam's face and clamped her lips shut.

'I could come with ye,' Mam said.

'No. Harry will be here soon enough. I'll go over and put some tarpaulins on the hay, try to keep it dry.' He saw Aoife watching. 'Don't ye be following. The storm has knocked down a few trees between the house and the cowshed. It's dangerous out there.'

Aoife ate her breakfast. Da was gone a while. When he came back and asked if Harry had arrived, she said he hadn't.

'Has the man himself even bothered to ring?'

'No,' she said.

Da cussed a bit and went outside to have a smoke. After a time, he came in and dialled a number on the phone. 'No answer.'

He went outside and headed along the cattle race towards the road, before disappearing. He might be checking for trees that had fallen across the road. He was gone a long time and when he came back, his trousers were tucked into his gumboots and the boots muddied all the way up to the top. 'River's flooded, and mud and debris is everywhere. Even dead rats, big ones. Branches down. A right mess.' He sat down and tapped the table with his fingers with a rat-a-tat sound.

Aoife went back to her bedroom and picked up a Nancy Drew book she was halfway through. It was called *The Strange Message in the Parchment*. Nancy and her friends were trying to uncover a mystery connected to a letter. There was also a kidnapper. Aoife sat on the sofa in the corner but couldn't concentrate on reading because Da kept standing up to dial the number and getting no reply. He went to the window and peered out. 'More coming this way, I reckon.'

Mam was folding the washing. She looked at him sideways. 'Nothing ye can do?'

Da shrugged. He grabbed his tweed cap from the hook, went outside and kicked a tin bucket across the lawn, like something he did when he was angry. Aoife returned to her book. The morning dragged by, until eventually Harry came.

'Sorry, mate,' he said to Da. 'Old man Barker got on to me to fix the drains at his place. Storm water flooding. Said it'd only take a half hour. Took forever.'

'Ye could've said no,' Da said sharply.

'Yeah, well, you know I do a lot of work for him. If I said no, he'd just as easily lay me off, not get me in again. He's like that.'

'Yeah. No loyalty.'

Aoife glanced quickly at him. She had a feeling he meant something else by this. Harry didn't take any notice. 'Shall we get over there? The shed, I mean? See what needs fixing?'

Harry and Da had been gone more than an hour when Mam told Aoife to take a basket with a thermos flask of tea and buttered soda bread to them. 'It's cold enough out there. This will warm them up.'

Aoife dragged her feet in her cold gumboots through the mud on the track as she walked to the barn. She thought she could hear shouts but Da often shouted. He had a loud voice. He'd even sometimes shout at her for reading her book by the fireplace when he came in from working. 'Go outside and find yeself something to do,' he'd say.

By now, she had almost stumped her way to the haybarn.

Up closer she could see Da standing outside. He was definitely shouting at Harry who had done something wrong and Da was letting him have it – guns blazing. She had heard that expression in a story on the radio one time and tucked it away to use again. Neither of the men noticed her come towards them. Aoife put the basket on the ground.

'You arrived so bloody late. If you had got here when I asked you, none of this would've happened. Now the bloody hay bales are ruined. Soaked through. No use to anyone. They'll fall apart if I try to pick them up. Waste of bloody space.'

Harry held a hammer in his hand. He lifted it up to his shoulder as if he hadn't realised he was holding it. 'Jack, man, you're out of order. Getting stewed up. This would've happened any time.' He waved the hammer back and forth like a weight. 'You should've been checking the iron on the roof a long time back. Not waited till there was a bloody great storm.'

Da snarled at him and grabbed the hammer. He tried to swing it. Harry wrestled it back, held it high for a second or two and brought it down towards Da, the claw end of it narrowly missing his chest. He tried to bash Da's hand with the hammer but Da was the stronger. He seized the hammer and held it high as if he were going to bring it down on the little man.

Aoife screamed. 'Harry. Da.'

It made no difference, neither of the men seemed to hear her. Da flung the hammer across the yard, turned towards Harry and took hold of him by the throat. 'Listen here, you little toe-rag. You piece of shit. You and all your excuses can go to hell as far as I am concerned. Fight like a man, you little toady.'

Harry struggled. He batted at Da's face with his balled-up hands.

Da flung him to one side. Harry got up and began to run away and Da raced after him, cursing. Harry bent down and picked up a large grey rock, holding it high, ready to aim.

Panicking, Aoife screamed. She didn't know whether to run for Mam to stop the two men or to run to save Da. She stood, swaying, trying to make up her mind. Silent in her rubber gumboots, she ran behind Harry and tried to pull him away by tugging at the back of his jacket. It was no use.

Da had the same thought. He strode to Harry and reached for the front of his jacket. The material bunched in one hand and he dragged the little man towards him. Harry flailed at Da, dropping the stone. Da's clenched right fist met Harry's cheek, smashing down on to it. Harry stumbled. Da fell on him, pinning him to the ground, punching him in the face again.

'You little bastard,' Da shouted.

'Da,' Aoife said loudly. She didn't want him to hurt Harry. If only Mam were here. 'Da, stop,' she cried again. What if he killed the other man?

A big dark cloud passed over and a noise as a truck drove up the cattle race and stopped. She turned to see a man get out. Suzie's father. Mr Barker was tall and strongly built. He marched right up behind Da and wrenched his arm back. Da spun around in surprise and raised his fists, thrusting wildly at him.

'Stop it,' a voice commanded. Matiu's grandfather clambered down from the passenger seat in the front of the truck. He ignored the three men and limped slowly across to where Aoife stood. The men pulled apart and watched him. 'Matiu's missing. He's been gone all day. We can't find him. Someone thought they saw him heading down the side road to your farm.' He looked hard at Aoife. 'Missy, would you know?'

Aoife looked down at the ground. Did she? There was a place she knew Matiu could be fascinated by. 'I might.'

'Well, tell us where, please missy. And hurry.'

'He might've gone to the swamp in the gully at the back of our farm. Mam said it was dangerous but ...' Aoife hesitated, unsure of what to say. 'He went in there one time. I reckon he might have wanted to check it out again.'

Mr Henry shook his head. 'I was worried about him missing his mother but this ... Can you take me there?'

Aoife looked at Da. He was breathing heavily. Sweat was running down his body and his singlet under his open jacket was soaking wet. The two other men had their heads down, like boys when they were in trouble at school.

Mr Henry followed her gaze. 'Your father will be fine. They're big lads. Let them sort it. Come on, young missy, show me where he is, please.'

Aoife nodded and started walking towards the gate, leaving Mr Henry to follow. She led the way down the cattle race towards the back of the farm. Mr Henry was breathing heavily behind her, using his stick to make progress.

They had walked almost to the end of the farm when she saw two figures in the distance, near the swamp. The man from the shelter and Matiu. She turned to speak to Mr Henry who was still pacing behind her, head down, his breathing even harsher now. Ahead of them, the man called Michael carried Matiu towards the shelter. She broke into a run and raced towards the pair, hearing her own breath coming out all ragged.

'Matiu,' she called.

Matiu's body was limp and soaking wet, and Michael was cradling him. What had he done? This was all her fault. She should never have told Matiu about the man in the shelter and she shouldn't have let him go in the swamp. She ran even faster. Michael reached the shelter and lowered Matiu's body onto the ground. He disappeared inside the opening of the shelter, intending to get something, she thought. The mug of water?

A shout came from behind her. It was Da. When she turned back, the other three men were all catching up. Aoife began to cry, a weird high-pitched shriek. She pushed herself on, breath grinding in her throat. 'Matiu.' She reached him first, ahead of the other men. 'Is he all right?' she asked Michael quickly in Irish. Before Michael could say anything, Da pushed her aside and tried to bundle Matiu into his arms.

Matiu's grandfather caught up with them. He gave a low moan. Was Matiu dead? Aoife's stomach lurched. Mr Henry shoved Da, thrusting him away from Matiu. He laid Matiu on his side like Aoife had seen Mr Kirton do that day in the class-room and let out a long keening noise. 'All right, boy,' he said softly over and over.

Da reached out and touched Matiu's chest. 'We need to get him to hospital.'

'No,' Mr Henry said. 'No.'

The men looked at him.

'He may have hit his head,' Da said. 'The boy looks to have been knocked out.'

'No, he's had a turn, that's all,' Mr Henry said firmly. 'He'll come to. Give him a few minutes now. It's happened before. I need to get him back home. He can sleep it off.'

Water. Aoife remembered the water. She moved her hand around inside the shelter, found the tin mug of water, and took it back to Mr Henry. He splashed it on Matiu's face and touched him gently. 'I'm here, boy. You'll be all right. We need to get you away from this place.' He turned to glare at the area of the swamp. 'Not a good place for anybody.'

A shudder went through Aoife. She looked around for Michael but he was nowhere to be seen. She began to sob. After a long while, Matiu opened his eyes.

* * *

Matiu didn't come to school on the Monday and he was off school for a week. One of the boys said his koro had taken him over to the east coast someplace.

When Matiu returned, Aoife saw him kicking a ball around at playtime with Felix Jackson, who was in their class. She went over to stand on the side of the playground, watching, and waited for Matiu to notice her but he paid her no attention.

After the bell rang, she followed him towards the classroom.

'What happened in the swamp that day?' she said.

Matiu began to walk faster. He tossed the ball to Felix and reached out to catch it when it was thrown back.

'Something happened,' Aoife persisted.

Matiu stopped and turned to face her. 'My koro said for me to keep away from your farm. He's forbidden me to go there.'

'But why?'

'He said bad things have happened there. And he says you see things you shouldn't see.'

'No, I don't.' Why would his koro say that? How would he know?

'Yeah, you do.'

'That's ridiculous.' Aoife stomped her foot. 'I told you the swamp could be bad and not to go there. Now you're blaming me.'

'Yeah, well.' Matiu seemed to hesitate. 'Now you know. It is bad.'

'But what did happen to you in there?'

'Nothing.'

'Did you see someone? Did you see the man I told you about?'

The bell sounded. 'Matiu. Come on, mate,' Felix called.

Matiu turned on his heel and marched off. Aoife had never felt more alone.

IMOGEN
Taranaki 2018

My phone rang early in the morning while I was out walking. I had got into the habit of making my way towards the back of the farm in the mornings. It gave me an opportunity to keep my steps up but also to clear my mind.

I was pleased to see it was Zoe calling.

'Your mum phoned this morning,' she said.

My heart skipped a beat.

'Like you thought, she had lost her phone. She couldn't find where she had written your number, so she phoned the office number on our website.'

I was impressed by my mother's detective work though I was also apprehensive. I hadn't told her what I was up to and she might have worked out where I was by now. 'Did you tell her I was visiting Jack?'

'No. I wasn't sure you really wanted her to know about that. I fudged things a bit. I said you'd gone to New Zealand to visit Rebecca in Wellington for a well-earned holiday.'

That could work. Aoife had met Rebecca when she'd come to Melbourne for our class graduation. 'Did she give you her new number?'

'She did. I'll text it to you. She said she was in town buying supplies and she'll try to phone or text you later. She did add there wasn't a lot of reception where the farm is.'

Good. That still gave me a chance to come up with a story if I acted quickly. I wasn't ready to let her know what I was up to yet; the Rebecca alibi would have to do for now. 'I'll text her later.' After I had time to think.

We spent a while talking about work projects. Changing the subject, she asked if I had made any progress on what she had taken to calling my 'shortlist of suspects' (with the emphasis on 'short', it occurred to me). Before I could reply I spotted two men near the stream at the back of the farm. 'Possibly more to add,' I said jubilantly, 'if the two men I see ahead of me are anything to do with it.'

I began walking faster. 'Hey, you,' I shouted at the men, still clutching my phone in my hand.

'Wha-at?' Zoe's voice echoed shrilly on her end of the phone. 'Don't do anything silly.'

'You can bet they're something to do with the Barkers,' I said before telling her I'd call her back.

Puffing from walking so fast, I marched up to the pair – two Filipino men in khaki overalls. One of them was digging with a shovel and small stones and soil from the bottom of the stream were piled up on the sides of the stream. The stream itself looked higher than usual. 'What do you think you're doing?' My voice came out bossier and louder than I had intended.

The man stopped working. He looked at me awkwardly, embarrassed. 'The boss sent us to take a look. We've got a problem downstream on the farm below.' He gestured towards the side road that ran along the boundary to Jack's farm, the one I'd seen on my first day. 'Flooding. The water's backing up. Something in the stream.'

He continued to dig, looking down. He hauled up a carcass,

the remains of a dead calf, its head so smashed and jelly-like I was immediately nauseous. My mood changed back to anger and I said icily, 'I don't care what has happened. Or what you've found. You're trespassing. This is not your land to be on.' I flung one arm out, pointing towards the farm they had come from. 'Get out of here or I'll call the police.'

One of the men looked stunned. 'Miss ... Please. We're just checking the stream. You can see for yourself. But if you want us to go.' He began to step away, his footsteps getting faster as he walked. The other sent me a sullen look and also moved away but I saw he had pulled out his phone and was speaking into it.

Let them report me to their boss. How dare they! I watched them go, turned and marched back towards the house. A sense of satisfaction came over me as I stomped one foot after the other. I mightn't have dealt properly with Aoife but I could control these men. This was Jack's land, and I wouldn't let anyone onto it. I might not have found out yet who'd been harassing him but at least I'd taken charge with these men who had no right to be there. The Barkers' men.

Jack gave me a long hard stare as I walked into the kitchen. 'Your face's red, like a strawberry.'

'So?' I slumped into a kitchen chair, let my breath even out. 'There were men down the back of the farm. Digging in the stream.'

Jack sighed. 'I know. I just got a call from Andrew Barker. You told his men you'd get the police to arrest them?'

'Not exactly.'

'Well, you made an impact. Frightened one of the guys. He has family dependent on him back home and he needs this job. He can't do anything that could get him arrested and affect his visa status. I guess you mustn't have known that,' Jack's tone was dry, 'or you wouldn't have threatened him like you did.'

I had been so riled up at seeing them I hadn't given it a thought. 'That isn't the point. Are you happy to have them trespass on your land? You let the Barkers run roughshod over you after all that's been happening?'

Jack opened his mouth to reply, but instead turned towards a banging noise coming from the back door. After what he had said, I expected Andrew Barker to barge in, not Nathan. He took his boots off at the door, almost as if he were biding his time before he came in.

'What's this?' he asked. 'Sorry, couldn't help but hear you both. An Australian creating an international incident? That would be a first.'

'Ha. Very funny.' A pathetic attempt at humour, I wanted to say. Why did he always get me mad?

Nathan looked at Jack. 'Shall I explain, or shall you?'

'Explain what?'

Jack said nothing. He shrugged. He could have almost said the words 'Nothing to do with me' because that was the message I took from his actions.

'Andrew Barker sent his workers over to give a hand. He didn't want to bother Jack after all the stress he has been through.'

'And didn't let Jack know?' I glared at Jack.

'This is what we do in the countryside,' Jack said. 'I'm no fan of any of the Barkers, but he was just trying to fix a problem that was heading downwards to his farm on the side road.'

'And you're both ganging up on me now?' I could sense irritation, frustration – and hurt – welling up inside. 'Don't treat me like an idiot. Someone is doing things to cause you harm, and you won't let me find out.'

'Look,' Nathan said. 'I know you want to help, but antagonising Andrew Barker isn't likely to benefit anyone, least of all Jack. His sister's on the council in case you've forgotten. And if

Suzie Barker can get Jack for dirtying the water in the stream, she will. No matter a dead animal is not his fault.'

Jack nodded. 'Aye. True enough.'

'But what if it's the Barkers who are behind what's going on?'

Now both Jack and Nathan looked at each other, baffled.

'You can't accuse people of something like that,' Nathan said. 'Without any evidence.'

I knew that but his words still annoyed me.

'If it's them,' Jack said slowly, 'they could have asked to buy the land.'

'I thought they had asked and you said no.'

'Who told you that?'

It had been Daniel but I wasn't about to tell them this. 'Not sure now.'

Jack leaned forward and picked up a packet of tobacco off the table. He took a wad and placed it in his other hand. 'They don't need it right now. They'll wait till I get too old to run it and I've been carted off to some home then they'll put in a silly offer but they know not to try it on me right now.'

I stopped to consider this. How well did Jack know the Barkers?

'Anyway, these kinds of actions are too visible for them.' It was as if Jack had read my mind. 'They've got dirtier ways of doing things. Even through the law.'

I shuddered. What could be worse than damaging a prize bull to frighten an old man? I glared at Nathan. 'I'm getting a warning, is that it? To stop investigating. That's why you're here?'

Nathan pulled out a chair. He glanced over at the kitchen bench and said airily to no one in particular, 'A cup of coffee would be great. No, I'm not. I came here for another reason.'

Jack tamped at the end of his roll-your-own. He indicated by the flick of his eye that the electric jug was over there by the bench. I decided to ignore him.

'I came to invite you to a trip to the maunga tomorrow. The weather is supposed to be good.' I sensed him checking my reaction. 'It's not a good idea to climb it in the winter but you can get great views from some of the lookouts. We could go as far as the lower levels where there's snow.'

I looked at him in surprise. 'Why would you want to do that?'

Jack made a scoffing noise and I wanted to respond but I held back. Instead, I glared at him.

'Because,' Nathan said, 'we got off to a bad start, you and me. Think of it as an apology.'

'Did Shelley put you up to it?'

Now it was Nathan's turn to look surprised. 'Shelley? No, why would she?' His phone buzzed. He pulled it from his pocket and checked the screen. 'Look, I've got to go. Anyway, I can see you don't like the idea. Forget it.' He turned, put his boots back on, and strode away from the house.

I had given him a piece of my mind but he had had the last word. I stood still, trying to work out what I was feeling. Jack gave me a long stare. 'Like your grandmother,' was all he said before picking up the newspaper and choosing to ignore me. After a time he put it down. 'If you're planning on staying much longer, you should take that rental car back and use mine. It's out in the shed.'

I looked at him suspiciously.

'Get them to fix the tyre at the rental place.'

I knew it. That annoying Tamati had told Jack what had happened to my car tyre. Nothing was a secret around here. At least Jack had accepted I was intending to stay longer and was obviously giving his reluctant blessing. Now I had to let Zoe know, and send Aoife an innocuous-sounding text so she didn't start worrying about where I was. Or what I was up to.

AOIFE

Taranaki 1978

'Where's your da?' Mam asked.

Aoife looked up from her book. She had nearly finished it. 'He's over with one of the heifers. She's about to calve.'

Mam had been in one of her tidying moods, tossing newspapers and magazines and empty cardboard boxes into a cloth bag the potatoes had been in. She stood on a chair sifting through the papers, some torn from old magazines and others from envelopes, which got tipped into the narrow cubbyhole in the wall near the kitchen.

'God knows how this stuff gets in here,' she said through gritted teeth. 'This place is a complete tip.'

Aoife tried to return to her Nancy Drew mystery but when Mam was like this, it was hard to ignore her. She'd be demanding Aoife got off her arse and helped her sort things.

'Do ye want me to help, Mammy?' Aoife said before Mam had a chance to get mad at her.

'Yes, ye could take this bag outside for me. Put it in the old oil drum.'

Aoife stood up. Her feet were numb from sitting with her legs folded underneath her. She took the bag outside. The forty-gallon drum was empty so she tipped the papers out of the bag into it. Mam hadn't bothered to give her a matchbox to set it alight. If she forgot about it the rain would come down and wet all the papers. It had happened before during one of Mam's clean-ups. Aoife would be sent out to remove the wad of damp clumpy papers and there'd be nowhere to dump it except down by the swamp.

Matiu hadn't said anything more about that day when he fell in the swamp and she hadn't gone back there since. She went back inside to ask Mam for the matchbox.

Mam was muttering to herself, holding onto a piece of heavy cream paper. The paper had writing on it and looked official. 'What …?'

Aoife went closer to see what she was looking at. She saw the name Halliday's Law Firm typed at the top of the page and partway down Da's name and also Mr Murphy's but before she could read any more Mam pulled the paper out of her reach. 'I can't believe it,' she was saying, more to herself than Aoife. 'Where did you say your da was?'

'Helping the heifer calve over in the back paddock.'

Mam held the embossed paper out in front of her at arm's length. She began to walk to the door. 'Right, so. You stay here,' she commanded.

Aoife watched her mam go through the back door, past the cluttered gumboots and garden implements stacked higgledy-piggledy on the porch. She looked longingly at her book but this seemed serious. She couldn't let Mam storm off across the farm on her own. She grabbed a pair of gumboots and shoved them on her feet.

Mam was too angry to look back and see Aoife following her. She marched along the cattle race towards the paddock where Da was. The paddock wasn't far from the swamp and, too late, Aoife realised she could've brought the paper rubbish and tossed it in there. It would likely mush down into nothing. Now it would probably sit in the oil drum and get all wet and no one would remember about it. Not now.

Aoife was having to walk faster and faster to keep up with Mam. Mam was striding so fast it was as if she were marching towards Dingle all those thousands of miles away across the sea.

IMOGEN

Taranaki 2018

There was a funeral for a man called Harry on Friday. Molly had come over to ask if I could drive Jack to it. 'Someone Jack knew well.'

Not that Jack was ready to claim any friendship. He snorted. 'That cheeky little shrimp. Saw his death notice in the paper yesterday. No friend of mine. Let me down when I needed his help with the roof on the shed, the bastard. I had a big fight with the little rascal and nearly killed him.'

Another story about a fight. How many were there? Was Jack ever in the wrong?

'Same day young Matiu hid in the swamp and got himself frightened …' Jack appeared to be musing over what happened. 'Aoife was there. Or was that another day?'

Molly was brisk. 'I'm sure his relatives won't know that fight story and you could keep it to yourself?' She sent me a glance. 'You might have seen him outside the pub. He and a couple of the old fellows liked to hang about on the bench there.'

The old chaps I saw on my first day in Wexford. 'Of course. I remember them.' Though I doubted I would recognise which one was which. They'd reminded me of garden gnomes. 'I'll be happy to accompany Jack and drive him home.' He was still looking grumpy like a child who had been chided.

Jack glared at me. 'I'm not helpless.'

'The cops have been pulling up people for breath testing around these parts lately. They've had a real drive.' Molly went over to fill the kettle. 'A woman from Ōkato got caught last week, Jack. Someone said she used to be a teacher at the primary school years ago. Miss Anderson?'

Jack nodded. 'Taught Aoife when we first got here.' I was surprised to hear him remembering a detail of my mother's child-hood. 'Was a nice-looking young lassie in those days. Did her best, but some of those big girls she taught were right little madams. That Barker girl, the one on the council now, I remember she was trouble. Bit of a ringleader. I think she tried to bully Aoife when she first started school. Kids,' he said dismissively.

'Interesting,' I said. 'I'd picked that Barker woman for a bully.' I didn't add the Aoife I knew would never let anyone even try to bully her. That was one thing about her. She'd never have let that little snake put her down like that; those were the exact words she used when I finally told her what had happened with Gavin. Aoife was not one to feel sorry for anyone. She told it straight.

She hadn't been that taken when I told her I had started seeing Simon and got that look on her face. 'He's not divorced? Hardly serious then.' I knew what she'd say if I told her we'd broken up.

'I'll be off then.' Molly cast a glance at Jack. 'Imogen, I've got some newspapers for the fireplace if you want to come and get them from the car.'

Outside, she lowered her voice. 'Listen, if you're wanting to head back to Melbourne, you mustn't worry about Jack. I'm around. He'll be fine and he wouldn't want you to ignore your own life because of him.'

'Thanks, Molly,' I said. 'Zoe has got everything in hand at work. It's fine as things are.'

'So long as you know.'

I watched her leave. I had no intention of leaving. Not right now. Not before I had got to the bottom of things here.

The funeral was at a small wooden church in Ōkato. A group of men who were gathered outside stopped talking as we walked up the path. A couple of them greeted Jack, while a few still gave me a look that said, 'And who are you?'

Jack appeared to enjoy the service despite his initial negative comments. He laughed quietly as people related stories about the man who had died. It was obvious he had known him very well. Afterwards we went to the hall for refreshments, where Jack was happy with a glass of whisky and a chair to sit on. Some of the women I had seen at The Empire that night passed around hot meat savouries and club sandwiches.

It was odd Aoife had lived in this district yet had never mentioned childhood friends. So far, the only people I had come across who had once known Aoife were the rude Barker woman and Matiu.

I recognised a voice behind me.

'Ladies,' Nathan greeted the women behind the counter. 'Sorry I couldn't make the service.' There was a little flurry as the women vied to offer him a drink and a plate of food. He accepted a small plate of sandwiches, a scone and a can of lemonade. I noted all this without realising I was noticing.

'How are things going?' he said to me. He spoke politely but I could feel how distant he was.

I matched his tone: 'Busy.'

'Work?'

'I've been looking into what's been happening to Jack. That's more important right now.'

'Look, I've told you what I think.'

I nodded. 'You've made it perfectly clear what you think.'

'But it's not what you want to hear?'

Jack looked over, caught my eye and waved. He either wanted another plate of pastries, or to go home. I was glad to have the distraction and walked across to him. Let Nathan find someone else to talk to.

It was much later that I helped Jack, who had made the most of the whisky on offer, into his car and drove him home. He was happy to let me take his arm to lead him into the house and into the sitting room. Once we got there I knew something was wrong. Someone had dumped the contents of an old bureau in the corner onto the floor. Papers fanned out, envelopes strewn everywhere. The glass doors of a china cabinet had been flung open and pieces of the china were smashed – a teacup and saucer I recognised as the dainty, green-and-white Irish Belleek. It would have been my grandmother's.

I found a chair for Jack to sit on then strode off, intending to check his bedroom. I stopped short in the hallway when I realised a picture was missing from the wall. The big, framed photograph of Duke, the ancestor of Jack's beloved Champion had gone. I heard a noise and turned around. Jack was following me.

'No, Jack, stay there,' I called. I didn't want him to see the blank space. Too late, Jack was already behind me.

He paused and stared intently at the wall. 'What the hell?'

I took his arm. 'Someone's been here, looking for something of yours. You've got to tell me what's going on. What do they want?'

Jack had gone pale. He put his hand up to his face. 'What do they want?' He repeated my words slowly, his voice dull. 'I don't know.'

'Who are they?'

'I don't know.' He sounded even weaker now, not so much in control.

I let him be. There was no point in haranguing the old man.

Further down the hall, the intruders had also attacked Jack's bedroom. They'd pulled out the drawers and left them. They'd flung open the wardrobe door and pulled shoeboxes down from the top of the wardrobe. They were definitely after something. I led Jack back to the veranda, sat him down and got him another whisky before heading to check my own room. My laptop, thankfully, was still there, tucked beneath the middle of the mattress where I stowed it whenever I went out. I couldn't tell if anyone had gone through my things.

In the kitchen, I took Jack's list of local phone numbers from the wall and looked for Nathan's number. He couldn't put this incident down to the forgetfulness of old age. This was real and I had proof – Jack had been out with me all afternoon – he couldn't have done this. I grabbed my phone to call him. He was quiet while I described what we'd found when we arrived back at the house. This time there was no discussion about Jack having a memory lapse.

'Don't touch anything,' he said. 'I'll be there as soon as I can.'

My next call was to Molly, who was still in town at the vet's practice. It was Daniel who arrived first, asking me what all the shattered glass was doing on the path outside.

Nathan was next. He avoided meeting my gaze. *See*, I wanted to crow. I'd been right. I had known there was somebody behind it all. It took one look at Jack for me to know this wasn't the time to score points. This was about Jack, not Nathan and me.

***

When I arrived at the rest home early the next morning, Hayden Ward didn't look at all surprised to see me again. If anything, he looked pleased to be interrupted from completing a crossword puzzle. 'Stuck on a clue, fourteen down. Ten letters.'

I ignored the newspaper page he held out. 'Something's happened. Someone broke into Jack's yesterday afternoon and went through everything. Papers flung everywhere.' I took a breath and went on. 'Nathan came around to check. He said they must've worn gloves because he couldn't get any fingerprints.'

'That's not good.' Hayden leaned forward to put the newspaper down on the small table beside his armchair, looking at me steadily. 'Not good at all. Go on.'

I paused to take another breath. 'They've been after something. Some information. It made me think.' I stopped, trying to sort out what I wanted to ask him. 'The land. You said it belonged to Murphy?'

'I did.'

'So how did Jack come to own it?'

'Ah.' The old man looked away, seemingly organising his thoughts. 'Depends on who you ask. There were rumours he won it from Murphy in a poker game. That rumour got around fast and to tell you the truth, I don't think Jack minded if people thought that. He didn't want people knowing his business – where he got the money to buy the farm or put a down payment on it. He could be very cagey about such things.'

You wouldn't have to know Jack for long to realise this. 'I've been asking him to let me in on what's been going on since I got here. He clams up.'

Hayden nodded. 'The thing is, the sale of the farm didn't go out to the market, and I don't think the price Murphy sold it for was as good as it could have been. In fact, you might say he almost gave it away but the prices of land were down a bit at that time; there was a slump and no one was buying. Those that sold did it because they had to. All in all, I reckon Jack did get it fair and square.'

'How can that be fair? Wasn't it taking advantage of Murphy because he wasn't with it?'

Hayden looked away briefly. 'It wasn't the most Christian thing to do to someone who had taken you in and given you a home and work. I'll give you that.'

The words he used made me think of Molly and Daniel, to whom Jack had also given a home and work.

'I know it doesn't seem right but you weren't there that night,' Hayden went on.

'And you were?'

'Yes. I was there with Smiley Webster. The four of us. I used to stay a night every few weeks at The Empire when I was making my sales visits. I'd go from South Taranaki, calling in on farms around the coast behind the mountain, doing long days. I used to look forward to spending an evening in Wexford before heading back to New Plymouth on the Saturday morning. I liked the people I met around here. They were good sorts.

'That's how I know. It was a strange old situation to be in, I can tell you. I heard Jack ask Murphy a couple of times if he knew what he was doing. Murphy was known to be a drinker but, you know, I didn't think that he was drunk then.' He paused, deep in thought. 'Look, I can see that night as clear as anything, even if it was all those years ago. It was almost as if Murphy wanted shot of the farm, wanted to be gone. He didn't care about the farm or how much he got for it. Enough to live on would do him, he said.'

'Did you do anything to stop it?'

'I tried to say something to Murphy, but he paid no attention. The next day I went to Jack's place. His wife had gone out somewhere, taking their daughter, and he was on his own at the house. I gave him some frank advice. I said I knew what went down but when other people heard about it they would be bound to have it in for him.'

'How did he react?'

'He didn't take much notice but Jack never did. He was his own man. He told me to bugger off and stick my nosy beak where the sun don't shine. I didn't believe there was much else I could do.'

'Anything else you recall?'

'Just what I told you. Murphy said he had no family to hand it over to or leave it to. Murphy himself had never married. I heard Jack could've been a distant cousin of some sort. You could say he kept it in the family.'

Hayden cast his gaze around the room. It rested on a framed painting of the mountain, the building I recognised as The Empire in the foreground. 'Found it in a second-hand shop one time,' he said when he saw me looking at it. 'By the end of the week, Murphy had shot through. Went to the South Island, or so I heard. He'd been there before and liked it.'

'After that?'

'Never heard anything much about him till we learned he had died. Darned if some of us hadn't thought of him as old Mr Murphy all that time but, I guess, he wasn't as old as we picked. I would've thought the drink would've killed him long back. He could've given up the drink after he got rid of the farm. Sometimes I wonder if something about the farm had spooked him and he couldn't wait to be rid of it. Now we'll never know.'

I frowned.

Hayden caught my eye. 'What are you thinking?'

'I'd say someone's not happy about what happened back then. Jack must know more about this than he's letting on.'

'You think so?' Hayden leaned forward eagerly, almost touching my knees. For an elderly man he was certainly agile.

'I'm not sure.'

What I did know was his words had given me an idea of where to search next. I remembered that day at the beach Shelley had talked about old newspapers. I wished I had thought of this earlier. I stood up. I needed to get back to the house to make sure Jack was all right. I texted Aoife another invented update about my holiday in Wellington with Rebecca. I should be ashamed of myself, I'd become adept at lying – spinning the truth – but the times were desperate. And I remembered when I had last heard that expression – from Michael Flynn, the odd character who had accosted me in the street in Melbourne.

Early next morning I drove to the library at New Plymouth and soon found the local history floor. The room itself was quiet enough when I ventured inside, with one staff member at a desk in a corner. I turned to the one at the desk in the centre, her name tag identifying her as Abby.

'Can I help you?' she smiled.

'I'm looking for information about the ownership of a farm in the Wexford district from the early settlers' period,' I told her. 'I already know the name of the most recent owner and the one before him, a Mr Murphy. I've tried looking online but it looks like I can only access the information from the old records of Lands and Deeds through the library.'

Abby beamed, clearly keen to help. She had a nice smile. 'I can search this for you. I'll need the address.'

I gave it to her, got out a notebook and waited quietly while she checked her screen. She scrolled through screeds of information, sometimes peering in closer to read what was on it.

'It was a Denis Murphy,' she said at last. 'His name is the earliest recorded from the time of the settlements here by Europeans. His entitlement to ownership of the land was recorded on February 4, 1867.' She gestured at the screen, turning it around so I could see it. 'If you look here ...'

I leaned closer to read the small type. Fifty acres of land in a part of the district of Wexford in the foothills of the Mt Egmont Ranges had been given to a Corporal Denis Murphy in payment for his services to Her Majesty's Government as a member of the Taranaki Militia. I wrote this in my notebook.

'You can see here he was born in Ireland,' Abby said, pointing to his place of birth on the document. 'County Kerry, Ireland. Many of the soldiers at that time were from England or Ireland.'

'As payment for services,' I read aloud. 'Was that usual?'

'Yes. In fact, I've researched this period in my library studies.' She said this proudly. 'It was a period of financial depression in New Zealand at that time and the government didn't have enough funds to continue paying the soldiers. Makes sense. They had confiscated all this land, might as well ensure it went to army men as payment. I guess it was a solution where it looked like everyone benefitted. Plus, they'd now have even more men prepared to settle on the land.'

She leaned forward, eager to share her knowledge of the local history. Judging by the emptiness of the room I guessed she might not get called on to do this too often. 'It would've been covered in native bush. It can't have been easy to break in and turn into farmland but few would have had an opportunity like this before.'

I was sure she had more to tell me. 'Go on.'

'Well, from what I've read, it would appear most of these soldiers were fighting because they needed the money, not for the glory and not because they were loyal to Britain.'

I thought about this while she glanced at the computer screen again. 'We can also check the online marriage records to see if Denis Murphy married. In later years there will have been electoral rolls he'll have been named on if he continued living in the area. I know a lot of the men gave up on the land pretty quickly. Too much work. They sold it and returned to where they'd come from or headed to Australia.'

As it happened, Denis Murphy had got married, about five years after he was given the fifty acres, to a young woman named Johanna Harrington, also from Ireland. Had he sent for her, or had they met in the immigrant circles of those days? The couple, according to the Births Register, had produced two sons.

'Which means one or both inherited the farm,' I said, 'and it was a Murphy who owned it back in the 1970s. Could it be the same family?'

Abby flicked back to the other screen with the Lands and Deeds information. 'All the first owners we have listed after Denis are Murphys. Just to let you know, the records here don't include modern times. Only the old Lands and Deeds paperwork.'

I glanced at the scribbled notes I had written in my notebook after meeting Hayden Ward. The Murphy of the 1970s had been an old man, a bachelor, with no known close relatives. I thought of a couple of my former workmates in Melbourne. Both were from extended Irish families and were never short of distant cousins they were happy to claim. Either Mr Murphy liked to live, as did my mother, as if he had no living relatives or he had forgotten about the many distant cousins he might have back in Ireland, until one day someone must have informed him Jack would be turning up with his wife and daughter.

'Do you have any information relating to the conflicts the earliest Murphy fought in?' I asked. 'I'm interested to learn more about this period in history.'

Abby nodded and led me to a full shelf of history books. I could see the words Taranaki and New Zealand Wars on the spines of some of the books.

'These should do,' she said. 'You can take them into the reading room over there.'

Inside the room I sat down at a table and opened the first book I came to, not sure what I was looking for. I flicked through it and skim-read sections on preparations for war, the soldiers' way of life in their camps, and other material that caught my eye. It was interesting and I read on, though at the same time I had a strong sense of something waiting there for me to find.

I stopped skimming and began to carefully read a section on the destruction of a pā, the senseless killings by both sides of the skirmish. Some of it was gruesome reading. I tried to imagine these things happening in the very district I was staying in. So much of the forest had been razed for farmland all those years ago and now dairy workers were milking one thousand cows a day. The only thing that had stayed the same was the looming mountain, standing sentinel over the lush green paddocks and herds of black and white cows and, of course, the river.

My hand moved to my necklace. I checked the time on my phone. This had taken longer than expected and I'd left Jack's car on a metered parking spot. I still wasn't sure I had found what I had come for.

I opened another book to see a number of pages of colour plates depicting artists' representations of the men in the British Army and other troops that had been in Taranaki during those war years. On the next page, more grainy pictures of men in their uniforms.

The necklace tingled against my chest. The pictures showed men in odds and sods of uniform fording rivers, tramping through the bush under the mountain ranges, and setting up camp in the middle of nowhere. Interesting stuff. I was about to turn the page when I stopped myself. If it had been at all possible, which it wasn't … was it? It couldn't be. I leaned forward to take a closer look.

I recognised the clothing; a couple of men in dark-blue loose smock tops over trousers, others in big blue overcoats, some with rolled blankets slung around their chests. All these years later, the clothing could easily match what the man called Michael Flynn was wearing the day I met him. The oversized navy jacket had made him look like a beggar decked out in op-shop gear. His clothing had been too warm for a Melbourne day, even in mid-winter, but appropriate for the icy chill of winter on the slopes beneath the Taranaki maunga.

I felt myself shiver as I tried to think about what this could mean. A soldier. A fighter. The kind of man who might have fought hard against the Māori in the forest on what was now Jack's land. Like Denis Murphy – only not Denis Murphy. A man called Michael Flynn. So, what did he have to do with Denis Murphy? Or the farm? Or anything else for that matter?

My phone buzzed, startling me. It was a text from Daniel saying he was nearby. He'd spotted Jack's car parked on the street near the library and would hitch a lift home whenever I was heading back. It was unsettling to know I hadn't been able to escape the farm without someone seeing me in the city. I could hardly avoid him now.

'Meet you at the car,' I texted back.

I found Abby at her desk, told her I had to go and thanked her for her help. She handed me a sheet of paper with a list of websites. 'I printed these off for you,' she said. 'Some useful articles on the New Zealand Wars and the Taranaki conflicts in particular. Oh, and this.' She reached for a pad of large yellow sticky notes. She scribbled a few words on one.

I squinted at it as I took it from her.

'Papers Past on the National Library website. It's another good resource. You can look that up yourself on your own computer. It's available to the public online. You might find scans of old newspaper articles that mention your Denis Murphy. You'll need to key his name in and an appropriate year range.'

'Thanks,' I said again. 'I'll look it up.' I stuffed the sheet of paper and the yellow sticky note in the side pocket of my bag. It had been a profitable day. Now I knew who the original owner of the farm was, I had something to follow. I was sure of that.

Heading back to the car, I could feel the adrenaline race through me. It was like old times pulling out the threads of a mystery, finding out things bit by bit and seeing where they connected, getting the story. This time, though, it would be different. No one could stop me and I definitely wouldn't let anyone know what I'd been doing.

I'd tell Daniel I had whiled away a couple of hours traipsing through the nearby art gallery and reading glossy magazines in the library. I could say I'd been making enquiries about getting an out-of-town visitor's library card. It would be easy enough to come up with a suitable story because right now I didn't want anyone at Wexford knowing what I was up to.

AOIFE

Taranaki 1978

Dusk was settling in and along the power lines birds were lining up, making their evening calls, shrilling out to each other. Aoife followed Mam to the back paddock. Da was leaning against a fence watching the in-calf heifer. He had a roll-up smoke in his hand and had taken a puff, the smoke curling in the air above him.

Mam waved the bundle of heavy parchment paper at him. 'What in God's name is this?'

Da glanced at the papers, avoiding her gaze. 'I was going to tell ye, Peggy, honest I was.'

'Tell me what?' Mam spat the words out. 'And when? I can see the date on this, ye scheming bastard. I can see it clearly.'

Da sighed, then tried to smile. It was a weak smile. 'Listen now, Peggy, it's all fine. It's only paperwork. It won't make any difference.'

'To whom?'

Da leaned on the fence. 'To Murphy, if that's who ye are worried about. Nothing will change. I'll be running the farm and he'll still have the little cottage down there on the road to come back to. He'll have plenty, don't ye worry. He'll want for nothing.'

Mam stamped her foot. 'How did ye manage this? Get him drunk? Has he even seen it?'

'He signed it at the lawyer's. His lawyers, they are, too. It's all above board, I can assure ye.'

'Indeed,' Mam scoffed. 'With ye nothing is above board. I know that meself. Tell me the truth now. How did you do it?'

'It was fair and square, love.'

'Really!' Mam stamped her foot again. The gumboots didn't make much noise, more of a squelch on the muddy soil. 'Title deed papers, is it now?'

'Right, so.' Da sighed. 'It was after the poker game. We had a few whiskies, and he was letting on how he wanted rid of the farm. Murphy said the place was fair spooking him out and he should've left years ago. He wouldn't say any more than that. He didn't want to be stuck with the place any longer. If there was anyone he was happy to pass it to, he said, it was me. Us. As how ye and Aoife had been good to him.'

For someone who often didn't say much, Da was sure gabbing. He couldn't wait to spit it all out. Mam stared at him with a strange expression that Aoife couldn't quite work out. Da peeked at her from under his bushy eyebrows.

'We don't have the money to pay for a farm.'

'That's just it. He doesn't want much, only a down payment. I'll pay him off as we go along. He doesn't care anymore. He wants rid. Land isn't fetching much at the minute anyway. I have to give him enough money to buy a little caravan in the South Island.'

'How are we getting that money?'

Da looked away and it seemed an age before he answered. 'Remember Barry? I told ye I'd be asking me cousin, the one who's done well in America. He stumped up. It's not a lot. He owes me. Ye know that. I took the rack for his little shite of a brother, the one I told you about. He was there in the bank that day. It was Barry and his uncles that sent the messenger.' He took a long breath and raced on some more, words tumbling out as if he were pleased to have them in the open, as if Mam would now understand. 'They made me do it. They're big in the division. They give the orders. Top of the tree in terms of commanding officers. They gave me no choice. Someone had to play the guilty party and it wasn't going to be that little scoundrel. The gardai up north have a file that big on him. They were out to get him for what happened in the bank.'

'Well, that's worse. My God, taking blood money and cheating Murphy. Wrong on all counts. Why would ye even want this place? Aren't we planning to go back home soon enough? Hadn't it all died down like you promised me?' Mam's voice rose higher and higher in her agitated state. 'Or are ye meaning to make a quick buck by selling the farm once it's yours? Wouldn't put that past ye now. I can't believe anything ye say. Ye always were a liar. My own da didn't warm to you from the first. I should have listened to him and saved meself a lot of trouble.'

The heifer in front of Da moaned. It was a long-drawn-out moan, and Da cast a quick look at her. He put out his hand, touched her flank and ran his hand over it carefully. He rolled up the sleeve of his jacket. 'Soon,' he said softly to the cow.

Mam took no notice of the heifer. 'Well, and I can tell ye what ye are going to do. I want ye to listen now. Ye are to go back to that lawyer and tell him ye both made a mistake. Rip up the agreement. The land belongs to Murphy and that's whose hands it will remain in.'

'No,' Da said firmly, looking up at her. 'No, it's done now. Signed, sealed, and done. Nothing can change that. This is our land, and it is rightfully our land.'

'We could go back home,' she pleaded.

'Ye know we can't. We can't be creeping around there, fearful of being dobbed in by a little shite of a cousin or two. Someone will know what happened. There's always a fellow who will talk. Ye can bet on that.'

'But what will people say when they find out?' Mam was despairing. 'No one likes us here in the first place. And now this.' Her voice rose again plaintively, louder than the cries of the birds that lined the wires.

'Well,' Da said. 'Murphy reckons he will tell people he lost it in a poker game. That should shut them up. He likes to gamble. Everyone knows that and on the night, I was the better man for the gamble.'

'Ye will get it changed back.'

'No, I won't.' Da began to walk away.

'Now listen to me.' Mam looked about her and caught Aoife's eye. It was as if she had only then noticed Aoife. She took a long breath. 'In that case, if ye won't listen then Aoife and I will be leaving.'

'Peggy ...' Da began.

'I mean it. I've had a gutsful of your antics. Come on, Aoife. There's nothing to be done here.'

The heifer let out another long moan. A mournful panicky moan. Aoife saw a tall shadow come out of the gloom and stand near the cow. When she looked across at Da, he seemed to be torn – eyeing the heifer, while also trying to keep Mam in sight.

'Come on, Aoife,' Mam said again. She began to walk away to the other side of the yard.

The shadow became Michael, the man from the shelter. He looked across at Aoife as if wanting her to take action but what could she do about anything? The cow moaned again. Da looked down at the animal, suddenly aware of what was happening.

'All right, all right now,' he murmured to her.

He reached his arm into the back side of the heifer and pulled. After a struggle a leg covered in a gooey substance came out. Reaching closer he grabbed the leg. The cow gave a deep moan and a sleek sticky creature whooshed out and slumped to the ground. The heifer put her head down and began to lick the damp body of the calf.

Da wiped his hands on his trousers. He sighed, then hurried after Mam. The stronger of the two, he gripped her arm. 'Peggy, don't be so mad at me, woman.'

'Leave me be,' she said sharply.

It was Mam who lashed out first, not Da. He responded, or that was what it seemed like to Aoife. All the same, she cried out when her mam fell to the ground. Da's fist had collided with her jaw. Mam held it as she tried to push herself up. 'You bastard. My tooth could be broken.'

Da swore. 'The feckin heifer distracted me.' He reached out to touch her face, but she elbowed him away.

'That's it. It's all over. No more,' she said. The words came out oddly through her jaw. Blood started to trickle out the side of Mam's mouth.

'Come on, Aoife.' She began walking back to the house. 'Come with me now. This place is not for us. There's evil here. I knew it from the beginning but I couldn't see it. Or wouldn't.'

Her voice grim, she stepped up her pace. Aoife went after her. She turned back to see Michael was following them, a few steps behind. The evening was turning dark now with a half-moon appearing from behind clouds. When they got to the house, Michael stayed outside.

Mam told Aoife to gather some things – her clothes, anything else she wanted – and put them in the small suitcase. 'Quickly now.' She was on the phone to someone. Aoife could hear a woman's voice asking questions on the other end. There was a rush of Mam looking for things, their paperwork, passports.

Mam picked up the suitcase Aoife had packed. 'Outside.'

'Mam,' Aoife began, 'we can't ...'

Mam spoke over her, flinging things in another small bag. She seemed to be talking to herself. 'We should have gone ages ago. I was too patient. I've known this for a while. Passports. What else do I need? Cash. Where did I stash it? Under the mattress.' She swung around, saying to Aoife, 'Go on.'

She went outside as Mrs Greene's car drove up the track and stopped in front of the house. Michael came around to where Aoife stood. 'Please, Miss, don't leave. You must know I tried to protect you.'

Aoife glared at him and scoffed. 'Protect me. Why didn't you protect Mam from being hit? Stop them fighting?'

'I couldn't. I can't explain. I tried to help you but nothing happened. I was frozen, like the snow on the mountain there.'

Aoife didn't want to hear his excuses. 'I gave you food and water. I wanted to help you that day. You did nothing for us. I hate you. Get away from us.'

'You don't understand. I couldn't. Not anymore. I couldn't do anything.' He sighed heavily. 'There was some other power at work.'

What was he talking about? It was nonsense. Aoife turned her back, crossed her arms, and ignored him. When she turned around again he had gone. A flash of gold glinted on the track and she bent down to pick up the object: a gold necklace with a locket. Could it belong to Michael? Should she call out to him? She looked in every direction but there was no sign of him. She was left holding the necklace as her mother came out of the house and told her to get in Mrs Greene's car, the woman's pale face watching them curiously.

Aoife didn't want anything of his. She thought to toss it to the ground though her grip tightened around the chain, the little heart-shaped locket. She heard her mother tell her again to get in Mrs Greene's car and that they were leaving. Quickly, she pocketed the locket and did as she was told.

She and Mam stayed the night at Mrs Greene's house. In the morning, Mrs Greene took them to the airport at New Plymouth. Aoife looked out the window for the mountain but the cloud cover was low and she could see nothing. Like last time, there was no chance to say goodbye to anyone. In Auckland, they boarded a bigger plane, bound for Sydney, Australia. Aoife knew about Australia. It had kangaroos, koalas and snakes that could kill you.

AOIFE
Alice Springs 2018

Her phone had been out of action since she'd dropped it in a puddle on the farm. They were a fair distance from civilisation. Rusty, the farmer who employed her, had said they'd go into town for supplies and she could get her phone fixed but, so far, they hadn't been anywhere. Too much to do, he told her.

She should have known it was a mistake taking on a job like this one. She hadn't been sure whether to believe he had hired other workers to share the load. 'I'm waiting on a couple of them to get in touch about a start date,' he said. Yet there had been no sign of anyone else since.

Rusty reminded her of her da. He was a big man with a larger-than-life air about him that suggested you couldn't believe all he had to say. She didn't really believe any of Rusty's stories about his time over in Asia in the army, stationed in Singapore, though she pretended to listen.

If she could persuade him to drive her to the nearest town or let her use his truck she could look for another job. She could go to the library and check websites for rural workers. Even if she had wanted to borrow his old computer – a dinosaur if she had ever seen one – the Wi-Fi out here was shit useless.

It was times like this made her think about her life before, and even what kind of life Emer and Lucy, her two close friends back home, had now. Were they still in Ireland? It was so long ago. Why would they even remember her? She had been the girl who disappeared with her parents in the middle of the night, never to be seen again. That was what they would've said about her in the years after they left. People liked to gossip in their village – it was kind of the lifeblood of the place. There'd have been all kinds of stories, the same as when she and her mam took off from Wexford, also on the quiet with only Mrs Greene knowing what they were up to.

They had never gone back to Ireland, she and Mam. After they arrived in Australia Mam had found a job on a farm miles from anywhere, sorting sheep wool. There had been a new school to go to. Another place to explain how Aoife was pronounced. Another crop of suspicious girls, reluctant to move over and let her join their circle. She knew what to do now, how to keep them at arm's length. On her first day at school, she refused to join in and simply scowled at anyone who looked at her. She thought back to the two big girls on the bus and how they had carried themselves on their first days and she copied their style. She walked to and from school on her own, with no trouble.

So it began, moving from place to place. After a while she'd got used to it. Aoife's accent became more Australian and no one asked about her name or where she came from. She was sixteen when Mam got the cough that wouldn't go away. By that time she was also working alongside Mam on farms in the outback; fruit picking, hay making, sheep shearing, she'd tried them all. After Mam died in the little hospital miles from the farm they were on, Aoife carried on working. There was no time to mourn. Seasonal work was about to begin. Again moving from place to place, it was all she knew. It was a long time before she even began to think about how she could see her da again.

In the end, she returned to Taranaki hoping it would feel a bit like home. Not Ireland, but still.

From New Plymouth, she hitched a lift in a newspaper delivery van to the farm, walked up the farm track and told Da she was back. Once there, she kept herself occupied in the house the first couple of days, sorting out the stuff in her bedroom, the dolls, the clothes. She put it all in boxes by the front door to drop off at a charity shop next time she went into town. She had started to do the same with the woollen jerseys and shoes her mam had left behind – all the stuff she couldn't fit in her suitcase that night – but Da came in and got angry, told her to leave her mam's stuff alone and to quit interfering, and that pissed her off in turn.

She wasn't afraid now to face up to him, nor was he prepared to back down. She yelled at him that it was all his fault Mam had died and stormed out of the house, got in Da's little truck and driven to the pub.

When she walked in, people seemed to be eyeing her, trying to work out who she was. She got a vodka and tonic, found a quiet table and ignored them. People in this district always had a look of the family they came from, and she was sure some of the faces matched those who had gone to school with her. The Martins, for instance, there had been a big bunch of them, and two guys standing at the bar had the same dopey country expressions on their faces that the Martins had had.

A man came out from behind the bar and began setting up microphones at one end of the room. It was band night and four guys came out and took their places. Aoife got herself another drink. It was going to be a long evening but she didn't plan to head back to the farm any time soon. When she and Da had that almighty row, she thought he was going to hurl the bottle of whisky he'd been holding through the window, he was so mad.

It took a while to realise the slim guy in black top and jeans playing the bass guitar kept glancing her way. Not that she cared. Another drink was more important right now and she had no intention of going back to the house sober.

The band wasn't bad, better than okay. Ages later, when they finished the final set, the guy who had been looking at her came over. He didn't seem to be local, now she thought of it, though she did know him.

'I'm Matiu,' he said. 'I'll drive you back to Jack's. Let me have your keys.'

Aoife had thought to protest but gave up. 'How will you get home?'

'I'll get one of the boys to follow in the van.'

She was nearly sick on the way back, retching into the foot-well. After that, she didn't expect to see him again but he phoned the house the next afternoon. He said he'd given her time to get over her hangover.

Matiu suggested a meeting place. She knew immediately where he meant and it shouldn't have surprised her. Who else would know of it?

The place was overgrown but the shelter was still there and Matiu was standing near it. He waved and when she caught up to him, he gestured for her to go ahead of him and crawl inside like they were children again. There was barely room for the two of them, and she had to bow her head to get through the entrance. Inside there was no sign of Michael, of course, the man she had once found in it – no item of clothing or a tin mug. She'd often thought of him watching her and Mam leaving that night, helpless even though he wanted to help. Useless bugger, as Da would have said.

She tried asking Matiu again what had happened to him that day in the swamp, and he said he couldn't remember. His face seemed to shut down. He had once been her only friend yet all these years later, he still didn't want to be asked difficult questions.

Instead, he reached out to touch her necklace, undoing the clasp of the locket to reveal the pictures inside. 'Who's this?'

She retaliated then by pulling it away from him. 'None of your business,' she said, sounding mean, like she had all those years ago. She and Matiu were like two parts of a broken vessel, neither willing to give in to the other. She relented. 'I found it. It belonged to the man here, the one I met in the shelter.'

When he reached out for her a while later, she responded. It had been nice to be with him that afternoon, good to feel wanted after Da had treated her so callously, though that wasn't going to change her mind about heading back to Australia as soon as she could. She asked him if he would drive her to the airport and he said he would. After her row with Da all she cared about was leaving, getting as far away as she could.

She'd managed it, hadn't she, spending part of the summer on a kibbutz before realising she needed to go back to the harsh arid outback, the one place she thought of as home. Aoife put all thoughts of Wexford and the people there behind her. It hadn't worked out and she had no intention of ever making contact again. Yet somehow, being here with Rusty seemed to bring it all back and that wasn't good. It was never good to dwell on the past.

It was Imogen she needed to worry about now. She'd been thinking about her a lot lately. Was it that crazy habit the old Irish had of suddenly being drawn to thinking of people when they were in trouble? Her grandmother and the great-aunts back in Ireland used to go on about it. 'I only thought of him and would ye know, he died the next day. He'd fallen off the roof,' her great-aunt once said. There was always a tragedy or some terrible injury. The others would nod in understanding. So now Aoife knew something was going on with Imogen, even though she didn't know what it was. She hoped it wasn't as serious as the things that happened to people her great-aunts knew.

It could be that useless boyfriend, Simon. She had got his number from the few details Imogen had let slip. Thinking he was weak – running back to his wife all the time – she'd wanted to warn Imogen though her daughter was another one you couldn't tell things to. She didn't want advice, at least, not from her mother. In fact, Imogen preferred to give Aoife advice, as if she couldn't think for herself. It was an odd sort of mother-daughter relationship at the best of times.

Meanwhile, she'd give Rusty another nudge about going into town.

IMOGEN
Taranaki 2018

It was Saturday afternoon and Molly had gone to New Plymouth with Daniel to see a movie. She asked if I wanted to go with them and I'd said no, because I needed to sort out a work problem. I sat in the kitchen, my laptop open on the table. The wind had picked up and the pine trees in the unkempt garden at the front of the house roared.

'You sent me the wrong file,' a client complained in an email which had come an hour before. 'Not my project at all.' I had no excuse for the error. I hadn't been concentrating on what I was doing and needed to send him an abject apology soon. I was focused on this when the landline phone rang, startling me.

Jack, who had been reading the newspaper at the other end of the table, picked it up. The caller said something. 'Where?' Jack responded sharply.

I could hear the reply, though couldn't make out the words.

Jack replaced the receiver. 'Wrong number,' he muttered, and started heading towards the door. 'I'm going to drop off some old mail at the Post Shop, pay a few bills.'

He grabbed a handful of envelopes with typed addresses on them from the sideboard. I imagined he still paid his bills over the counter by cheque. 'Shall I drive you there?'

'No need.'

'Okay.'

I turned back to the email. I had work to do – and quickly if I were to remedy an embarrassing situation.

After Jack had gone, I wrote my reply, trying to make it sound suitably apologetic but without accepting any blame. Feeling at a loose end, I began pacing the room, aware the wind had begun to howl. The windows rattled and cold air was sneaking in beneath the gaps under the doors. Unable to concentrate, I started to straighten up the clutter on the table.

Something was wrong, I wasn't sure what exactly, though I felt a sense of foreboding. And gloom. Aoife always said her bones got chilled before the icy winds even arrived. She knew the temperature would change before it began. Now the wind started to bluster even more loudly. The iron sheets on the roof seemed to be banging as if lifted by the wind. The gale was sweeping around the house, bashing into things as it passed by. A bolt of lightning lit up the grey sky, followed by a roar of thunder. A sudden downpour of rain hit hard outside making me move away from the windows as it pelted onto the glass.

The landline rang again. 'Imogen, you're there.' Matiu sounded relieved. 'Thank goodness. The Met Office has put out a tornado warning. I think it will hit your end of the valley fairly soon.' The fast pace of his speech was a strong contrast to the measured tone I'd heard when we'd spoken at the bridge.

'It's already a gale outside,' I said.

'Tell Jack to put some boards up on the windows at the back of the house where the winds will get high. He'll know what to do.'

'He's not here. He said he was going out to the Post Shop in the village.'

'It won't be open. Closes at midday on a Saturday. He would know that.'

Was Jack getting forgetful, as Nathan had suggested? A thought struck me. I hadn't heard Jack's truck start up after he left.

'Hold on a minute while I check if his truck's gone.' I placed the receiver on the table and went to open the back door. The downpour had stopped. The truck was still in the shed across the yard. As I came back to the phone a howl swept around the outside of the house, a big gust of wind seeming to shake it on its foundations. Where could Jack be? 'The truck's still here. He hasn't taken it.'

Matiu was quiet, perhaps thinking through the possibilities. 'Does that mean Jack's out on the farm?'

'He got a phone call and he went out. He said it was a wrong number.'

'Do you think he's gone to the back paddocks? Has he got his dog with him?'

'Bandit wasn't at the back door just now.'

'Okay.' Matiu seemed to consider. 'Look, these tornadoes can get bad – blow windows out – big enough to send roofs flying. They can overturn a tractor.'

Now he was frightening me. 'I'll go out and look for him.'

'Wait. He'll know to take shelter somewhere. I'll drive him back from town if he's there.'

'No, don't do that. The roads might be blocked.'

I put the phone down. I had come all this way to help Jack and so far I hadn't been much help. This time I couldn't let him down. I picked up a torch from the kitchen bench, grabbed an old raincoat and a rain hat from beside the door and, in the porch, pulled on a pair of gumboots. As I left the house, the glass in one of the windows shattered. An old pine creaked painfully, then crashed against the fence. I struggled to walk in the rain, water trickling into the wide openings of the gumboots, and the boots themselves slippery on the ground. The wind tore at the raincoat as if it were trying to rip it off me.

Should I run back inside to safety? I could crouch behind a sofa in the lounge for protection if the windows got blown in, but no, I couldn't do that, not when Jack was still out there somewhere. I struggled on and began to shout out Jack's name but the words came echoing back at me. A sudden gale lifted a sheet of roofing iron from the nearby shed into the air and it whirled past along the side of the house, startling me and making me shriek.

Jack must know what powerful damage the storm could bring. With luck, he'd already taken shelter. I began to run along the cattle race, pitting my body against the wind. Massive branches roared and swayed on the pine trees. An even louder whistling noise tore through the air and a huge gust which came with it almost forced me off my feet.

'Jack,' I shouted again as I kept on moving, one foot in front of the other, my feet sloshing around inside the gumboots, which now had a lot of water in them. I was partway down the cattle race when a huge gust of wind barrelled over my head and flung me to the ground. The wind whirled and spiralled and roiled like it was alive. I lay on my back, terrified, as I watched it race ahead, felling a huge tree in its path, sending it splintering onto the track. Should I return to the house? My body heaved with sobs of fear. I shouldn't be out here in this wildness. I didn't know what to do. I was no use to anyone. I cried out, 'Help me, help me,' but no one was there. In the distance, I saw a bolt of lightning and then another.

As the icy gale swept past me again, my fingers became blocks of ice. I tried without success to get up but my energy had gone. I was going to lie there and die. People would find my stiff body and they'd know I'd been stupid, careless, heading out into this terrible storm. I had been determined to help Jack but I'd achieved nothing. Now he was in danger somewhere out in the paddocks and I was about to freeze to death. I lay on the muddy track, cursing myself for my stupidity. Why had I turned down Matiu's help? What made me think I was anyone's saviour? My actions made no sense at all.

Strangely, I felt my body lifting up as if a kind of energy force wanted to heave me off the ground and drive me to my feet. I found myself standing, light-headed and wavering, trying to get my balance. Crashing sounds came from the direction of the cowshed while sheets of iron swooped high into the distance. I plunged forward.

Stumbling against the wind, I made my way to the old cowshed. At the entrance, I had to shove aside a pile of fallen barrels and sodden sacks before I could get any closer. I stood looking for any sign of Jack, terrified his body could be lying on the concrete floor. No one was there.

I remembered that the room with the milking machinery was at the back of the shed. I waded across the wet and sodden floor towards it. Over the wind, I heard a man's raised voice. I peered around the side of the open door and glimpsed Jack and two men. He was slumped low in a steel outdoor chair. One of the men was a giant, somebody I hadn't seen before, the other wore a leather jacket. I could see a long one-word tattoo that seemed to run down his neck inside the jacket. He was the man I had first seen at the café, ignoring the pleasantries of the German waitress. I'd seen him twice since.

'That's all you have to do.' I remembered that voice, too, the tone of contempt in it. He held a pen in his hand and a sheet of paper. 'Sign there and there. Tiny here will organise the rest.'

'I want to see Bandit,' Jack said. His voice was weak. 'I told you before. What have you done with him? You said you had him.'

'Sign the paper and then we'll give him to you. First things first,' the tattooed man said.

Tiny growled. 'Give him a whisky from your flask. That'll get him going. The man likes his whisky, doesn't he? If that doesn't persuade him to do the right thing, then it's goodbye to his beloved Bandit.' He chuckled and cracked his knuckles.

'Hey now,' the tattooed man spoke up. 'No need for that, Tiny. Jack will do what's right, won't you, old man? And then everything will be fair and square like it should be.'

'Wait,' Jack began again. 'I need time to think.'

The man with the tattoo shoved the pen towards Jack. 'You've had plenty of time. Shit loads of it, and now it's up. C'mon, get on with it.'

He reached out his arm to hold back his mate who was hovering menacingly over Jack. 'Hold your horses, Tiny. We'll do it my way.'

Tiny took no notice. He slung an arm around Jack's neck, forcing him to face him. Jack spluttered. 'Listen, stupid, you had your chance. Time to do the right thing or you're a gonna, mate. No mucking around. We'll be outta here and no one's gonna find you till it's too late.' He pulled at him again. 'Too late, mate.'

'Hey, I'm in charge here,' the tattooed one said. 'I've warned you, Tiny.'

How dare they threaten an old man? They were nothing but bullies and I'd had enough of bullies. I couldn't throw my arms up in despair and walk away like I had with that dickhead Gavin – so much more was at stake now – I couldn't watch passively. What could I do? If I shouted for help, who would hear me in this terrible storm and in this derelict shed? It was tempting to turn and run away, to run back to the house, to phone for help.

I heard a voice in my head. *You might be on your own*, it said, *but you must help Jack. There is no one else.*

The rifle was on the floor by the side wall. Jack must have brought it to defend himself with but it was of no use to him now. The men clearly weren't bothered by it. Their brutish strength was all they needed. Could I get to it? And what did I hope to do?

An icy blast brushed past me. I turned and saw Michael standing in the open doorway. A mixture of relief and anger that he had taken so long to make himself known went through me. Except maybe he'd know what to do, how to save Jack. What he did next was a complete surprise.

Michael moved swiftly, his black hair flying, and swept silently across the room. His movement, like a gust, sent the paper the man was holding into the air. It seemed to float for a moment before falling to the stone floor. I watched, doubt coursing through me. How was that supposed to help?

Surprisingly, it made an impression, taking the attention of the two crooks away from Jack.

'Shit. What was that?' said Tiny. 'How the fuck?' The paper lay on the floor motionless yet both men gazed at it as if it had a life of its own. He reached down as if to snatch the paper.

In that instance, Jack came to life. He reared up out of the chair and shoved the man with the tattoo out of the way, surprising the man and knocking him, impossibly it seemed, so he faltered. As the man stumbled, Jack raised his fist and hit him in the chest. Jack let out a massive roar, swung his arm back and hit him again – hard. He was like a man possessed with the energy of a twenty-year-old. I remembered his story of threatening the haymaker with a shovel.

I reached forward and grabbed the rifle and handed it over to Jack. If anyone would know how to use a rifle it would be him and I was right. He held it by the barrel and smashed the wooden stock down on the tattooed man, hitting him in the chest, winding him. The man curled up on the floor coughing, trying to catch his breath. Jack lunged on top of the man, whether on purpose or from sheer exhaustion I couldn't tell. He lay half on him, holding him down with the rifle flat against the man's body, trapping him there, wheezing heavily, his body a dead weight.

It all happened so quickly.

The huge accomplice went to pull Jack off his partner, then clearly thought better of it.

Instead, with a grunt, he reached for the paper Jack had been meant to sign. Yet the paper suddenly lifted into the air, as if picked up by a breeze, floating away and rising high above Tiny.

Was it Michael's doing? He was standing almost flattened against the rear wall, his expression impassive as he watched the action.

The man swore loudly and gave up on the sheet of paper as it bobbed near the ceiling. His mate meanwhile was struggling ineffectively beneath Jack who was still holding him down. Tiny looked like he didn't know what to do next, as if waiting for instructions from the tattooed man, and glanced at the doorway, about to take off and get the hell out of the place.

Outside there came another crack of thunder and rain thudded heavily against the tin roof. I edged towards where Jack held the rifle and saw Michael give a nod. Quickly, I tugged it out from under Jack and aimed it at Tiny. I hadn't held a weapon since the time I went rabbit shooting with the Carrington boys on their farm, when Aoife and I were living at their parents' place in the outback. I'd been too squeamish to pull the trigger then, to actually shoot a living creature. Was the gun loaded? What if it went off in my hands and I killed someone?

I shook my head, that wouldn't happen. Michael, across the shed, responded with a firm nod. *Yes. Do it.* Had he said it aloud? I couldn't be sure though it felt like he had shouted the instruction at me. My hand tightened around the barrel of the rifle, my finger on the trigger. I had never shot anyone in my life and didn't think I could do it now. I stepped forward as a streak of lightning lit up the milking shed through the door opening. In the distance, there was a rumble and a clap of thunder.

It jolted the big man out of his stillness. He came to life, lunging at me, grabbing for the rifle to seize it from my grasp. Things were happening in a blur. I tried to fight him off and hold onto the rifle, but it was no use. I didn't have the strength against such a big man. I fumbled with the gun and, too late, he wrestled it off me easily, then grabbed my arm with his thick hand.

You can do it. The voice in my head was Michael's. He was still standing by the wall. *It will have to be you. You're the only one now. You can do it.*

I heard a harsh grunting sound and saw that Jack, suddenly invigorated, had locked his arm around Tiny's leg and was hauling him away from me. The big man shouted and attempted to pull out of his grasp but Jack's hold on his leg forced him to lose his balance and stagger. As he fell awkwardly, Tiny landed hard on the stone floor with a sickening crack. Concussed, or at least in a daze, I couldn't be sure which, he lay there motionless. I picked up the gun from the floor and held it closely, my hands shaking. Jack grunted again before subsiding, all his energy gone.

Michael's voice was suddenly near me again. *Use the rope,* he urged. *Tie him up.*

Rope, what rope? Glancing around in a panic, I saw a couple of coils in a corner. I put the gun down nearby and tugged the end of the rope towards me. It was old, hardened from lack of use, and my entire body was trembling so much it made things more difficult. I managed to get it around one of the big man's wrists and finally, after a lot of effort, the other. He was now tied up. I wanted to relax, but my body continued to shiver with fear and adrenaline as I grabbed the gun again.

At almost the same time, Jack rolled himself off the tattooed man. The man shrank in fright when he saw that his mate was unconscious.

Tie him up as well, Michael ordered, his voice stern.

I took the rest of the rope and managed to loop it around the man's hands and pull it tight. Both men were now looped together, sharing the same rope. The tattooed man's groaning subsided.

Picking up the gun and aiming it at the thugs, I looked over at Michael. Time to speak properly with him at last. I might have been pleased to see him, yet there were things I needed to know. What was he doing here after all this time? How did he know to come to help? I wasn't sure he had been much help but still, without his guidance, I wouldn't have known what to do and he was here, wasn't he?

'I told you there was trouble,' he said quietly. 'I thought you didn't believe me but you did, and you came in time. You were as good as your word. Leave it to me, you said.'

Except I hadn't meant those words, had I? I'd said it to get rid of him.

'What do we do now?' I asked, exhaustion taking over from the adrenaline that had kept me going all this time. So many questions were swimming around in my brain. Who were these men? What had they to do with Jack?

'We wait.' Michael was calm, too calm almost. 'For further assistance. It will come soon. Like the mist on the mountain.' He ran his hand over his face and it seemed to me his whole body faded in and out, weary now – as exhausted as I was. 'You have done your bit.'

'Imogen, are you all right?' said a voice from behind me. It was Daniel's. Before I had a chance to reply, he swore. 'Shit. What the hell? What's happened?' He strode towards the tattooed man and bent down to him.

'Don't. Don't touch them. Either of them. This man has some explaining to do,' I said to Daniel, the gun shaking in my hands.

'Dad?' Daniel was still leaning over the tattooed man. It was a question yet I could hear a resigned tone, as if he didn't need to be told. Suddenly I wasn't surprised at learning who the man was either; it was all beginning to make sense. 'What have you been up to?'

'Just doing what had to be done. I told you I'd sort it.' The man's voice was thick, his breath harsh. 'What do you think it looks like? He was happy enough to cheat another man all those years ago and keep quiet about it. Now he's getting pay-back.'

'I dunno what the hell you were thinking, Dad.' Daniel turned to see if Jack was all right.

'Leave him,' I said again to Daniel. 'He might be dazed. Especially after the ferocious fight he'd put up.'

A door banged outside somewhere. It sounded like the wind was still tearing through the paddocks. It whined and howled. Yet I heard another noise – heavy footsteps. What should I do? The doorway filled up. It was Nathan in wet weather gear, his hair soaked. Behind him were Tamati and two men I didn't recognise. Farm workers from the Barkers' place? One had Bandit by the collar. Bandit's fur was also wet. The leash was broken in half as if the shivering dog had escaped imprisonment from someplace where he couldn't be heard in the storm.

All shall be well now, Michael said in what seemed like a whisper. Had I imagined his words? In the few seconds it took for Nathan and Tamati to reach the two crooks, I turned to reply and found he had gone.

The man holding Bandit took him over to Jack. The dog began to whine. Jack was still breathing harshly as Bandit licked his neck and face. The other man crouched down. 'He's fine. Just needs to take a few slow breaths. Got knocked around a bit, eh? Let's get him up.'

As he reached out to stroke Bandit, I could see colour returning to Jack's face. The two men lifted him to his feet. Nathan stepped over to me and eased the gun from my hands.

I turned to face Daniel. I couldn't find the words, but the anger in my voice would've told him what I thought of him. If I could find the strength I would've thumped him in the chest. 'Look at me, you … you … Do you have any idea what they were going to do to Jack? They were forcing him to sign his name on a piece of paper or they'd kill him. What the hell was that about?' I snatched it up from where it now lay, damp and marked with traces of dirt from the stone floor and tried to read it. 'A change of ownership? Are they mad? You do that for cars. Nothing legal about it, besides, any agreement signed under duress would get thrown out of court. What did they think they were doing? And who did these idiots want the farm to go to?'

Daniel's cheeks reddened. I thought he might cry. 'Look, I can explain everything. Honestly. I know it looks bad, but …'

'You better had explain. And fast.' I knew that voice. Molly was behind me, glaring at Daniel. She was talking to Daniel's father, as I now knew the man with the tattoo to be and her voice dripped sarcasm. She did not like him, that was clear. 'I should've known you'd get yourself involved in something that's no business of yours. When there's trouble you're never far away. They let you out of prison, did they? Or are you on a break?'

Nathan had pulled a set of handcuffs from his belt and was now putting them on Daniel's father. Tamati, arms crossed, had boxed the other man, the big scary one, into a corner and was holding him there. Was this how people in a rural district dealt with trouble? Quietly and efficiently with no need for a huge police presence. Nathan spoilt my fantasy by putting in a call for back-up.

'Trees down on the cattle race, so you'll have to leave the car on the road,' he instructed and turned to me. 'Good job, Imogen, but how the hell did you and Jack manage to overpower two big guys like these?'

I saw the other two men look up and nod, as if they had been thinking the same thing.

'A hell of a lot of luck,' I said. 'Jack did a great job tackling that one, and somehow I got lucky with the other. I never thought hitting someone on the cheek with a rifle could cause such damage. Never used a gun before but they were going to hurt Jack. They were forcing him to sign this paper they thought was legal, and without his agreement. I couldn't let it happen.' Was I explaining too much? Casting suspicion on my actions?

'I did have help,' I said, looking at Jack. Had he seen Michael? Would he say anything? 'You should've seen Jack. He was like a champion fighter in a boxing ring. He still had it in him.' I heard pride in my voice. An elderly prize fighter, but still. Those stories I had heard from Hayden Ward about Jack in his fighting days rang true.

Jack's face was blank. He wasn't about to add anything. Hard to believe now, as he watched us so innocently, that he was a man who might have hit another man with a shovel and had in this very room hit someone with the butt of a rifle. We both had our secrets.

Nathan fixed the other men with a stare. 'Unbelievable.' He looked back at me. 'Unbelievable.'

There was no way I could tell him or any of them the real story.

'I mean, sure Jack knows how to defend himself.' Nathan wasn't ready to let it go. He regarded me curiously as if continuing to assess my and Jack's ability to take on two large men and beat them. He wasn't a police officer for nothing. 'Still. He's getting on a bit. No offence, Jack, but I think Imogen's right. You both got lucky here, God knows how. The outcome could have been a lot more serious. For both of you.' His voice was stern. 'If Matiu hadn't phoned me to say Jack was missing back of the farm somewhere, that there was no sign of the dog and you might have gone looking for them …'

Jack grunted.

'Let's get him home,' added Nathan.

I looked around the room at the people in it. Jack and Nathan. The two men I had suspected of not wanting to help me, one I had actually accused of not wanting to help. The horrible two in their handcuffs and Daniel. Had I got everything so wrong?

Daniel. I looked at him, wondering why he would betray Jack like this.

It seemed to take us forever to trudge through fallen branches and over roots on our way back to the house. The paddocks were stripped of many of their trees, the ground muddied and dangerously slippery.

Back at the house, Molly, silent and suddenly awkward, made a pot of tea. Daniel looking stricken, his face white, sat watching the door. No one said anything. Jack sighed a few times. It was as if we were waiting for an order to go ahead. It was going to be a long day.

The door opened and Nathan came in. 'My backup has taken those two.' He pulled out a notebook. 'Now, Daniel, it seems to me you might have a story to tell us.'

Daniel reluctantly dragged his gaze away from the door, as if he might still be able to make a run for it. 'So … well … well …' he stammered. It was unlike him. 'One of Dad's old mates managed to track me down for him. He asked for my mobile number and when Dad came out of prison he texted me. We talked a couple of times and arranged to meet up. He asked me a lot of questions about why we had come here, to Wexford, and … well, I told him.' He cast a quick glance at Molly. 'You know, why we had come.'

So why had they come? I was desperate to ask but around me there was silence. Nathan kept his head down, eyes on his note-book. Jack said nothing apart from making a humming noise under his breath as if his mind was elsewhere.

I thought about the story Daniel had told me about how they had come to Wexford and by chance met Jack. A lie. They had been looking for him. 'You didn't happen on Wexford by chance, when you were traipsing around a cold and gloomy north Taranaki in winter in your campervan, did you? Like you told me. Nice story, by the way. I never doubted it.' My voice was harsh and I hoped my sarcasm reached him. In fact, why hadn't I doubted him? I should have, I realised now.

'Sort of.' Daniel looked uneasy. 'After Mum found out …'

Spit it out, I wanted to shout. I had a hunch that I knew what – or who – his mum had found out about. The thought hadn't occurred to me before but now it had I could see it made sense. 'You came straight here?'

Nathan caught my eye. He frowned, a warning.

'Yeah.' Daniel refused to look at me.

'And you knew exactly where …'

'Imogen,' Nathan interrupted. 'Let the lad tell us himself.'

I heard myself snort. As if. Molly had her head down. There was a long silence. I wondered who would be the first to try to make excuses, give their side of this whole horrible tale.

Finally, Molly sighed. 'Listen, Jack, we did come up here to find the farm. It was – it was after I learned Bryan Murphy had owned this farm. He was my father. I had come across an old friend of his, a man called Neville Shuker. He told me a farm in Taranaki had been handed down the Murphy line for many years, since the early days, and Bryan was the last Murphy to own it. He said for some reason, Bryan had passed it on to a Jack Maguire.' She was speaking faster now, recalling this information. 'So I decided to check out the farm. My roots. Get an idea of it. That's why we came up here, Daniel and me. That's the absolute truth, I swear to God.'

'You wanted to see what you had missed out on, you mean?' I didn't try to hide the acerbity. I was bitter, damn it. Let her see what I thought of them both.

Molly ignored me and continued to address Jack. 'Neville said there was more to it, how it happened. It sounded a bit fishy, he said. Look, it's true, it didn't seem fair to me but when we met you, I realised you were a good person. I wanted to tell you who we were, from the first, only then I got this crazy idea. I thought we could help on the farm.'

'You did and I was grateful.' Jack nodded at her.

Tears glistened. 'I thought that if you saw what a great worker Daniel was, how good he was on the farm, you might look at taking him on full time.' Her voice went up an octave. 'Running the farm even. Especially when you learned about his relationship to my father – to Bryan – that he was his grandson. I was going to tell you. I know it sounds ridiculous but you had no one, no family to care about you anyway, and you were getting older and …'

'Then you learned he did have family?' I asked. 'When I turned up?' Had I turned up because I cared about this old man

I never even knew existed? Or for my own sake, to find out more about my father?

It struck me how odd this all was. Mr Murphy was said to have no close family and the same had been thought about Jack. The whole situation was a mess. It seemed the farm had never really been Jack's, either, not properly. He had been quick enough to take advantage of Mr Murphy wanting to get shot of the place and head down south. Was it any worse than what Molly had intended to do? I shook my head. Thieves and vultures. The sooner I went back home to Melbourne – my real home – the better. God knows what I was going to tell Aoife about all this. Maybe nothing at all?

I had another question and I wasn't going to let anybody try to lie to me again. 'You can prove this relationship to Mr Murphy?'

Molly had the grace to look me in the eye. 'I knew he was my father all right. My mother had told me who my father was ages ago. Plus I did a family history DNA test and my results got matches in common with distant relatives of his of the same name in Ireland and America.'

A DNA test. Simon had encouraged me to take one, too, one time when I told him about my unknown father. I hadn't wanted to, as it hadn't felt right somehow.

'My mother said Bryan upped sticks before I was born and went roaming in his caravan. She never heard from him again and I didn't ask her any more about him before she died. When Neville told me Bryan had owned land in Taranaki – home to all his forebears – I started making enquiries, doing some research into the farm ownership and, okay, it just seemed odd that he would have passed it over to you, Jack, the way he did, from what I've heard. That's all I'm saying.' I thought I saw a glint in her eye. She stood her ground, her voice firm. She would be a match for Jack, I could see that.

Nathan stood up. 'Listen, guys, I think we could all do with a cuppa.'

I noticed he avoided looking at me as he said this. Molly went over to the sink and ran water into the electric kettle. The water was starting to boil when Nathan's phone rang.

He took it with him out to the veranda. 'Hang on, I'm actually at Jack's right now.' He was silent while the other person spoke again. 'No, stop work immediately. I'm bloody serious. It could be a crime scene.' He had raised his voice, speaking in a commanding tone I hadn't heard him use before.

He came back inside to collect his jacket and began to walk out of the house. At once, without speaking, everyone else followed him, me included. Nathan marched ahead along the cattle race, saying nothing. When we drew near to where the swamp was, I could see the same workers I'd yelled at the other time. Close by was a digger which they'd brought through the dismantled Taranaki gate. They must've been trying to clear the roots of a felled tree to prevent the stream flooding again. Andrew Barker stood looking into a big cavity in the dirt, phone clutched in his hand.

Nathan strode over. Jack did the same.

'That's not a crime scene, lad,' Jack said. 'That's a grave. An old one, by the looks of it.'

'Don't disturb it any further,' Nathan ordered in the same authoritative tone. 'We need to leave it untouched.'

He took his phone from his shirt pocket and called someone. 'Matiu,' I heard him say as he moved away from the group. He began explaining the find. I heard him say 'likely ancient' and 'yes, can you bring him here?'

'Matiu will contact Mr Katene,' he said to the little group gathered around him. 'He's the kaumātua of the tangata whenua here. The elder of the local iwi.' I got the impression he had added the explanation for my benefit, for the Australian outsider. Perhaps that was what I would always be to the people around Jack. I told myself to not be so sensitive.

He used the phone again and spoke to a colleague back at the office. Again, he mentioned the words 'likely ancient'. He added, 'We'll need to get the forensic pathologist out here. So we can be sure.'

Jack sighed heavily. 'Young Tamati was right, sure enough.'

'About what?' I asked.

'He told me he'd been doing research. Looking at maps, I think. The old people all knew about this place, he said. It was here on the farm all the time.'

'A burial ground?' Nathan asked. 'An urupā?'

Jack hesitated. 'An old pā, I thought. I didn't take much notice. There've always these stories around here. I thought he was spinning a bit of history malarkey to …'

'To persuade you to give up the farm?' I couldn't resist asking. So I had been right to have been suspicious of Tamati.

'No, I mean I didn't know what to make of it, that's all,' Jack said. He sounded so much like an old man, his voice drained, all fight gone, the voice of a man who had been battling demons on all sides. 'I didn't know what he wanted from me. There were the messages. I thought … I thought it could be someone from home. Ireland. Settling scores? I didn't know who to trust.'

'Threatening notes? Destroying your cattle? Burning your hedges? Breaking into your house?' What else had been going on that Jack hadn't told us about?

Nathan whirled around and glared at me. 'You knew about threatening notes and you didn't bother to tell me? We could've fingerprinted them.'

I shrugged. 'I wasn't sure at first and you thought Jack was losing his marbles. So, no. And anyway, the one time I caught him with one of these notes Jack burned it before I could do anything.' I didn't mention the one I found on the rental car.

'Okay, let's not play the blame game.'

I wasn't sure who he thought I was blaming, himself or Jack?

'I remember now,' Jack said. He straightened, his brow wrinkled in thought. 'He said there had been a pā. A fortified pā. I thought he meant the people had moved on, gone back to the other pā, the one that's at the end of the town, the marae. He could have mentioned an urupā, as you call it, now I think of it but I don't remember. I'm getting old.' He sounded defeated.

I remembered the stories about ghosts walking through the land and its buildings and I thought of the dream I had had. The hallucination. A tremor ran through me. 'Do you think the people here had been killed? Not died of natural causes?'

No one replied. The silence itself felt eerie. I began to shiver again.

'Shock.' Nathan put his arm around me, holding me in a strong grip as if he thought I might be about to fall over. His body was warm against mine. He looked closely at me. 'No wonder. You rescued Jack. You fought those two crooks. That was brave. You're a real hero, Imogen.'

Jack nodded as if he agreed.

The real hero was Michael. I owed so much to him. He'd done more than his share and disappeared quietly and unobtrusively as ever. Yet some caution held me back from mentioning his name or indeed how he had helped; now was not the time nor place, who would believe it?

Nathan's grip tightened around my shoulders. 'Listen,' he said awkwardly. 'We got off on the wrong foot in the beginning. You were only doing your best to help Jack.'

I thought about how I might reply but I was too worn out

by all that had happened. I wasn't prepared to apologise. I had done nothing wrong. A little part of me, which I did my best to ignore, said I could have given Nathan more of a chance but I dismissed this. Now wasn't the time. Even so, I liked the strength of his grip. It felt safe.

Eventually, the silence was broken by a vehicle. A black Jeep came through the gap in the hedge on the side road which the Barkers' farm workers had used for their digger. The Jeep made its way across the paddock towards the grave. Matiu, Tamati and an elderly man got out. A second vehicle, a van, followed, carrying more people. The group made their way across the paddock towards us. Two women, both with wreaths of greenery adorning their hair, began a high chanting call that gradually fell then rose again as they approached the grave. Our small group looked on as the kaumātua, Mr Katene, tears flowing, addressed the grave in Māori. One of the women began to sing. I didn't know what the words meant but I could feel the sadness and the power of it all.

A tall figure in a dark woollen jacket appeared nearby. It was Michael. He didn't interfere but instead watched, staring into the deep chasm. He had an unfathomable expression on his face, a mixture of sadness and relief. He bowed his head, touched his forehead and chest, making a sign of the cross, picked up a handful of dirt and cast it down. He looked down into the trench as if he were saying words of farewell and remained still for a time, bearing silent witness to the events of the past.

Tamati moved over to face Jack. He patted him gently on the arm. My grandfather nodded silently. Something passed between them, an understanding. The women began to encircle Tamati and Jack.

I felt a rush of air race past me and I realised Michael had gone. I knew I had to chase after him. My heartbeat sped up as I ran. Ahead of me dark, luminous trees, bent by the storm, swelled and swayed. I caught up to him near the entrance to the swamp. It smelt damp and fetid.

'You were going to leave without telling me,' I protested. 'I knew it.'

'I'm sorry,' he said. He gave a shiver, as if something untoward had passed him by. 'The right thing has now been done.' He pointed back towards the urupā, to the grave where he had appeared to communicate with the people buried there. He bowed his head, as if in prayer. 'Their souls are at rest. I have tried to help so many people but found I couldn't do it alone. Nor was I successful. Then you came and now there is no need for me here. What is done is done. You know what to do. After all –' He took a breath and stretched out his right arm, palm up, in the direction of the grave. 'These people are your own people. They need to be recognised, their rights returned. You will know what to do from now on.'

Now it was my turn to shiver. His words had gone straight to my heart.

'Yes,' I said. So much made sense now. It was as if I had known, somewhere deep in my consciousness, who my father's family were. I remembered how on the first day as I reached the gates to the farm I had a bad feeling. I recognised it now as an overwhelming sense that people – *my* people, if this was the meaning of Michael's words – had suffered loss and worse on this land but I hadn't been able to voice it.

My mind was racing now with so many questions. 'How did you know where to find me? In Melbourne?'

He seemed to hesitate. 'The necklace, it led me to you.'

I recalled how he had stared at it that day.

'Do you still have it?' Michael asked.

'I do.' I lifted it out from beneath my shirt.

'It was given to me by a person who is very dear to me,' he said and his voice broke. 'She thought it would keep me safe. I wasn't sure it had but I am still here now and speaking with you. I wonder, miss, if I might have it back? It is very precious to me and I would like to give it back to her.'

'Of course.' I reached up and undid the clasp of the necklace, handing it over to him. 'I've looked at the pictures many times and wondered about them. I hope it'll protect you now.'

Tears welled in Michael's eyes. He opened the locket and gazed at the picture of the girl and the woman inside. 'Aye, that it will. That is what Eliza told me. I have to believe it.'

'You need to return to people you love.' I looked into his eyes and knew what I was saying was truth. 'And someone who loves you.'

'Finally,' Michael agreed, 'and I hope t'will not be too late for me. I have been trying to make my return for so long, hoping to earn my passage.'

Did he mean payment? I thought about it. 'Through good deeds? Being able to return was dependent on you helping others?'

He nodded. 'That is what I believed I had to do but I didn't succeed very often. Not even this time.'

We were both silent and I saw him brush a tear from his eye.

'Oh, but you did,' I said. I sensed he was ready to leave, though I had a question for him. It had been preying on my mind. 'Michael, did you meet Aoife, my mother?'

'The young girl who lived here, Jack's daughter? Yes.'

'So she saw you, too? Talked with you?'

He smiled. 'Yes.'

'But not the others?'

His expression grew serious. 'Only those who had the gift. You and Aoife both have the ability.'

I remembered what Matiu had said about my being able to

sense things – that Aoife had it, too. All this time, I had never much claimed my Irish heritage. I knew, however, that a belief in the supernatural had been a common property of the Irish people over the centuries and still existed in some parts of the country today. People sensed spirits and told stories about seeing ghosts. I was, after all, my mother's daughter.

Michael waited. I half expected him to do that little jiggle from foot to foot as he had when we spoke in the street in Melbourne. 'Safe journey,' I said. 'Wherever you are going.'

Michael smiled. 'Thank you.' He turned away from me and then he was gone from my sight. A chill flooded through me, then a strong sense of grief. I knew in my being I wouldn't see him again. I hoped his loved ones were waiting for him.

I walked back to where the others were. Someone took my arm. It was Jack. 'Let's go home.' It surprised me a little how my heart went out to him.

Back at the house, I settled Jack in the corner in his armchair. He seemed happy to sit quietly, exhausted from all the tumult, his eyelids drooping as if he might fall asleep. It was probably too much to take in. He'd been through a lot. The threats, the violence that he had kept hidden. A thought occurred to me: at the river, Matiu had recognised the gold necklace. I realised this had also been in the back of my mind for a while but I hadn't followed it up with him. How had he known about it? When had he seen Aoife wearing it? Now might not be the best time to ask but I needed to know.

'Did Aoife ever come back here after they left?'

Jack, who had drifted off to sleep, stirred. He looked guiltily at me. 'Aye, so she did.'

'And?'

'Well, you know your mam.'

'And you?' I could well imagine the two of them. A pair of hotheads.

'We quarrelled. She was only young when she left with her mother. She thought I was to blame.'

'For what?'

He frowned. 'It was her mam dying in Australia. That was the hardest for her. She thought she'd come here, maybe to honour her, I'm not sure. All I know is returning didn't work out. She wasn't here long before we had words. She blamed me for every-thing that had gone wrong for her then and ever since.'

He was quiet for so many minutes I thought he must've fallen asleep, then, with a start, he turned to face me again. 'Like I said, we argued. She packed up and stormed out into the night before I could stop her. She was a grown woman, what could I do? She said she was never coming back and she didn't.' He was quiet, reflecting on what had happened.

'She met with Matiu while she was here, didn't she?' As soon as I asked the question, I knew the answer. I remembered Hayden Ward explaining whakapapa to me. How it had seemed to be to do with knowing your roots, your history, who your ancestors were and perhaps finding your place with it. Now, deep in my spirit I began to understand why knowing one's whakapapa was so powerful.

The look of surprise on Jack's face couldn't be faked. 'So that's who she took off with that night? I should have guessed. I heard a car start up down at the gate. I should have gone after her.'

Had Matiu suspected anything when he met me? Had he made the connection that day at the bridge? When I told him the old kuia had thought I was Ana? His half sister? Knowing him as I did now, I could see how he might be reluctant to bring up such a sensitive conversation with a woman he had never met before. A woman young enough to be his daughter. 'I think there's a lot that needs to be talked about,' I said. Of us all, I had no doubt it was Aoife who was the one who should do the talking.

Days later, I sat in Aoife's old bedroom waiting for Zoe to return my call. Catching sight of my handbag, I sifted through my wallet, planning to ditch any stray New Zealand coins that'd be no use in Australia. A yellow sticky note in the side pocket of my bag caught my eye. It was the note the librarian had written the website on. I typed in the URL and when the website came up, entered Denis Murphy's name and guessed a year of birth. After scrolling, an article caught my eye.

Denis Murphy: excerpt from 'Reminiscences of the War Years', memories as told to Moira Kelly and published in the North Taranaki Historical Society Newsletter, 1906.

The young Maori lad who found me, half-dead and dehydrated in dense bush at the bottom of a steep hill side, was proud of himself. To him, I sensed, I would be proof that he was now a warrior for capturing an enemy. He hallooed for support, probably to his young friends who may have gone on ahead. I listened out for my horse yet there was no sign of him. The lad lashed a piece of flax rope around his wrist and mine and pulled me behind him.

It was shameful though I had no strength left. I had no idea of how much time I had spent lying there in the bush, unable to get up. It must have been days. After I stumbled a few times, he stopped by a bush and pulled berries from it for me to eat; further along he found a wee waterfall and allowed me to drink some fresh water.

He kept a careful eye on me, watching my every movement. I drank the water so greedily I began to choke. He pulled on the rope and indicated for me to follow him again. He held me up as we stumbled through the bush, pushing back branches of heavy green-leafed trees and ferns.

I had shooting pains all over my body from the tumble down the bank. A branch or sharp stick encountered on that fall had pierced my skin, along the side near my ribs. When I touched it, I knew it had narrowly missed my heart, or where I imagined my heart to be.

I could not do much about it, he had me trapped, but still my pride was too great to give up. I limped along, bearing the pain in my side. Tho' I also made sure to observe the lad's movements. He wore a tool slung carelessly from the waist of his clothing. I sensed he wasn't yet one of the warriors of the tribe. More of a young 'un, learning the ways of war from his elders. He reminded me of my own younger brothers back home, full of bravado and no doubt anxious to prove himself.

That may have explained why he was here in the bush on his own, running a message perhaps. Or like Michael, my friend and fellow army man, he had taken it on himself to venture forth into the darkness. I, of course, had been stupid enough to follow Michael in the hope of making him return to camp.

We stumbled on for what was, in my injured state, a long way through the thick bush. But for the occasional high-pitched calls of birds, it was as if we were in a church, such was the silence and solemnity.

Oft times, the lad spoke words to me in his own

language and I spoke back to him in my Irish tongue. Things might have continued like that with him as my captor but there came a moment when he stopped to relieve himself against a tree trunk and I saw my opportunity. I swung back hard against him, knocking him down. Despite my weakness I was stronger than him and it was to my advantage when he fell awkwardly face-down.

He hit his head on a big root sticking out of the ground. He moaned and lay still. I could see my opponent was only a boy, barely out of childhood. I was not able to tell whether he was dead or in an injured state. I knew I would have to make a choice. Stay or run. I would have to leave him if I wanted to save my own skin. If he was dead, there was no helping him. I crossed myself and intoned a prayer I knew was said for those who had died. It was all I could do. I reached down again and grabbed the rough weapon which hung from a belt on his skirt. It was made of bone, with a sharp tip on the end. I used it to cut through the rope that tied us together and began to run. I followed my instincts, nothing more.

Avoiding the paths in case someone else was following or tracking me, I stumbled on, cutting at the swathes of branches with the sharp end of the club I had taken from the lad. When night came, I hid beneath a pile of leaves and slept fitfully. Daylight was shining through the treetops in the morning when I heard the sound of hooves. I listened carefully, not intending to rush out to see who it was. It could be the army, or it could be a warrior on horseback. I stayed in the bushes and waited.

After a time, a horse appeared on the path. It was a big black horse and I waited until I could see the rider. As he got closer, I saw he wore a uniform. Not my uniform. I stepped out onto the track.

The man riding the horse reined it in. 'Good God, man, who are you?'

I told him.

He nodded. 'Captain James Hooper,' he said in return. 'Are there any more of you?'

I wasn't sure who he meant. 'I got separated from my troop, back there some ways.'

He was looking hard at my muddy, bloodied uniform. 'How in hell did you manage to escape alive?'

I didn't know what he meant. 'I caught a young warrior sneaking up to our camp at night and I chased after him into the forest,' I lied. 'Then I fell down a bank and was injured. I don't remember much more.'

'We found your troop,' he said as if I hadn't spoken. 'Or what was left of them. It wasn't good. We helped patch up the wounded.' He scrutinised my face, looking for something in my expression. 'Sent them on their way back to New Plymouth with a number of our men. It was fortunate we happened to come across them. Extremely fortunate. Few of them would have lasted the day otherwise.'

What could I say now? I didn't want to say I hadn't been there. I didn't want to incriminate my good friend Michael – nor myself for that matter.

'God, what a bloodbath it must've been,' he said. 'How did your captain let it happen? Why were so many unarmed, resting without their weapons?'

I had no idea. 'What happened?' I asked, bewildered.

'We couldn't get much out of the survivors,' Captain Hooper said as if I hadn't spoken. 'There weren't many and some couldn't bring themselves to tell us what had happened. They were in shock. We helped them pack up their tents and sent them on their way, back to camp, with a convoy of our men.' He frowned. 'The badly wounded had to be carried on stretchers.'

The captain got down from the horse and pushed me up onto it. 'You've been injured.' He tugged at the bridle and led the horse back along the path. I thought of the young man, dead or alive, I had left behind to his fate, and a pang made my chest feel tight. It was too late. I could do nothing.

'When did you find the camp?' I asked.

'Last Friday,' the captain said.

'What day is it now?' I asked.

'Tuesday.'

I thought about the days that must have passed. Where had I been? Was it even possible? An awful weary feeling came over me and I must have drifted off. When I came to, I was being held on the saddle by the captain. I could smell fire and smoke in the distance and then we were in a clearing. There were other men in uniform, my first opinion of them being they were a raggle-taggle bunch.

The captain led me to a tent and called for someone to tend my wound. 'And broth, if we have it.'

Later, after all this was done, he came back to squat beside my cot. He must have been mulling over what I had said. 'Tell me again how you left camp? Who authorised it?' He glared at me. 'Or did you run when you had the chance? Leaving your fellow soldiers to face the music?' A disgusted look came over his face. I was sure he had summed me up as one of the worst of the worst, a deserter. You couldn't get anyone more low life than that, and the penalties were severe.

'No no,' I said, 'it was not like that.' I went to speak but then fell silent. I had more to care about. 'Did ye come across an Irishman, Michael Flynn?' I asked instead. 'A lad with black hair and a beard? He was riding on horseback on the way to the camp but he never got there. I think he took a wrong turn and they got him. The Maori warrior party.'

The captain wasn't paying attention. I sensed he was thinking about where he found me, how far away from camp I'd been. He had more to say and I could only wait for him to continue with his deductions. He moved close to me, his breath fetid as his spittle landed on my cheek. 'So, you absconded, did you? Instead of aiding your fellow fighters? Wait here.' He beckoned another soldier over. 'Guard him. I am placing him under arrest,' he said curtly.

I wanted to protest, to explain my innocence but I did not have the energy. Nothing he said made sense and nothing I said would change his mind. Back at camp in New Plymouth, I would be court-martialled as a deserter. Another thought occurred to me. What if Michael hadn't survived? What if he were one of those bodies the captain had mentioned?

The captain strode away, leaving me to my fears and the man guarding me came closer to speak in my ear. 'You should come with our troop,' he said, 'and see some action. We'll pay them back for what they've done to your lot.'

I didn't want to tell him I had seen more than enough action.

He started to tell me about the chief whose tribe they were going to fight and what that same man had threatened. I didn't want to listen yet he carried on anyway, gleeful as if this were a great tale to retell. 'We'll vanquish him and his followers, don't you worry,' he said.

I thought of Michael and how he had tried to tell me what we soldiers were being asked to do was wrong. That a wise old Maori man had told him promises by the government to the Maori leaders had been broken. I hadn't wanted to listen. That kind of talk could only lead to trouble. 'Keep your mouth shut and follow orders if you know what's good for you,' I'd said. I wondered if Michael had been right all along, but now was not the time to dwell on it.

I said I needed to rejoin my own company. 'They'll be looking for me.' I knew they wouldn't because any survivors of the raid likely thought I was dead, but I would not tell this man that.

I was suddenly extremely tired and requested to lie down before I fell. I don't know how long I was asleep, but awoke to the captain's return. As he did so, an officer started shouting to take up arms. A raiding party had charged its way into the camp. The captain swung around to shout orders and, in the midst of the confusion, I rolled off the cot and ran.

As soldiers began shouting out warnings to each other, the captain hurried towards his men. By now I'd found a hiding place behind one of the tents under the trees. The Maori warriors were well-trained men. The soldiers scattered as they ran though the camp. I saw a tall warrior capture the captain and drag him away, his body thumping on the ground. I hadn't liked the man but I felt sorry to see this. I didn't want to imagine what might happen to him now.

I managed to retain my hiding place during all this time by playing dead till the warriors left. Two other soldiers had also hidden and the three of us headed off to make our way back to the army camp at New Plymouth.

On my return, I recited the same story – that I had got lost from my original troop in the forest while chasing a young warrior before being found by the now-captured captain and his men. This was accepted without too much questioning. The camp commanders were more interested in why my old captain had lacked caution in allowing his men to sleep without their guns close by. He must have had his reasons but we were never to find out why. It's possible he was drunk and gave orders no one could disobey. Or he had decided his troops had vanquished so many of the local warriors they were now invincible. At least for one night.

At the camp, the same commanders transferred me to another company. I spent the next year with them before joining the militia. There was nothing back home but poverty to return to so I took up the government's offer of fifty acres of land in payment for my army service and for being available to fight to protect the other settlers whenever required. When I thought of Michael from time to time, I remembered his passion when he compared what was happening to the native people here to what had gone on in our own country. I remembered what the visiting priests had told us under cover of the hedges about the English and their domination of our people. I've kept my mouth shut but now I am of an age where I must face the golden years of my life and I want to give a truthful account of what went on.

I never saw Michael, my best mate, again. To this day, I don't know if he was killed, his body mutilated beyond recognition. Or maybe he was fighting under an assumed name, because even when I asked the booking clerk at the shipyards to check for me, he didn't come across the name Michael Flynn on record as being a passenger on any ships leaving the shore. There were many things to ponder about the man I still thought of as my friend. I missed him and each night said a prayer for his safety. On occasion, I also said a prayer for the young lad who through no fault of his own had encountered me in the forest. If his body weren't found, his spirit would linger amongst the trees. Somewhere a mother would be mourning him without a body to hold, much like my own mam had no doubt thought of me as dead to her.

I never did return to my home in Ireland. I had hung up my guns for good, and from then on was known as a respected settler farmer, adding to my land as time went by.

I sat for several moments reflecting on what I had read and felt a pang of sadness for such loss of life, and for the young men who were part of this war. I called Molly. This account was part of her family history, and Daniel's. I found Matiu's phone number on Jack's list in the kitchen and sent him the link to Denis's account of his war experiences. This was part of his iwi history, too. After this I went out to the sitting room to Jack.

* * *

It had been an effort to persuade Aoife to come back and she made many excuses which delayed our trip to Wexford. She couldn't leave her boss in the lurch, she said. He was a hopeless old bugger, couldn't manage without her. I nearly laughed. She could have been describing Jack.

In the end, I got on a plane and headed to Alice Springs to meet her. The farmer she worked for had, to my relief, made himself scarce. One troublesome old man in my life was enough to deal with.

Aoife had never been one to confide in me and I didn't expect to learn too much. She told enough for me to picture her life when she and her parents lived on the farm at the foot of the mountain. I could see my mother as a young girl, torn between allegiance to a parent she loved and love for the other, the one left behind. It couldn't have been easy.

'And then in Australia you lost your mother,' I began. 'I can't begin to imagine.'

Aoife's eyes filled with tears. 'Things happen,' she said.

'Later when you went back to see your father ...?' I was prompting her, almost as if I were interviewing her for an article. I reminded myself not to force her, to let her take time telling her story in her own way.

Her lips tightened. 'It wasn't good.'

'He's sorry, I know what he's like but I believe he is sorry.'

Her expression hardened. 'You weren't there. You can't know.'

'I know he's a difficult old bastard, but he's more than that. Hear him out. Give him a chance. It's the truth that's important.'

'That's rich, coming from you,' Aoife said. 'After lying to me about what you were up to over here.'

'Well, I had no choice.' She was a fine one to talk. She had lied to me about my grandfather. 'We're as bad as each other then.'

She had also lied to me about my father all those years ago. It was time to ask her again, this time to insist she tell me the truth, though I found myself picking up my glass of wine to avoid confronting her. Aoife had been through enough; she had suffered enough, losing both her father from her young life and then her mother. There would be time to deal with this and I sensed that back in Wexford would be the right place to do so. There had been more than enough hurt and secrecy in that community. What was needed was healing, not more blame.

Instead, I handed her the printed pages. 'I brought this for you to read.'

I sat quietly while she read Denis Murphy's account of his war years. Tears welled up in her eyes as she read and she placed her finger under the lines that mentioned Michael. After a time my mother carefully placed the pages beside her on the couch and looked at me for a long while.

'The necklace you gave me,' I said. 'It belonged to Michael Flynn, didn't it?'

Aoife frowned. She was silent, considering how to answer, still wanting to keep things from me. 'Poor Michael,' she said quietly, 'he was so lost.'

I thought about telling her how he'd found me in Melbourne. Instead I said, 'I gave it back to him, so he could finally leave.'

'Good.' She clamped her lips shut. She wasn't going to ask any questions and clearly intended to say no more. Would we ever speak about him further? How much more did Aoife know? How much did I know about Michael? A man who shouldn't have been in our world at all. Another secret, like those embedded in the land we had both got to know.

Aoife was watching me closely, biting her nail. Then, unlike her, she reached out and gave me a sudden hug. Family. They were all different.

'So you'll come back with me to see Jack?' I asked.

'It looks like I have to,' she said grudgingly, yet I thought I saw her smile.

I had finally made plans to spend a few days in Wellington with Rebecca after Taranaki. I was hoping for a relaxing time, the two of us on our own but, with Rebecca, I knew anything could happen. She was already planning to introduce me to her boss. One thing at a time was my mantra for now. There were still things to sort out in Wexford first.

Nathan had taken it on himself to Skype me in Melbourne regularly and keep me informed of all the goings-on. I'd told him about my efforts to contact Aoife, and how, when I got hold of her and asked her to return to the farm with me, she'd given me all the excuses under the sun. Till now.

'I've won her over,' I said, 'finally.'

Nathan said Jack had been meeting with members of the iwi to discuss officially returning the old pā site to the local people so everyone could have access. It was important to him that this should happen. 'While I'm still alive,' Jack had told him.

'They've been having preparatory talks but he's waiting for you and Aoife to be here before going ahead,' Nathan explained. 'The local council want to put up a memorial sign on the road with directions to the old site. That will mean people with family ties to the iwi now living in other parts of the country or overseas can find it when they visit Taranaki and learn the history.'

He fell silent. I tried to think of something to say and realised I was trying to prolong the conversation. 'What does he intend to do about Molly and Daniel?'

'Ah.' Nathan looked thoughtful. 'I think Jack's hanging on till you get here. It will need the wisdom of Solomon. He said me that whatever happens, "What they do after I'm gone is up to them, but I hope people will do the right thing."'

I guessed he meant all four of us. I had no idea what Aoife would want to do but it seemed to me Molly might have a legal claim to the farm that was once her father's. If the farm was handed back to Molly, then it could be up to her and Daniel to decide on its future. 'I guess we can talk about it when we get there.'

'Yeah,' Nathan said. 'I'll call tomorrow, see how things are going your end.'

'We're making progress.'

Nathan sent me a smile. 'Talk tomorrow.'

I could almost get used to it, I thought, these late evening chats.

I turned the rental car into the driveway and paused at the open gate. The 'Owner has gun and will use it' notice had disappeared.

'Ready?' I asked.

'As ready as I will ever be,' Aoife replied stoically.

Getting Aoife and Jack together and moving towards a reconciliation was a priority, even if at the moment neither might see it as such. It was what Michael would've wanted too, I was sure. He had tried so hard to get me here to help Jack. I wish I knew why helping Jack had become so important to him. Was Jack a part of Michael earning his return home? Was this all a form of reparation? He had needed to make amends and if he could achieve this by helping an elderly man he thought was in danger, maybe he had been successful. Now I would never really know. I wished Michael and I could have talked more though I was sure it wasn't to be.

When the plane had landed at New Plymouth airport earlier this morning, we'd had a clear view of the mountain. There was sun on its slopes, and it stood white and majestic surrounded by clear blue skies. As I drove along the back roads to the farm, the long row of ranges stood out clearly, also outlined in snow. Nathan had once invited me to a trek up the mountain and I'd turned him down so sharply that I could still picture the look on his face, both angry and hurt. I hadn't known then that he was someone you could trust to do the right thing. A good guy. I'd been suspicious of him, of everyone. It seemed ages ago now when that had been my normal default mode. Thinking about this, it hit me that I hadn't given a thought to Simon for a long time.

I parked the car on the track at the side of the house. After we both got out, Aoife hesitated, looking towards the house. I wasn't sure what memories she would have of the place. I had so wanted it to be perfect, this return home. She took a step and together we began our journey along the path.

This time Jack knew we were coming, so neither of us was an unexpected visitor and he'd mustered the troops – whether as support for him, or to welcome our arrival I couldn't be sure. Molly and Daniel were waiting with him on the veranda. Tamati was there as well. I found myself looking for Matiu, then I realised that might have been expecting too much. Time for that later.

My attention was drawn to the tall man who wandered out from the shadowy end of the veranda and stood where I could see him. It was as if he was in no hurry to meet me. His face broke into a crinkly smile as he held up a pair of tramping boots. We had unfinished business and it was clear Nathan had no intention of letting it go. I would finally be doing the tramp up the slopes of the mountain with him. A strange sense of relief went through me and I found myself smiling back. I turned to smile at everyone else.

All this time I had wanted a family – and maybe this was it. Not the family I might have imagined when I was a child but mine, nonetheless. I watched as Aoife moved ahead of me and reached for her father to give him an awkward hug, one Jack accepted without a fight. I thought of Michael Flynn, part of me wishing he were still around, caring so much for us.

I moved onto the veranda to greet the people that I, too, had come to care about.

AUTHOR'S NOTE

Michael Flynn is a fictional character. However, the inspiration for him came from a real person, also a soldier from Ireland, Michael Begley, the brother of my maternal great-grandmother.

After a stint on the Otago goldfields in the 1860s, Michael Begley became a private in the Taranaki Military Settlers. In return for service protecting the settlers, the Military Settlers were given land previously seized by the Crown. Along with other military men, Michael was awarded a tract of land (usually 50 acres per soldier) in the Ōkato area of Taranaki. He died of TB at the age of 38. He left the farm to his sister, my great-grandmother. She, her husband and their five children made the formidable journey by sea from Dingle in Ireland to claim it.

The fictitious Michael Flynn is a youth in Ireland when the novel begins. He too, via the goldfields (in his case those in Victoria, Australia), is recruited to join the Crown in the fight against the Māori inhabitants of Taranaki. From the 1840s onwards, the Crown had confiscated substantial areas of Māori land throughout New Zealand, including in Taranaki. The colonial and other troops were tasked with quelling a people the Crown saw as rebels but Māori were, in fact, fighting to protect and retain their own land.

Michael Flynn, like many of his Irish compatriots, would find himself going to war against people who reminded him of his own people back home in Ireland ('them with their potatoes, and fish, and children'). He would ask himself why he was fighting for what to him was an English army, thereby helping oppress a people who, like the Irish, were being colonised by the English. When Denis, his soldier friend in the army, tells him his family barely scratches a living on their land near the bogs rented from the English landlords, Michael is reminded of the history: that following the Irish rebellion of 1641, the English politician and republican Oliver Cromwell passed a series of Penal Laws against Catholics and confiscated almost all land owned by them.

The novel is set in Taranaki around the base of the maunga, the mountain. However I invented the district of Wexford, along with the Boulder River, as well as the sites of the pā beneath the mountain that the soldiers came across in their forays into the hinterland. The descriptions of fighting and action are derived from my reading of the histories of the time and are typical of what happened in other parts of the country, not just Taranaki.

The New Zealand Wars left a long memory in the Māori community, and reportedly Pākehā also did not remember the Wars with any enthusiasm (this can be found on Te Ara online). A character in the novel comments, 'Things are never fully forgotten. The old people who endured this treatment may have passed on but not before giving their accounts and then the history itself is there forever.' Accounts of what happened and the brutality inflicted by both sides paint a bleak and horrifying picture; but, as many in New Zealand have come to accept over recent years, it is a history that can no longer be hidden away in some dark forgotten place.

In this novel there is much reference to ghosts and the meaning of their appearances. I have been intrigued by this idea since I was young, after overhearing my mother talking about a family in which some members died of mysterious illnesses and it was believed this was because their farm was haunted. When my cousin from Ireland, Noel O'Mahony, wrote me an account of the many supernatural events that had occurred in the O'Mahony ancestral home in County Kerry, I wanted even more to include ghosts in my story, but in this case on the farm in Taranaki.

The farm in the novel is situated beneath the slopes of Mount Taranaki. I grew up in south Taranaki with the splendid conical mountain in full view across the farm paddocks, covered in snow in the winter, bare in summer. At times, the mountain would be shrouded in cloud, sometimes for days on end until the weather changed (the grass is green in Taranaki for a reason).

In Taranaki and beyond, the mountain has long been treasured as a sacred icon to both Māori and (more recently) Pākehā.

SOURCES

The following were useful sources of information about these times:

Cowan, James. *The New Zealand Wars: a History of the Maori Campaigns and the Pioneering Period, Vol. 1*. Government Printer, Wellington 1922, 1955, 1983.

Gretton, G. le. M. *The Campaigns and History of the Royal Irish Regiment, Vol. 1: From 1684 to 1902*. William Blackwood and Sons, 1911, pp. 193–224 (available from National Library, Wellington, New Zealand).

King, Michael. *The Penguin History of New Zealand*. Penguin Books, 2003.

Ryan, Tim and Parham, Bill. *The Colonial New Zealand Wars*. Grantham House 1986, revised edition Wellington 2002. (An illustrated history with coloured plates).

Werry, Philippa. *The New Zealand Wars*. New Holland Publishers, London, Sydney, Auckland 2018.

Various websites, including Te Ara online. Two books by Māori historian Dr Danny Keenan are also recommended:

Wars Without End: New Zealand Land Wars – a Māori perspective. Penguin Group, 2021.

Te Whiti O Rongomai and the Resistance of Parihaka.
Huia Publishers, Wellington 2016.

For a Pākehā reflection on the history and meaning of Taranaki Anniversary Day:

'The Anniversary of our Amnesia' by Vivian Hutchinson in
E-Tangata, 8 March 2020, available online.

In my reading I came across the two comments below which record Irish soldiers' responses to the conflicts they were taking part in, and I have used a variation of them in Michael's conversations:

'Those women and children could have been our own
mams and sisters. They were poor enough as it was. And
we've escaped from the burnings of cottages and the
evictions back home only to force it on these poor divils.'
– The words of an Irish soldier, quoted in various historic
accounts of the time.

'Surely these people are no different from our own
people back home, them with their potatoes, and fish,
and children.' – The words of an army surgeon, cited in
A Sketch of the New Zealand War by Morgan S. Grace,
(published by Horace Marshall and Sons, London 1899).

I also came across an anecdote about a young sentry shooting at an intruder to the army camp and finding instead he had shot a harmless pig. This was found in the published recollections of a man on my genealogical tree about his time in the Armed Constabulary in Taranaki in the 1870s – 'Living pioneers, reminiscences of an octogenarian' (J.C. Hickey), *Opunake Times*, 22 March 1927.

The scene that describes a young Irishman lowering his guard to turn away from an exhausted young Māori warrior is adapted from an account in *The Campaigns and History of the Royal Irish Regiment, Vol. 1: From 1684 to 1902* by G. le. M. Gretton, published by William Blackwood and Sons, 1911, pp. 193–224 (National Library, Wellington, New Zealand). The book was a useful source of the history of the time.

ACKNOWLEDGEMENTS

In writing this novel I was immensely grateful to receive a New Zealand Society of Authors CompleteMS manuscript assessment in 2020. Thanks to Philippa Werry, my assessor, for all your suggestions, which were most helpful.

Many people have helped me along this journey. My thanks to my supervisor Bill Manhire at the International Institute of Modern Letters at Victoria University for encouraging me to write a novel rather than short stories during my MA in Creative Writing, thus giving me a push towards that form.

Thanks to my early and later readers Linda Pears, Geoff Palmer and Rebecca Styles for their consistent support as I wrote this, and to my writing group Annette Edwards-Hill, Jennifer Lane, Janis Freegard, Jackie Owens and Piripi Evans for their invaluable feedback. Thanks to my Irish friends John Breen and historian Ida Milne for their advice on all kinds of things Irish, and to New Zealand authors Vaughan Rapatahana (for responding to a request about protocol when an ancient grave is discovered), and Cassie Hart. Thanks also to David Williams for his checking of the historic sections in particular, and to Jeanette Cook and Tina Shaw, my editors, for their useful suggestions. I am grateful to the former Irish Ambassador to New Zealand, Peter Ryan, for his encouragement to 'finish your novel'.

Thanks to my husband Michael Burrowes (who suggested the title of this book), my daughters Hannah Prebble and Sophie Hilton, and my good friend Mary Kriechbaum for their practical advice and support.

Thanks to the team at Cloud Ink – Helen McNeil, Tina Shaw and Dione Jones – for bringing *Secrets of the Land* into the world.

ABOUT THE AUTHOR

Kate Mahony is a long-time writer of short stories and flash fiction with an MA in Creative Writing from the International Institute of Modern Letters at Victoria University of Wellington. Her work has been published in anthologies and literary journals internationally and in New Zealand. Her fiction has been shortlisted and longlisted in international and national competitions. She has previously worked as a journalist in both London and New Zealand, and in communications roles. She grew up in Taranaki where her novel *Secrets of the Land* is set. She lives in Wellington.